"Tell me I

Jamison was smiling like he'd won a small victory, but the muscle in his cheek was twitching as though he was trying to hold himself back. "Tell me you don't want me to move closer. That you don't want me to reach my hand around your neck and pull you into me so I can kiss you."

Jamison Hunter wanted to kiss her.

She wanted to kiss Jamison Hunter.

And the problem was…?

"What if I'm not big enough for you?" It shouldn't have been a question, she thought. It should have been a statement, because it was true. Gabriella Haines was not *big* enough for Jamison Hunter. Not even close.

He scooted closer along the bench seat until their thighs were touching. He wrapped an arm around her shoulders and tugged her more tightly against him. Then he leaned back and looked out the windshield into the blackness. His relaxation made her relax by default. Not all of the tension dissipated, there was still the sexual kind, but the awkwardness of the date was finally behind them. Like they were starting again at a drive-in theater, watching a movie and it was the moment when the screen went blank right before all the action began.

Dear Reader,

People who know me, know I'm a huge golf fan. In particular, I'm a Tiger Woods fan. So on that fateful Thanksgiving day when his car crashed... or his wife took him out with his own golf club... I, like everyone else, was shocked and not a little heartbroken that my golf hero proved to be not very heroic.

In the years since, I've watched the greatest player in the game fall from the very top to the very bottom, and watching that fall of course made me consider all the ramifications of it.

Now, I'm certainly not justifying Tiger's actions, yet I couldn't help but imagine what a person would go through after such a collapse. More importantly, how a person might find it in himself to make his way back. This story is my spin on how sometimes the best thing that can happen to a person is to lose everything and try to earn it back. Including love.

I love to hear from readers! I can always be reached at www.stephaniedoyle.net.

Enjoy!

Stephanie Doyle

The Way Back
Stephanie Doyle

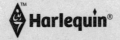 **Harlequin**®

TORONTO NEW YORK LONDON
AMSTERDAM PARIS SYDNEY HAMBURG
STOCKHOLM ATHENS TOKYO MILAN MADRID
PRAGUE WARSAW BUDAPEST AUCKLAND

Recycling programs
for this product may
not exist in your area.

ISBN-13: 978-0-373-71773-6

THE WAY BACK

Copyright © 2012 by Stephanie Doyle

ABOUT THE AUTHOR

Stephanie Doyle, a dedicated romance reader, began to pen her own romantic adventures at age sixteen. She began submitting to Harlequin Books at age eighteen and by twenty-six, her first book was published. Fifteen years later, she still loves what she does as each book is a new adventure. She lives in South Jersey with two kittens who have taken over everything. When she isn't thinking about escaping to the beach, she's working on her next story idea.

Books by Stephanie Doyle

SILHOUETTE ROMANTIC SUSPENSE

SILHOUETTE BOMBSHELL

Other titles by this author available in ebook format.

All backlist available in ebook. Don't miss any of our special offers. Write to us at the following address for information on our newest releases.

Harlequin Reader Service
U.S.: 3010 Walden Ave., P.O. Box 1325, Buffalo, NY 14269
Canadian: P.O. Box 609, Fort Erie, Ont. L2A 5X3

To Kevin, Trevor and Ryan

No matter where life takes you as you get older…
we'll always have the beach

CHAPTER ONE

"GABBY, I THINK you should do it. What do you say?" Melissa Smith, senior editor at McKay Publishing, sat at the head of the table wearing an expectant expression.

Gabby Haines looked at her boss. Oh, no. Melissa was talking to her. She expected her to say something in return. The proper response would have required listening. Probably not the best time to admit she'd been thinking about what she would have been doing at her old job at this time of day. Not when she was only two days into her new job.

"Well?"

Let's see, Gabby thought. She was a junior editor in her first editors' meeting and her boss was calling her out to do something. She was probably being asked to do a low and vaguely demeaning task such as fetch coffee. Best to simply go with it.

"Absolutely. I'm on board. Tell me what you need."

Melissa clapped her hands. "Excellent. Go bring back Jamison Hunters' tell-all biography with a nice pink bow on it."

Gabby blinked. Okay, she had not imagined hearing Jamison Hunter's name. No way would a conversation containing those two names, *Jamison* and *Hunter,* occur that her ears didn't perk up and her brain immediately focus. Not to mention other parts of her body.

"I'm sorry? Who…?"

Melissa smiled. "That's right. The elusive author we want you to track down is none other than Jamison Hunter."

"Jamison Hunter? The astronaut. The legend. The… cheating pig bastard?"

"That's the one." Melissa nodded as the other editors surrounding the massive conference table chuckled.

Apparently everyone was in on the joke except Gabby.

"You're the new kid on the block and we always send the new kid on the block."

"I went three years ago," Mary Jane, an editor who focused on cozy mysteries and self-help titles, chimed in. "Disaster. The man had me in tears in mach two seconds."

"I don't get it," Gabby said, trying to catch up with what she'd missed. "You want me to bring back his story? The autobiography of Jamison Hunter? He's one of the most reclusive people on the planet. He hasn't been heard from in years. I'm talking J.D. Salinger level hermit. You've got better chance of getting President Clinton to give us a tell-all about his days with Monica Lewinski than you do of getting this guy to talk."

"Yes, I know," Melissa agreed. "But here's the thing we have with Hunter, which we don't have with President Clinton—a binding contract. Hunter—in a major deal, I might add—agreed to give us his story. Granted, that was a few weeks before the scandal hit. Afterward, he tried to return the advance, but we refused it. We thought he might change his mind, might want the world to know his side of the story. And when that time came, he'd already be committed to us. Given the sizeable advance we paid him, we've got a lot at stake. So every few years we send an eager new face to meet him and personally give him a nudge."

Eager and *new* were not two words Gabby would necessarily associate with herself. *Washed up* and *worn down* were more accurate.

Get a grip, Gabby. You got fired, not murdered.

It was her inner therapist at work. Just because she lost the hottest job on morning television in Philadelphia to a younger, thinner, hipper version of herself did not mean her life as she knew it was over. Her ego had taken a punch was all. And her self-esteem. And her self-confidence.

And her wallet.

The truth was, she'd been lucky to land this job— even if it was an entry-level position. Even if at thirty-three she felt more like sixty-three working with so many young twentysomethings. Twentysomethings who were all ahead of her on the corporate ladder. Twentysomethings to whom she would have been teaching the ropes at her old job.

But after coming to the realization no other local morning programs were looking to hire a slightly overweight, aging host, she'd had to scramble for a new plan. Openings in her field of journalism were few and far between, so it seemed like a reasonable idea to try the other end of writing and look at openings in publishing.

Apparently publishing houses were often looking for junior editors. When they told Gabby what her starting salary would be, she understood why.

Still it was a job and a new start.

Plus there were advantages. Gabby loved to read. She could bury her head in books without anyone caring there were wrinkles around her eyes, or what clothing size she was currently wearing. She could earn enough money to keep her from having to move in with her mother—which, at her age, would be the most pathetic thing *evah*. Most importantly this job would give her time. Time she desperately needed to figure out what she wanted to do for the rest of her life.

And now, a handful of hours into this new career, Melissa was offering her the chance to meet Jamison Hunter.

Jamison Hunter, the epitome of all good things men could be. Proof that not all men were asses. The crush of her life, the man she'd idolized above all others… until he smashed every one of those romantic dreams with a single horrible press conference. He'd broken not only the nation's heart, but hers, too.

Jamison Hunter.

Huh.

Funny where life took you sometimes.

She was nodding before she let herself think maybe this wasn't the best idea given her particular mental state right now. Facing the man who had set her expectations about what a man should be, only to then confirm the worst of what she knew a man could be, would definitely be treading some rocky emotional ground.

Her mouth opened. The words came out. "I'll do my best."

Before she could reconsider Mary Jane leaned toward her and whispered, "Trust me. Take a box of tissues with you."

"WOOF!"

Jamie Hunter watched his ancient dog Shep slowly stretch and push himself into a standing position alerting him that company was coming. Shep sighed and creaked, but finally he was on all fours.

A second later the doorbell rang.

"Poor, Shep, you are definitely feeling your age, my man. There was a day you would have given me a five-minute heads-up." Jamie patted the loyal German Sheppard's head as he rose from his recliner—not as quickly as he once did, either.

Dropping his book on a table and removing the glasses he needed to read—as ridiculous as it was, he was slightly self-conscious about wearing them—the two aging warriors made their way down the hall to confront the intruder. After eight o'clock on a Tuesday night, it was a good bet almost every one of the eight hundred and twenty-two inhabitants of this island town were bunkered for the night.

Unless there was trouble. Jamie picked up his step.

"Yeah?" he said, opening the door half expecting it to be the sheriff asking for help with something.

The female face on the other side of the door was a complete surprise.

"Jamison Hunter?"

"You've got to be kidding me," he muttered. He took in the business suit, the low-heeled pumps, the hand thrust out in welcome. "Are you a reporter?"

It wasn't possible. He was old news. Yesterday's story. A forgotten has-been with a sad legacy no one wanted to remember because he depressed them. Unless someone had found out about— No. He wouldn't even allow himself to think it.

He noticed she was huffing slightly from the forty steps it had taken her to reach his house from the road. If she was a reporter, she definitely wasn't a beat reporter. Too soft.

"No, I'm Gabriella Haines. I'm from McKay Publishing."

He ignored the hand completely. "Oh crap, not you people again. When are you going to figure it out? I'm not writing the damn book."

She blinked twice. Okay, maybe he didn't have to be quite so harsh. It wasn't this woman's fault the company was so persistent. Not her fault at all. But he knew if he maintained his hard attitude, she would leave faster. He knew this from experience.

"Come inside. I'll write out the check. Again." He opened the door wider.

She didn't move immediately. Probably wondering if either he or Shep bit.

Shep had never bitten anyone in his life.

"Inside, lady. That suit you're wearing isn't warm enough for this weather. No doubt you're freezing."

She nodded and stepped inside. As soon as he closed

the door behind her she began to rub her hands over her arms. "It was sixty-five degrees when I left New York."

"And this is an island off the coast of Maine." If she'd checked the local forecast, she would have figured out to dress more appropriately. He walked toward the rear of the house to his office where he kept his checkbook. When McKay had refused to accept the advance the first time he'd offered to return it, he had put the money in a separate account he never touched. That way he would always have it at the ready whenever they came asking for it. He'd figured after a year or two they would come politely begging for the cash. He definitely hadn't anticipated their persistence.

"You should tell your boss I'm making a tidy sum off the interest," he said over his shoulder. "And I've got no qualms about spending that interest, either. It paid for a new deck last year. I'm almost sorry to have all that extra cash come to an end."

Jamie glanced up and saw she hadn't followed him. No doubt she'd stopped by the fireplace to warm up. He wrote out the check then tore it from the book and headed to the living room. As expected, he found her in front of the fireplace, her eyes raised to the skylights in the high, wood-beam ceiling.

Skylights so he could see the stars on a clear night.

With her jaw open and her arms crossed over herself, she looked more like a lost little girl than the grown woman she obviously was. Despite whatever protective instincts her appearance might spark within him, Jamie had no intention of being swayed. He didn't rescue lost little girls anymore and he certainly didn't rescue grown women.

"You know there's no ferry service back to the mainland tonight?"

She looked at him. "I know. I started driving early today, but there was an accident on the Tappan Zee Bridge and then I hit rush hour out of Boston. I saw it was the last ferry run, but I didn't want to stop. I felt if I stopped, I would…"

Jamie found himself wanting to hear the rest, wanting to know what she feared would happen if she stopped. She was dressed professionally with long dark hair loose around her shoulders. She appeared to have it all together, but somehow with the way her hair seemed to swirl around her—as though the brutal wind on the island had done a number on it—you knew there was nothing but chaos inside.

"They usually send the newbies to hassle me," he said. This woman was no newbie—in her thirties, if he had to guess.

Her lips curled. "Believe it or not, I am the newbie. At least at this job."

It made a little more sense. No wonder she wanted to keep going even though it was late. She had something to prove, lost ground to make up. He was sure of it.

Not that he cared, he quickly told himself. He was not about to get caught up in whatever her story was.

"Well, there is a B and B on the island. They'll have plenty of space this time of year. Follow the road into town, it's the biggest house. You can't miss it."

"Thanks. Yeah, I have a room waiting for me."

He held out the check. "Go on, take it."

She glanced at the check with a similar expression to the one he imagined he'd given her hand when she offered it at the door. Like he'd rather touch a dead fish.

"I'm not taking the check."

"Lady—"

"Gabby. My name is Gabby Haines."

"Ms. Haines, I don't have the patience for this. I really don't. Here is how this situation will go. You'll make your pitch and try to persuade me to write the damn book. I'll refuse—just like I've done since the first time I tried to cancel the contract and return the advance. You'll be stubborn, thinking that might sway me. It won't. We'll keep the stand-off going until eventually you'll break down, maybe even start crying, reminding me you're new and really need this job, and if you don't get at least a commitment from me to write the book, you'll be fired. There will be begging and pleading, maybe even some threats of legal action. None of that will change my mind. So let's save ourselves the aggravation, shall we?"

"Gee, no wonder Mary Jane cried."

"Huh?"

"Never mind. See, here's the thing, Mr. Hunter. As you so accurately pointed out I'm not some fresh girl with her first real job. I've wrestled with a tough subject or two. I've been to the top. I've been on TV. Until they ripped it all away from me."

He noticed her voice was gaining in volume and shrillness. Any second Shep would start whining.

"Now I'm starting over and you and your story might

be the thing that will change my whole life. During that ridiculously long drive, I thought about all the reasons why you might be resistant to doing this book. And one of the things that occurred to me was that you had discovered you can't write—or at least, not well enough to write an entire book.

"Well, I can solve that problem for you. I'm a writer. I majored in journalism. I wrote magazine columns and I blogged long before I started hosting a television show. Maybe what you need is someone who can bring a certain skill set to the table."

"I'm not telling my story."

"Don't say that. At least not yet. Think about it over night. I'll come back in the morning and we'll talk about this like reasonable people. You can be reasonable, can't you?"

"You clearly don't know much about me, if you can ask that."

This made her laugh. In fact, his comment made her nearly double over with laughter. He was obviously dealing with a slightly hysterical editor-slash-writer. Terrific.

"Oh, I know about you," she said, pulling herself together. "I know of you very well."

And there it was. That look he'd seen before in the eyes of women. Women who had idolized him or fantasized about him. Women who thought they loved him even though they had never even met him and knew jack about him. Women who felt as if he'd cheated on them, too.

Yes, Gabby's look of betrayal wasn't the first one

he'd witnessed. But hell, he didn't have to see it in his own house.

"Get out. Take the check and don't come back."

She didn't say anything for a moment. Then she took the slip of paper and flicked it into the fireplace. They both watched a flame lick up and obliterate it.

"I've got more checks."

"I've got nothing to lose."

He met her eyes again and saw it. A determination he wasn't easily going to squash. But squash it he would. Because he wasn't telling his story. To anyone.

"You can show yourself out." With that he dismissed her and went back to his leather recliner and his book. He held off putting on the reading glasses until she walked past him. A few seconds later he heard the door close behind her.

Gone. For now.

Gabby Haines. With the long dark hair that swirled around her shoulders. A sudden image of his fingers digging into her thick hair stirred something inside him and had him shifting in his chair.

Man, it had definitely been too long if he was getting turned on by some half-crazed New York editor who would probably make his life hell for the next few days until she ultimately gave up.

At least the next few days weren't going to be boring.

JAMISON. HUNTER.

She felt as though she'd met Tom Cruise, Brad Pitt and George Clooney all rolled into one perfect fantasy. She took a deep breath. She was supposed to be cool about this. She was a professional. She wasn't supposed to regress to teenage behavior, but...*wow.* Jamison Hunter.

And they had talked. Okay, mostly he'd dictated and postured. Then she'd gone crazy lady on his ass.

What had she been thinking?

She hadn't. That was the problem. She'd taken one look at the check and thought about returning to New York and her tiny cubicle, mission *not* accomplished. She imagined standing in Melissa's office admitting she'd failed. The awareness of how far she had fallen had hit her again and...she sort of snapped. She couldn't go down without a fight.

That idea she'd had on the long drive—offering to ghost write Jamison's story—was a good one. Maybe fate had sent him into her life for this very reason. Maybe she was supposed to do more than get a promise from him. Maybe what she really needed to do was tell his story. Write about his life and his downfall and finally give answers to all the questions everyone had about him. She didn't have to be the enemy. She didn't have to be some two-bit employee of a publishing company who wanted to use his story to make money.

Instead she could help him bring his side of the story to life. They could empathize with each other. Bond over tragedy. After all, she knew what it was like to be on top and have everything taken away. Not on his scale certainly, but on her own.

Unfortunately he didn't see things as clearly as she did. She would have to work on that. But she wasn't backing down.

Standing on the other side of the door separated from the fireplace's warmth, she quickly took a chill. He was right. Business suits and heels weren't the best for a Maine island spring. Luckily she had thrown some jeans into her bag. Melissa had given her a few days to work her magic and Gabby planned to do it wearing comfortable clothes.

The question was how long would Melissa give Gabby if Hunter did agree to allow her to help him write his story. Would Melissa even go for the idea? No point worrying about it now. First Gabby needed his consent, then she would work on her boss.

For now it was best to head into town and to her room for the night.

She thought about the mountain of stairs she'd climbed and cringed at how heavily she'd been breathing when he opened the door and she'd gotten her first look at him up close. But that was fine because it was all part of the master plan.

Step one: start new career.

Step two: get in shape.

Step three…

Well, the first two steps were fairly significant. Step three could wait.

Turning, she considered the long and winding wooden stairs which zigged right and zagged left over the jagged landscape. The light above the door gave her some guidance, but there was no railing to hang on to—nothing to stop her fall, should she stumble on the uneven surfaces. Coming up, she'd been fueled with fear, adrenaline, excitement and determination.

Going down was going to be a little harder.

Cursing even the low heels, she took her first cautious step. Only thirty-nine more to go.

What had taken her minutes to climb felt like forever to descend. Shaking with tension and cold and still reeling from the major life event of meeting an idol, Gabby finally reached the road again. She wanted to weep.

She got in her car and jacked up the heat waiting for the engine to respond to her desire to be warm. Rubbing her hands together she laughed to herself. She'd done it. She had a plan now. She wasn't going to sit back and passively take orders doing a job she didn't really want. She was going to remake herself. A *writer.* It was perfect.

All she had to do now was wear him down. Win him over with her charm and personality until he trusted her. Trust would lead to comfort and comfort would lead to his story.

Charm and personality. Two things she used to have plenty of. Surely she could drudge them up again.

One thing was for sure, she needed to get over this crazy starstruck feeling. Seeing him in person had been like fire bolt to her system. It had taken her ten seconds to remember her name and why she'd come. He might be halfway between forty and fifty, but, damn, he still looked good.

She'd met semi-famous people when she'd been the host of *Wake Up Philadelphia.* There had been the mayor of the city, the governor of the state, sports figures, local actors and performers who had made good. She'd interviewed Kevin Bacon for Pete's sake. Once you knew him, you were basically connected to everyone else in Hollywood. It was a known fact.

Jamison Hunter wasn't any of those people, though. He was more. At least to her. Growing up without her father during her teenage years, it wasn't hard to understand how she had formed such an attachment to a media figure—especially one who had seemed so perfect. A girl had to look for heroes where she could find them.

Of course, she hadn't been some silly twelve-year-old when Colonel Jamison Hunter first captured the world's attention. No, she'd been twenty-three, engaged and starting her career. She'd had the world in her hands and had believed her father's abandonment hadn't made a single dent in her perspective or her life choices. Maybe she wasn't the most romantic person, and wasn't overly sentimental. However, she had committed herself to a relationship. That was an achievement. Something to be proud of.

She really hadn't had a reason to fall into a crush with an image on the TV screen. Something about him had captivated her.

Air Force Colonel. Astronaut. American hero.

It was a story everyone knew. As embedded into the American psyche as Apollo 13, the Challenger tragedy and Neil Armstrong walking on the moon. Colonel Hunter had commanded a space-shuttle mission to help with repairs on the international space station. Once there, the crew of the station informed him the situation was more critical than first realized. In fact, they feared an imminent explosion would not only take out the station but the shuttle docked to it, as well.

In an unprecedented move originally not sanctioned by NASA, Hunter did the unthinkable with an unplanned, untethered, space walk. He set out to make the repairs, knowing if he didn't find and fix the problem, the lives of his crew and those on the station would be lost.

Gabby never understood all the specifics of what he'd done. Reporters explained the science, the possible complications and ultimately the risk he took, but none of it mattered to her. All she cared about was after he'd taken that brave action and was safely on American soil and she watched him being interviewed time and time again, she felt safe.

The world was a safer place because Jamison Hunter was in it.

Gabby wasn't alone in her hero worship of him. It seemed everyone had all come together to place him on a pedestal. It was one of the reasons he'd fallen so hard and so far when the scandal broke.

A sunny day in Florida. A motel not too far from Cape Canaveral. A picture of Jamison Hunter standing in the doorway of the room with a woman wearing only a sheet. Next to them stood his wife with a look of sheer horror on her face. His deception had crushed the world. It had devastated Gabby. How could a man capable of such honorable and heroic actions cheat on his wife? And if he could cheat on his beautiful, accomplished wife, what chance did an average woman have of preventing much less heroic men from doing the same? Gabby couldn't stop asking herself that question and becoming deeply suspicious of her own fiancé as a result. In retrospect that suspicion was a good thing... and warranted.

Finding her fiancé in bed with her half-sister might not have happened if she hadn't started looking for signs.

Gabby owed Jamison Hunter for saving her from a marriage with a cheating scumbag—something for which she was eternally grateful. But she also blamed Jamison for her inability to make any other relationship in the past ten years since Brad work.

"Stop it, Gabby."

The sound of her voice startled her. She needed the reminder though. She wasn't here to contemplate her life and dwell on her failures. She was moving on with her life. Fresh start, et cetera.

The drive into what the residents of Hawk Island considered town was short. The car had finally heated up, but still Gabby shuddered against the chill. It was late, she hadn't eaten since lunch and her stomach was grumbling so loudly she didn't think she could wait until the B and B's breakfast.

Of course she should. She had more than enough stores of fat on her body to hold her through the night. But the rational side of her brain reminded her starving wasn't a healthy method of weight loss. She needed to fuel her body at regular intervals to keep her metabolism up.

There weren't many options, though. The town consisted of four or five mom-and-pop shops—currently closed for the night—ranging from a small grocery, liquor and hardware stores to an antique toy place and an exclusive clothing boutique. Obviously those last two were targeted to the tourists who were starting to discover the charm of an island situated off the coast of Maine.

No fast food. No twenty-four-hour grocery stores. Everything was locked up and dark.

She spied one place that still had the lights on. Pulling up, Gabby peered through the window, which was painted with the name Adel's. She could see booths lined up along the window and a counter with stools suggesting this was a diner. Food. According to the sign that dangled from the doorknob she had seven minutes to get some.

Hopping out of her car and sprinting as fast as she could, Gabby reached for the door and heard the satisfying ring of a bell overhead.

"Oy, you've got to be kidding." The tall girl behind the counter stopped wiping the surface in front of her and scowled.

"The sign says you're still open."

"For only seven more minutes."

At first the Gabby didn't understand the woman, then she realized what had sounded like *meenoots,* was actually the word *minutes.* "I'll be quick."

"You'll make a mess."

"No, I swear I'll order only a salad."

The girl huffed and rolled her eyes. "Sit."

Gabby didn't have to be told twice. She plopped her butt on a round stool and tried to appear super hungry so the server would understand that she wouldn't have come in here unless she was really desperate.

"Adel, there is someone here who wants food."

An older woman pushed her way through a swinging door, carrying a tub of what appeared to be clean coffee cups.

"Oh, crap."

Gabby shifted. "I'm sure you all don't mean it but I'm starting to feel a little unwelcome."

Adel plunked down the tub with a rattle. "No, sign says we're open until nine, so I guess we're going to have to feed you. Coffee?"

"Please." She saw the young girl pour what was no doubt multiple-hours-old coffee dregs into a cup, but Gabby didn't mind. It was piping hot.

She shivered as the heat transferred from the cream-colored ceramic to her hands. It had been spring in New York when she left this morning. She was sure of it. She took a tentative sip. It was as foul as she expected but it warmed her throat all the way down.

"What do you want?"

This was easy. She'd already committed herself to a salad so there would be no reason to look at the menu and tempt herself with any of the other offerings. *Willpower, Gabby. Willpower.*

"House salad, oil and vinegar dressing is fine." Then she caught herself. "On the side. I need the dressing on the side."

"Oy." The girl rolled her eyes. "One of those. On the side this, on the side that. If you want it all on the side to put together yourself, go buy groceries and do it at home."

Said the girl with the long legs, tiny torso and high cheekbones. She was gorgeous—model thin with long, straight brown hair that looked as though it might actually touch her bottom.

Gabby naturally hated her on sight.

"Zhanna, give it a break." Adel finished stacking the cups under the counter and stared at Gabby for a moment. "You look hungry. You sure a salad is going to be enough to hold you?"

"Absolutely." Not. But this is what happened when you let yourself get careless. When you enjoyed food instead of counting calories. When you didn't accept you were thirty-three and not twenty-three and couldn't shed five pounds in a weekend. When your metabolism worked against you, but no one let on there was a problem until it ended up costing you your job.

A woman had to pay the price.

Gabby felt her price might have been slightly steeper than any another woman's, but those were the breaks. Especially in television.

"A salad is fine," she said.

"Right." Adel exited through the swinging door and Gabby was left with the decidedly unfriendly Zhanna. If she was staying on the island for a while, it would probably help to make an effort to get to know the locals.

"Zhanna, that's a beautiful name. Where are you from?"

Zhanna stared at Gabby as though trying to discover her true intention in asking. She must have concluded it was no more than mild curiosity because she answered, "Russia."

The way the R rolled off her tongue was dramatic and Gabby couldn't help but be a little impressed. She was just chubby Gabby from Philadelphia. While this girl was the exotic Zhanna from Russia. That comparison made Gabby wish she had more of an accent. "How did you find yourself here?"

"How did you?"

Not exactly a conversationalist, this Zhanna. "I took the ferry."

"Me, too."

Small talk over. Okay. Clearly, this local wasn't someone Gabby was going to win over. After a few minutes of silence, the kitchen door swung open again. Adel set the large plate of green stuff in front of her.

Gabby wished she could be more excited about it, but veggies had never really done it for her. Still, she needed to fill her stomach, so she started eating. Halfway through she was actually starting to feel better. Then Adel came out of the kitchen carrying a slice of pie.

Hot apple pie if the smell and tendrils of steam emerging from it were any indicators. To compound the evil temptation she scooped up some vanilla bean ice cream—the easy-to-detect brown bean flecks suggested it might be homemade—and plopped it on top.

"Figured you ate the salad, you might as well have a little pie."

Don't do it, Gabby told herself. *Do* not *eat that pie.* Being forced to eat the pastries, the gourmet cupcakes

and all those delightful things the local chefs who were
featured on the show's kitchen segments had ended up
killing her career.

Gabby didn't think she wanted to ever return to television to expose herself to that scrutiny again, but she
couldn't shake the feeling she had been responsible for
destroying her life and not the show's executives.

"It's not going to kill you," Adel said as she simultaneously slid the pie in front of Gabby while she cleared
the salad plate. "It's pie. Not poison."

"You don't understand," Gabby said wearily. "I'm
trying to change my life."

"Really?" Zhanna asked, leaning on the counter.
"Your life? Why do you need the changing of it?"

Oh, sure, Zhanna couldn't talk about making her
way from Russia to Maine, but Gabby was supposed
to come clean with all of her secrets. The odd thing
was, late at night, alone in a café with a girl who rolled
her R's and a woman who looked as though she knew
what a lifetime of hard work meant, Gabby found herself wanting to confess.

"I got fired from a morning talk show because I put
on too much weight and I'm getting too old."

"Bastards," Adel hissed. "A woman's always got to
be young, thin and beautiful. Is that it?"

"For men," Zhanna said. "Yes. Go on."

"I realized I had nothing in my life but the job.
Which meant without it I had nothing. I was nothing."

"Tragic." Zhanna's face was a study of sympathy.
"Russians, we understand tragedy."

"I needed a job, so I took this entry-level position at

a publishing company, but I know it's not where I want to be. I feel like an old lady among kids."

"You must find a new path for yourself."

"Yes," Gabby declared. "That's what I want to do. I thought this job would help me buy time, but now I think it's given me something even better to do. I think I want to write."

Adel leaned on the counter next to Zhanna. "Writing. Interesting. What are you going to write—murder mysteries, thrillers, romance?"

"I love the romance books," Zhanna said. "Especially the American ones where nobody dies at the end."

"No, I'm not a fiction writer," Gabby said. "I was sent here to get Jamison Hunter's story and damn it, I'm not only going to get his story, I'm going to tell it."

At the mention of his name both women straightened. Zhanna scowled and Adel frowned. Gabby was trying to figure out what she said to garner this reaction when Zhanna grabbed the plate of pie and dumped it under the counter.

"On second thought, you don't need the pie."

CHAPTER TWO

GABBY FOLLOWED THE scent of coffee downstairs the next morning. She could only hope Adel and Zhanna hadn't made it a point to stop by the B and B to rat her out to the owners. Their reaction to the news she wanted to write a book about Jamison was startling, and took her completely off guard. She understood wanting to protect a friend's privacy, but their instant hostility had been extreme. Even after explaining she wasn't some seedy journalist from a trash magazine, or a person looking to earn a quick buck by writing a lurid tell-all, the two women had still been cold. They'd accepted payment for the food, but had refused to take any tip.

Gabby had left the café with her head down and her enthusiasm for a new start somewhat diminished.

She'd left without a taste of that gorgeous pie, too.

Based on their conversation last night when she'd checked in, the inn's owner Susan had seemed like a nice middle-aged woman with a gift for making people feel welcome. Gabby didn't peg her as the type to withhold essentials such as coffee and toast simply because she didn't like what Gabby was planning to do.

Unfortunately there really was no way of knowing. If Zhanna and Adel were any indication, Gabby probably wasn't going to be the most welcome person on the island.

But this was a new day and she'd woken herself up with a pep talk.

She'd been fired. Nothing remained to go back to so she needed to make this new job work. If she could accomplish what no editor had accomplished to date, maybe she could leapfrog over a few people in the company and have an above entry-level position. If she actually convinced Jamison to tell his story to her while she wrote it, maybe the publishing company would line up more biographies for her. *That* was a role she could get behind.

Jamison's biography, as written by her, would hit bestseller lists. She would be back on the talk-show circuit, only this time as the interviewee. A sneaky thought drifted through her conscience, pointing out this crazy need to have more instead of being happy with what she had, but she squashed it before it fully formed.

Gabby stopped at the bottom of the stairs and poked her head into the dining room. There was one table for all the guests and on it sat a pitcher of juice and what appeared to be a pot of coffee. With not a little awkwardness, she took the seat over the single place setting laid out and hoped it was for her. Then the door on the opposite wall—that presumably lead to the kitchen— opened and Susan entered wearing a crisp white apron which made her look like a young Julia Child. She set a basket of assorted breads next to Gabby and smiled.

"Good morning."

Gabby felt a little more confident now. The diner women had not been in contact. "Good morning."

"I hope you don't mind eating alone, but you're my only guest right now."

Actually, Gabby preferred it. She'd been living on her own since she was eighteen—except for that brief stint with Brad—and she'd always felt mornings were sacred time. Silence was needed to get your head straight for the events of the day. Silence was also needed until the coffee kicked in.

"Not a problem."

"Now there is juice and coffee…"

Gabby didn't wait for the rest. She turned over the cup in front of her and reached for the pot. The smell of it as it poured out was life changing.

"Here are some pastries. But what can I make you? I can do eggs and bacon. Or, if you don't mind waiting a bit, I can do homemade French toast."

Gabby tried to pretend her mouth wasn't watering over the French toast. Strength. Willpower. "Just wheat toast if you have it. Dry."

Susan's expression fell. "Dry wheat toast? That's it?"

"I'm watching my figure." Gabby patted what she considered to be an only slightly larger than average hip.

"Oh, don't be ridiculous. Your figure is fine." Susan sighed. "But I suppose if it's all you want, then that's easy enough. You know, this isn't a normal time of year for vacationers. Not that I've ever had that many. Even in the summer the water is too cold to swim in, which puts us low on most people's lists of vacation spots. But in the fall folks like to come for the foliage. You're darn near my first guest in the month of April."

"Do you run this whole place on your own?"

"Yep. Just me. My husband—sorry ex-husband—used to be around to help, but it wasn't his life. He said, 'Susan, I'm not living my life.' I said, 'George, then you go do what you need to do.'"

Gabby nodded as she sipped her coffee. Her separation from Brad had been slightly more acrimonious with a great deal more foul words.

Even before Susan spoke next, Gabby could sense her purpose. "Back to you, April is somewhat of a strange time to take a trip north."

"Actually, I'm here working."

"Oh. That makes more sense. Working on what, dear?"

"A novel," she lied. "I'm a writer. Fiction. Pure fiction. I want to set my story on an island, so I came here to do some research."

Susan clapped her hands. "Oh, isn't that fascinating. A writer. Have I heard of you?"

Gabby wondered how much trouble she would get into if she lied and said her pen name was Nora Roberts. Best not to go too far out on the limb. "No, I'm just starting."

"Well, good luck to you. You're welcome to stay with me as long as you like. I've got no reservations for at least the next six weeks, which means you're going to be spoiled, spoiled, spoiled. I hope you don't mind."

Spoiled, spoiled, spoiled. That would be a first for Gabby. One of the downsides of living alone was you had to do everything for yourself. She never minded it really, but she also had no problem trying on spoiled to see how it fit.

Susan left Gabby to her coffee and thoughts. She'd gone to sleep last night thinking about what her next step should be. Obviously, Jamison wasn't open to the idea of his story being told. And as obviously, some of the locals were hostile, too. That meant she was going to have a hard time getting people to talk about him. It would be a lot easier to write this book with his buy-in.

A story like the one she imagined McKay wanted would have to be big in scope. It would need the color and depth of the perceptions from the locals who he'd lived among for the past eight years to help shape it. That wasn't going to happen, not unless she got him to trust her.

The next step was clear then. She needed to get to know Jamison Hunter—not as an editor who had an agenda, but as a person he might consider working with. She needed to let him see she didn't intend to sensationalize him or vilify him. Gabby wasn't interested in salaciousness for the sake of selling books. Of course, McKay might have a different view—scandal sold. But she imagined anyone interested in the story of Jamison Hunter was looking for more than a few sordid facts about his infidelity.

People wanted the truth. They knew *what* he did. What they wanted to know was *why*. Why a man of seemingly high honor and definite bravery could become a lying, cheating scumbag. It was the contradiction that made him so fascinating. That's what she wanted to write about. That's what she wanted to *read* about.

She needed to go to his house. At the very least she wanted to get a sense of how he lived and why he chose to live here. Not that it was all so far-fetched. Hawk Island was a perfect backdrop for a recluse. Accessible from the coast only by ferry, it was almost its own country separated from the U.S. by a couple of miles of cold north Atlantic water.

Where else would a man hunted by the world go to hide? Anyone not a local was easily identifiable. And if he'd done something to win over the locals here, which he'd obviously done with Adel and Zhanna, they could take extreme measures to make life difficult for anyone trying to pursue him.

Like denying people pie.

Adel and Zhanna. What had he done to win them over? Given his reputation it wasn't outside the realm of possibility that he'd seduced them. Adel was close to fifty if she was a day, but she was lean and strong and probably closer to his age than Zhanna.

But Zhanna was young and beautiful and exotic. The perfect target for a man on the prowl. Had he had his way with both? And if they were that loyal, did it mean he was *that* good?

Gabby shook the image from her head. Sex—especially Jamison having sex—was the last thing she needed in her head, combining with all the stuff about him in there. She'd had a crush on him, she'd been hurt by him. She'd even cried tears over him. Hell, she'd had a whole relationship with the man and she'd never met him until last night.

Bottom line was none of it mattered. Her crush, her anger, her wounds…none of it. She was over him, over the infatuation. She needed to be if she going to be objective in helping him tell his story.

Gabby Haines was a professional and she would act like one. Even if it meant working with and getting to know a man who was—she had to face it—a liar.

Gabby hated liars. She'd had enough of them in her life. From the father who always said he would come to see her after the divorce, but didn't, to her fiancé who said he loved her, but didn't, to her half sister who said she hadn't meant to fall in love with Gabby's fiancé, but did.

When Susan brought the toast out it was exactly as ordered—dry and consequently difficult to eat. Or it might have been thinking about Kim and Brad that left a bad taste in Gabby's mouth. Fortunately, the quality of the coffee almost made up for it. Either way she had enough fuel to start her day.

Brand-new start plus good coffee equals a great day, every time.

She had parked the rental car on the street in front of the B and B, but that didn't seem to bother anyone. There were no posted signs about places and times to park. Definitely not like Manhattan where there was a plethora of signs telling people where they couldn't park—among other things—and people choosing to disobey those signs.

Looking at the practical beige Ford rental, Gabby

couldn't help but remember the powder blue Beemer with gray leather interior she'd bought herself as her thirtieth birthday present. It had been a declaration of her success and she loved driving it. But once she'd decided to move to New York City, it was clear she didn't need a car. So, her heart breaking one more time, she'd sold it and used the money to help pay the rent on her apartment in Brooklyn until she found a job.

Besides, after losing her job, she'd felt like a fraud in the car. It was a reflection of everything she had been, but no longer was. Its perfection ridiculed her whenever she got behind the wheel.

Look everyone. See how far Gabby Haines has fallen.

Not allowing herself to descend into doom and gloom mode, she focused on the task at hand.

Jamison's house was about ten minutes up a winding road from where the main street cut through the island. On the map there were only four documented roads that crisscrossed the island leading north, south, east or west from the main street that occupied the epicenter. In reality, there were also a number of smaller roads that looked more like paved driveways, which led to the scattering of homes and cabins peppering the tiny island.

Jamie's house was situated on what must be the highest point of the island. That position probably guaranteed him a view of the water from the second level of the house. It also set him far apart from the other homes guaranteeing no neighbors within at least a half a mile of the place.

Perfect for a recluse.

Parking the car where she had last night, Gabby didn't relish climbing the stairs again. Nor did she anticipate a friendlier welcome simply because it was morning.

So how did a person go about striking up a conversation with someone when said target would not allow her into his home?

Confront him outside his home.

It seemed plausible. Your basic run of the mill, bump into you, hey, good to see you again, type of moment. Gabby peered through the windshield and spotted the dirt path which must be his driveway. She could hang out in her car, wait for him to leave, follow him to wherever he was going then pounce when he least expected it.

What if he'd already left to go to work? Did he even have a job?

She would ask him when they spoke. She couldn't imagine what he would do on this island. The man had been an astronaut for crying out loud. How did anyone, disgraced hero or not, come down from a job like that?

She didn't picture him selling screwdrivers in the local hardware store or flipping burgers for Adel. There wasn't much else in the way of labor on the island. It was possible he ferried to the mainland daily, but the commute would be enough of a hassle to outweigh the privacy of island living.

Since there was no point waiting for someone who wasn't even home to leave, Gabby got out of the car.

Wind whipped around her and she snuggled into

her winter coat. She'd worn jeans and a sweater today, adapting to the local climate. But the only real practical shoes she had were her loafers. She had packed sneakers since step two in her new life was to transform her body and she had the vague notion that daily, hour-long speed walks would accomplish that. But she couldn't fathom the idea of using them for any other purpose than to work out. Did Barbara Walters interview people while wearing sneakers? Did Oprah? Certainly not.

Her feet managed to go from cozy to frigid in minutes, but she didn't let it stop her. She walked up the dirt driveway making sure to stay to one side in case a vehicle came down and she had to make an emergency dive into the bushes.

She laughed at that image of herself attempting to hide in the foliage as Jamison approached. She suspected her feet in the air might give her away. Still she clung to her plan as she climbed—or more accurately *stumbled* since the loafers provided little traction—up the driveway.

Gabby couldn't help but wonder what type of car he might have. Something sleek and fast. High performing and responsive. A man who had flown jet fighters would need something to keep up with him, wouldn't he?

What if he had a motorcycle?

The image of him on a bike, flying down the road without fear or caution seemed accurate. Definitely a motorcycle, she decided. Or, at the very least, a convertible.

Which is why the old white truck was such a let-down. It sat alone at the top of the driveway parked a short distance from the house. Gabby remembered the dog from last night and listened for the sound of barking to announce her presence, but she heard nothing.

A dumpy, old white truck. Not fast, sleek or high performing. Maybe when he'd walked away from his former life he felt he needed to go to extremes. This truck was it. And a pretty good symbol of a man who once had everything and now had nothing.

Yeah, when they did finally talk, they were going to have a lot in common.

A muffled woof startled her. The sound wasn't close and followed by an even softer bark, so she could tell it was moving away from her.

Circling the vehicle she looked toward the house and could see the new deck extending from the rear. The deck McKay Publishing paid for apparently.

In the summer it would provide a magnificent vista of green leaves and blue water. But the leaves had yet to come out and all she saw was a barren landscape leading down a hill to what she imagined was a narrow shoreline. The gray water seemed to blend with the overcast sky.

"Shep. Come on, old man."

Gabby instinctively ducked at the sound of Jamison's voice, not sure she was ready to announce her presence. She could see he was already heading down the hill that ran away from his house. She spied the top of his head, then a few seconds later his dog followed.

The dog stopped briefly, turning his head in her direction, but another command from Jamison had Shep moving forward tentatively, until eventually his master met him on the path, picked him up and carried him out of sight.

The plan had been to wait for Jamison to leave the house then meet him on neutral ground. A beach was fair game, wasn't it? Gabby couldn't imagine he owned all the property from the house to the water, so it wouldn't be trespassing. She was just a regular tourist, out for a walk on the beach on a blistery April morning in Cole Hahn loafers.

Okay, not great. But it was better than if she'd been in stilettos.

Scrambling, she reached the edge of his deck and saw a path down the rocky hill. She waited a good two minutes to follow because she didn't want to risk him spotting her on the approach. Not to mention each *oomph, ow, oh, yikes* she muttered as she tried to descend would certainly give her away. By the time she actually reached the beach, which was no more than a stretch of rocky pebbles approximately twenty feet wide, her ankles, calves and thighs were screaming.

"Don't suppose you're lost?"

Gabby shrieked at Jamison's comment. There he was standing not ten feet away with his arms crossed over his chest.

He looked different in the daylight. A little older—maybe because of the gray hair. But there was nothing old about his physique. In a tight zip-up jacket and jogging pants he looked younger than she did. Lean, fit and strong. Definitely strong.

He should have been several minutes ahead of her

on the beach by now. The fact he wasn't meant stealth was not her strong point.

"You heard me coming."

"Even Shep heard you coming."

The brown and black German Sheppard tilted his head in acknowledgement.

"I was out for a walk." Gabby tried not to cringe at the way her voice went up at the end of what should have been a statement.

"You were trespassing. We do have a sheriff on the island. I have every right to call him and have him pick you up. A few hours in a holding cell in the mainland might cure you of your curiosity."

"Please don't." It seemed like a silly plea but she couldn't stop herself. She'd made all that effort to get down the stupid path. Her feet were like blocks of ice. Here closer to the water the wind had picked up and was throwing her hair all around. And she was hungry because she'd only eaten dry toast for breakfast. So, no. Being arrested was not a good way to start her life over.

"Look, lady—"

"Gabby. Remember? Gabby Haines."

"Gabby, I'm not going to give you what you want."

"Why not?"

That seemed to give him pause. He opened his mouth and then closed it. "Because." Then, as if realizing it was a ridiculous answer, he added, "What makes you think I would?"

"Because it's been, what? Eight years?" she said taking a step forward. The dog let out a warning growl and she stopped. "It's time people heard the whole story.

There were so many rumors, so much speculation. You walked away without any explanations and left people assuming the worst about everything. As bad as what you did was, I can't imagine you were as awful as the media painted you at the time."

The rumors had been awful. He was cast as a high-flying jet jockey with women all over the world. Illegitimate children spread from Russia to China to Brazil and beyond. Alcohol, drugs, sex. One article said he used to take cocaine before getting in his F-16 to fly missions over Iraq.

He grimaced. "I never— Some of those rumors— Well, some of them weren't true."

"I know. Talk to me. Tell me who you were. Let me tell others."

"What makes you think anyone would even care? Like you said it's been ten years since the space station event, eight since my personal life imploded. Other stories have come and gone. The days of my infamy are long over."

Gabby nodded as if in complete agreement. But they both knew he was leaving out a very significant reason why people might be interested in Jamison Hunter again.

"You've heard the reports about the trouble they're having with the Space Station again. I know you have. Even on this island they must have cable."

"Satellite. It's the only way to go," he muttered. "You think NASA might come and call me out of retirement for one more space walk, huh?"

"You don't?"

He shook his head. "You don't get it, lady—"

"Gabby or Gabriella," she corrected. She wasn't sure why she offered him her full name. Nobody ever called her by it.

"Sorry, Gabriella. I'm an old man. A washed-out hero whose day is over. They have younger and more qualified men and women for whatever space mission they are cooking up. Trust me."

"You talk like you're ready for the nursing home. You're forty-five."

"I might as well be eighty-five to NASA."

"John Glenn went into space when he was seventy-seven."

"I'm no John Glenn."

"No, you aren't," she admitted. The sad fact of his disgrace would forever separate him from the other astronaut heroes. "But you did what Glen didn't do. What so many astronauts before you never did. You saved fourteen lives that day. You should be remembered for your achievement."

"Isn't that what the internet is for?"

Gabby sensed a stalemate approaching. She had to be happy she'd gotten this far. They were talking. Communicating. She'd made her opening pitch. Now it was time to back off.

"You don't have to make any decisions today."

He chuckled. "I've already made my decision."

"Look, can't you take some time to get to know me? You'll see I'm not all that bad and I'm not out to destroy you or rehash the terrible things said about you. Maybe you'll come to trust me."

"Doubt it," he said. He considered her for a moment, but she had a hard time interpreting the gleam in his eye. "You want me to get to know you, huh? Are you asking me out on a date?"

As if. Gabby couldn't reign in her laughter. *A date.* With Jamison Hunter. Yeah, right. Pigs could fly and the sky was green. *A date.* The word was so foreign to her it might as well have been…well, foreign.

"Uh, no."

His face fell a little bit then. "Right. No point in going out with someone you think will cheat on you."

That had nothing to do with her reaction, but now he said it she figured it was true, as well. Gabby had been down the betrayal path and had scars to prove it. As a result she'd spent every day since avoiding situations where she might be betrayed again.

Of course, that hadn't really worked out, either. Her boss at the station, a woman she considered a friend, had been the one to fire her.

"Can't we just talk a bit? I can go with you on your walk."

"I don't walk. But if you can keep up, you're welcome to talk." He turned and started jogging, his dog valiantly trying to follow close on his heels.

Seriously? He wanted her to jog with him? Actually, no. He wanted to get rid of her. He probably thought this was the best way. *Outrun the girl with the chubby cheeks, why don't you.*

A fit of anger overtook her. She wasn't an invalid for Pete's sake. She'd eaten a few too many French fries was all. She could run. At least as fast as that. Ready to shove his words back down his throat, she started off on a pace slightly faster than what he was doing so that she'd catch up.

The loafers on the rocky soil weren't helping though. After a few steps she could feel sand filling up the spaces around her feet.

Cursing, she stopped once to shake each shoe out, then started after him again. She'd almost caught up to the dog when she tripped. She stumbled on the ground, her hands sliding out to break her fall, collecting some scrapes along the way.

Jamison turned back, scowling at her the entire way. He lifted her to her feet as if all those French fries were a figment of her imagination. For a second their hands brushed and she tried to pretend her stomach didn't flip as a result.

"Are you all right?"

"I guess," she said grudgingly. Except she was embarrassed, her knee was throbbing and she suspected she was about to burst into tears at any moment. She'd fallen down in front of him. He'd had to pick her up. How much more pathetic did it get?

"If you can't keep up, you can't keep up. See you around."

Great, she thought as she stood there watching the man and his dog take off down the beach without her. She knew it was probably her imagination, but the dog's tail seemed to wag a little harder.

Even Shep was mocking her.

CHAPTER THREE

THE NEXT DAY, Jamison headed for his daily jog, but was stopped before he could even start. Perhaps he should have been surprised by the sight of Gabby on the beach waiting for him. He wasn't. As a man who prided himself with being honest—at least with himself—he had to admit he was…delighted to see her again.

He really didn't want to think about what that reaction meant.

Instead, right now he had the persistent editor who wanted to be a writer to deal with. He'd much rather deal with the attractive woman, but it was clear her professional persona came first.

Damn.

After leaving her in his dust yesterday, Jamie knew he hadn't seen the last of her. She'd been wounded and humiliated, but he got the sense she wouldn't quit so easily. He'd expected to find her stalking him into town. Or maybe hiding out in his bushes. What he didn't anticipate was her making a second attempt to keep up with him running.

Her hair was tied in a ponytail. Those long dark waves hanging down her back were giving him fits at night. He was imagining all sorts of dirty things he'd like to do with that hair. Not the least of which was grip it tightly in his hand while he thrust into her from behind.

Swell, he was getting aroused before his run. That was *not* going to be comfortable.

"I wasn't prepared yesterday so I went shopping," she said, indicating the Lycra running pants and pull-over she wore.

"I see that," he murmured. Her legs looked long in the sleek black material. The pullover she wore came down over her hips, which, like most women, she obviously wanted to hide. But the legs were all out there for him to see and they looked pretty damn good. "You think you can keep up now you have the right equipment?"

She raised her arms over her head and put one leg behind the other as if she was stretching. Then she switched legs after only a moment letting him know she had no clue what she was doing.

"I'm going to give it my best try. You did say we could talk while we run."

Right. He ran five eight-minute miles every day. As an obvious novice she had no hope of keeping up.

"That's what I said." Jamie bent to rub his dog's collar. "I'm going to do my usual pace, buddy. You can hang back with her."

The dog shook his tail.

"Yeah, I know you don't like it, but those legs are getting too old for the pace. At least today you'll have company." It bothered him that Shep was stopping earlier and earlier into the run. It didn't seem that long ago that Shep would outpace him for the entire five miles.

She hopped up and down a few times and he could see the cold air puffing off her lips. It wasn't frigid this morning but the coolness would make it harder for her to breathe. He couldn't help but wonder how long she thought she would manage.

He didn't wait to ask her. Instead he trotted down the beach at his normal warm-up speed. He could hear her crunching behind him, her rhythm quickly becoming erratic.

"You do this every day?" she called.

"Every day," he said without turning around. He didn't want to give her any encouragement although he wouldn't have minded watching the ponytail—or other parts of her body for that matter—bounce around.

"So if NASA did come calling, you could tell them you're in good physical shape."

"I'm in excellent physical shape," he said trying not to brag. "But it still doesn't mean I would be a viable candidate."

"Because of the scandal?"

He tried not to wince at the word. It was so dramatic. "Because I'm retired."

She was puffing now and falling back a few steps as he increased his speed. "But what if they really needed you?"

What if they did? Jamie shook his head. They wouldn't. There were always others to fill the spaces opened by those who retired. The finest pilots. The best minds. If the Space Station was truly in trouble and the

International Space Committee asked NASA for help, NASA had a rich pool of talent to select from.

Besides, he couldn't fathom any reason why he would put himself through it all again. The press. The media. The spotlight. Hell, no. Jamie Hunter's days of standing in front of a camera were over.

"Can you hold up a minute?"

He stopped and saw her several yards behind. She was bent over with her hand grasping her waist. Trying to breathe out a cramp no doubt. She'd barely lasted five minutes.

Rookie.

"Sorry. You know the rules. If you want, you can walk with Shep."

GREAT. THE DOG AGAIN. Gabby wondered how much insight into his master Shep could provide.

"I'm guessing not much," she wheezed. "Right. You're not talking about him, either. Oh, my goodness, this is painful." She was finally able to work out the cramp in her rib cage. Several deep breaths and she could stand upright. She thought about starting again, but her legs felt like rubber.

Best to walk it out for a while. As she put one foot in front of the other the dog came to walk by her side. Crazy, but she sort of liked the company and she felt sorry for a loyal friend who was getting too old to keep up with his master.

Her performance was pathetic. That she had deluded herself into thinking she'd be able to run with Jamison… Well, she would have laughed if she'd had the lung capacity. Intellectually she knew a person didn't get in shape overnight. Not when it had taken so long to get out of shape. She never really saw it happening. She'd never been a work-out fiend. In her twenties what she ate or drank never impacted her figure at all. A couple of times a week at the gym, thirty or so minutes on the treadmill or a stationary bike and she was fine.

It wasn't until her work weeks started getting longer and her trips to the gym grew fewer that everything changed. Gradually, the inches had packed on. Not enough to make her worried, but enough to maybe shop for clothes one size up than what she'd been wearing. Or to pick a top that hid the little extra around her middle.

Certainly there had to be some forgiveness. At that point, she'd been working harder than she ever had before. Giving more of herself to the show rather than her personal life. Yes, she knew the demographics and format were aimed at a younger audience. A local show competing against a major network had no shot of beating them, but it could target a certain age range.

The guest singers were in their teens, the actors promoting their TV shows and movies were barely into their twenties and Gabby never considered interviewing an athlete over thirty. Only really famous movies stars and the city's mayor could break the no-one-over-thirty rule.

It wasn't until last year that she finally stopped for a second and took notice of the people she was working with, the people she was interviewing, even the people she was working for. In an instant she felt older and bigger than she should. For Pete's sake, how old was Katie Couric when she landed the *Today Show?*

But Gabby Haines wasn't Katie Couric and *Wake Up, Philadelphia* wasn't the *Today Show.* And she'd gone up two dress sizes. When her boss suggested a Botox treatment Gabby had flipped. She was smart, she was personable. People opened up to her. She was a damn good interviewer. And they wanted her to inject poison into her skin to help the ratings?

After she refused she'd been fired.

"Fired," she sighed. The word still sat like lead on her heart.

Woman and dog made their way down the beach, which framed the north end of the island. Moving around one bend, the vista opened up for a piece. She could see a few docks stretching out into the water with skiffs and bigger sail boats tied to them bobbing with the ocean's movement.

Way up ahead she could see Jamison. Still running. Completely uncatchable.

No doubt when the dog tired, he would simply lay down and wait for his master to return. After about a mile or so the dog plopped down in the sand letting the sun warm his belly before resting his head on his paws.

"Yeah, I'm beat, too. You tell him, though, this isn't done. Not by a long shot."

At least she hoped it wasn't done.

"So how is it going?"

"Good," Gabby lied, glad Melissa couldn't see her wince. She knew cell phone technology was advancing so people could face time instead of just talk. Gabby had no plans to purchase one of those phones anytime soon. She'd been walking to her car when she got the call and picked up immediately the way any good employee would do.

Opening the door she sat on the driver's seat glad to no longer be walking. "We're talking," she added confidently. At least that much was true.

"Has he changed his position about writing the book at all?"

"Uh…" Nope. "I think he's looking at all the possibilities. Let me ask you, Melissa, who would do the actual writing? I mean, the man's an astronaut not a writer obviously. Maybe that's what is holding him back. A bad case of writer's block."

"We could hire a ghost writer. We do it all the time for celebrity autobiographies. Heck, we did an autobiography of a rock star who, I was pretty sure, didn't know how to read let alone write."

"How does a person get that job? Would she interview or provide some samples…what?"

"What are you getting at, Gabby?"

Apparently Gabby hadn't been very subtle. She could hear Melissa's sharp tone loud and clear even though the cell reception on the island wasn't the greatest. "You know I have a background in journalism. I'm a solid writer. I'm also a good interviewer."

"You want to write Jamison Hunter's story."

It wasn't a question—was that good or bad? She hadn't been working with Melissa long enough to tell. "Am I the first newbie to suggest something so crazy?"

"No. But you're also the only newbie I know who has actually gotten him to talk and hasn't been crying when I called for an update." She paused. "Look, Gabby, I can't promise anything. But if you can convince him to do this book and you've forged some kind of connection with him, well, that will definitely be taken into consideration. First things first, though—we need a commitment. A time frame. Something, anything we can plan with."

"I'm working on it," Gabby assured her.

"Do it. And Gabby? An FYI. You've basically let me know you have no real desire to be an editor. So you better make this ghost writer thing work for you because I don't know how much of a future you have as a junior editor at McKay Publishing. I know it sucks. But I don't need people filling in time here while they search for a different career. I need people who want to do the job they have."

Gabby swallowed hard before she could speak. "I understand."

"Okay, good. Now, get me that book."

Gabby ended the call and felt the air in her lungs swoosh out of her.

So this is what it felt like to burn a bridge.

IT WAS AFTER SEVEN o'clock at night and Gabby finally had to admit she was starving. After her jog-slash-mostly-walk, she'd returned to the inn to shower, change and then set about doing what she imagined most successful ghost writers did—research and write down observations she had about her subject.

She'd contemplated using a recorder to capture her thoughts, but having tried it once to prepare verbal notes for interviews, she knew she felt silly talking aloud into it. Not to mention when she paused during her thought process she made this weird breathing sound she suspected she made a lot but was able to ignore as long as she didn't hear it played back through a recorder.

Instead she typed random thoughts into her laptop and saved the document simply as Hunter.

Things she knew about him so far—he didn't want to be interviewed. He was shorter in person. He was hotter in person. She deleted that point. His natural instinct was to help her when she'd fallen even though he didn't want to be bothered by her. He drove a truck instead of a motorcycle. He spoke to his dog in soft affectionate tones, which made her shiver a little. She deleted that point, too.

Not exactly ground-breaking biographical material at this point but she was just starting out.

After the past hour of staring at the screen and telling herself her stomach wasn't growling, she finally had to admit it was. Which meant going in search of food. After the horror at the café two nights ago, she'd chosen a convenience store hot dog for last night's dinner. On the island there was one gas station with a small food store next to it. In the store there was a rotisserie containing three hot dogs she was fairly sure had been sitting on the rack for minimum of two years.

The store was down one hot dog and she was down about five Tums to digest the thing, which meant she wasn't going back.

Earlier in the day she'd tried to hint to Susan an inn that served dinner probably would be a smashing hit, but the caretaker merely smiled and said breakfast was her forte. But for a fine meal Gabby could do worse than the café down the street.

Unless the café people hated her.

There was always the hope she could be worried for nothing. Maybe Adel and Zhanna didn't work every night. Or if one of them did, maybe they would stay in the back and Gabby would have a different waitress serve her. Perfect. Where there was hope, there was food.

Gabby put on her sneakers. She concluded that as unfashionable as they might be, they were the only practical shoes she owned. Anything less than heavy socks and total foot coverage was plain stupid for as cold as it was. Bundling into her coat, she trotted down the street and crossed in front of the café. No jaywalking signs. No clearly marked pedestrian walkways. In this town you looked both ways and, if there were no cars coming, you crossed.

If there were, and you chose to ignore them, you got hit.

Seemed pretty straightforward to her and a lot simpler calculating if you could get across the street with the seconds counting down on the pedestrian traffic light.

The bell chimed as she stepped inside the restaurant and her hopes were quickly dashed.

"Oy, it's you again."

"Hello, Zhanna. Nice to see you."

"Sit," the girl said pointing to an empty booth. "I'll be with you when I choose."

Gabby took encouragement she hadn't been told to leave. If she was sitting, there was a good shot they would feed her. She didn't allow herself to reach for the menu. She didn't want to know the sumptuous specials they were offering tonight. All she needed was a salad. With the dressing on the side.

On the side. On the side.

"Don't let her scare you."

Gabby looked to the man sitting at the counter who swiveled his seat in her direction.

"Too late."

He laughed. "It's just her way. Deep inside she's got a heart of gold. I'm pretty sure anyway." He hopped off his stool and offered her a hand. "I'm Tom. I'm the lone vet on the island."

She shook it and answered his smile. It was nice to feel a little welcomed. "I'm Gabby. Nice to meet you."

"What brings you to Hawk Island?"

"She wants to expose Jamie to horrible ridicule and humiliation," Zhanna stated, her order pad in her hand as she practically pushed herself between Tom and Gabby. "You don't want anything to do with this one, Tom. I'm fairly certain she kills little animals for fun."

Gabby's jaw dropped. "I do *not*."

Tom chuckled. "Don't let Zhanna get to you. She's all bark, Gabby. Good luck with whatever."

"Do you want to get pie from me or not, Mr. Tom?"

His eyes twinkled. "Honey, I always want pie from you."

"Oh, hush now. Go sit on stool and I'll fix you something hearty. You are always too skinny."

Tom wandered to the counter and Zhanna's eyes stayed with him for a minute longer than was natural. Then, as if shaking herself out of a trance, she focused on Gabby.

"Now you. What do you want?"

"A salad. With the dressing on the—"

"Got it." Zhanna walked away before Gabby could finish speaking.

Digging into her purse Gabby pulled out a pen and pad and started writing. One of the keys to weight loss she read was to document everything she ate in a day plus her amount of exercise.

Dry toast again this morning. Extensive jogging for five minutes. Salad with dressing on the side…

Zhanna plunked a plate in front of her. It sounded much too heavy for salad. It smelled way better, too.

"You did say hamburger and fries, didn't you?"

"No." Gabby looked at the plate of food and nearly wanted to cry. A large patty with cheese drooping down the side mocked her. Lettuce and tomato were merely camouflage. The big soft bun was made out of white flour instead of whole wheat. Not fair.

She stared at it and tried to ignore the rest of the plate which was teaming with crisp golden French fries.

She was starving. It smelled delicious. These women were evil.

The door to the café opened and Gabby glanced up to see Jamison enter. Zhanna turned and gave him a silly half smile.

He walked to her and clucked a finger beneath her chin in greeting. "Hello, brat."

"Hello, my favorite customer." The tone was sarcastic but friendly. These two knew each other well. Not a surprise given Zhanna's loyalty to him. Once again thoughts of how Jamison might have seduced the young woman filtered through Gabby's mind. But watching them, she did have to admit there were no sexual sparks between them. More like easy friendship.

"Gabriella."

"Jamison." Great. The one person who knew she could barely run for ten minutes spotted her behind a plate of artery-clogging—and very delicious-smelling—food. She felt her cheeks flame up and she blurted, "I didn't order this."

He laughed. "Then why did Zhanna bring it to you?"

Gabby figured ratting out his friend probably wasn't a smart idea.

"Ah, I see," he said, grasping the situation. "And what did you order?"

"A salad with dressing on the side. I ordered it… on the side."

He nodded. Then gave Zhanna a slightly disapproving glare. "Having a little fun with the new person in town?"

"She wants to write about you," Zhanna said sulkily.

"I know. How was the burger done?"

"Medium."

Jamison lifted the plate and set it on the table in the empty booth behind her. "Bring her the salad, Zee."

"Oy. Always the forgiving one." With a huff she went into the kitchen.

Gabby could feel him settle down directly behind her. He wasted no time digging into *her* burger.

"Thank you."

Around a mouthful of meat, he mumbled she was welcome.

"You should know if you hadn't come in I probably would have eaten it. I don't have much willpower."

He didn't comment.

She wasn't sure why she felt the need to confess to him, but it was important she not seem hypocritical. At least with herself. She wasn't perfect. There was no point pretending she was. If he knew that about her, it might make it easier for him to trust her.

Adel emerged from the kitchen a minute later. The salad was big and brimming with vegetables. The dressing was in a cup on the side.

"Thank you."

"Yeah."

It seemed her relationship with Jamison's dog was the best one Gabby had cultivated so far.

The café remained empty except for the two of them in the booths and Tom at the counter who was definitely taking a very long time to chose his meal. Despite the impatient way she'd treated Gabby, Zhanna did not seem to mind his indecisiveness.

As Gabby picked through lettuce, cucumbers and tomatoes she could hear Jamison's fork hitting the plate and imagined him diving into those decadent fries. It seemed awkward to have him behind her. But he hadn't asked to join her and she didn't want him to think if she invited him, she was doing so only to get information from him.

She wasn't out for the story tonight. A little company, however, would be nice.

Picking up her plate and dressing, she moved booths and sat across from him before he could object. He raised his eyebrows to let her know she'd been a bit daring, but before he could speak she did.

"Relax, I'm not going to grill you for facts about your life."

"I wouldn't give them to you if you did."

She ignored that. "It seems stupid the two of us eating alone."

"I eat alone most nights."

So did she. Most meals in fact. She preferred it that way. Or at least she thought she did. It had been the idea of him being there, only a foot away from her, but still separate that had bothered her. Two days of trespassing, two days of being left in his dust, yet Gabby was beginning to feel a connection. Sort of.

"Can't we have a normal conversation?"

"We could. If you were a normal woman and not a writer. But then, if you were a normal woman, this might be a date and we both know you wouldn't consent to that."

Just the word *date* made her nervous. "It can't be a date if neither person asked the other to be with them."

"Right. You didn't ask. You barged. Kind of like you did when you came to my house, then again on my beach. You know you what you are," he said shaking a fry in her direction. "You're a barger."

"That's not a word. But I have a solution. Tonight I'm not a writer or a date. Let's call me a tourist."

"And what am I?"

"You're the local. You tell me what it's like to live on an island."

He pulled another fry from the pile and chewed while he contemplated her suggestion. Because she'd already told him she was weak-willed, she didn't feel guilty at all about snatching one of his fries for herself.

It was delicious. Maybe a little more salt.

"Please, feel free," he said as she sprinkled some salt on one corner of his plate.

"You want a cucumber in exchange?

"Is that a joke?"

"Right. So, tell me what it's like here."

"It's quiet. What you would expect. A few small businesses, but most of the folks here are fishermen. Lobstermen to be exact."

"Lobster. That's right. This is Maine." It was odd. Suddenly Gabby felt like Dorothy emerging from her tornado-tossed house. She wasn't in Kansas anymore.

He scowled at her. "You don't know where you are?"

"I know where I am," she snapped. "I guess it just occurred to me where the place was. I've been more focused on the journey. By way of Philadelphia."

"So what happened?"

She wasn't sure what he meant and her face must have shown that.

"You. Here. The big story. Something sent you on your way. Turned you back into a newbie."

She shifted in her seat. Telling him the story wasn't as easy as it had been telling the women. "I got fired."

"And you're here to start your life over. I knew it."

"Something like that."

He shook his head and pushed away the plate. He'd devoured the burger and between the two of them they'd eaten every fry. Gabby took another stab at a tomato to counterbalance the fat.

"I'm nobody's do-over."

"I didn't say that. Look, at first I thought this was going to be a simple retrieval assignment for my boss. But I realize there is something more here. Something bigger. I don't want to write anyone's story. I want to write *yours*."

"You'll need to get used to the disappointment. Since I didn't order the burger I figure dinner is on you."

Vaguely, Gabby wondered how she might sneak it into her expense report. Although she didn't imagine McKay would mind her buying their meal ticket dinner. "Done. But you need to leave the tip."

"Why?"

"They won't take my money."

He slid out of the booth and dropped a five dollar bill on the table. "You better get used to that, too. Folks around here won't take kindly to what you're doing."

"What are they going to do? Kick me off the island?" She thought she'd made a joke. But he didn't smile.

"They might."

CHAPTER FOUR

"WHAT'S THIS?" GABRIELLA held out the neatly typed piece of paper to Susan the next day so she could see it clearly. "I found it under my room door this morning."

"Yes, dear. It's your bill."

"But isn't that typically something you give to someone at the end of their stay?"

Susan smiled and shrugged her shoulders. "I'm sure you've seen all our little island has had to offer. Surely you have all the material you need for your book. Your *fiction* book."

The jig was up. Either Zhanna or Adel had talked. Or word got out simply because that's how a small town rolled. Now Susan was trying to be polite and sweet while at the same time kicking Gabby out on her ass.

"I'll go pack my things."

"Yes, dear. I'll have your dry wheat toast waiting for you downstairs for your last breakfast."

Gabby nodded and went to clean out her room. After choking down the toast, she loaded the rental car with her suitcase. She'd changed into her running clothes since the plan had been to attempt another late morning jog with Jamison. She could still meet up with him, perhaps farther along the beach. Her unphysical fitness would prove to be a blessing in this case because she didn't need to worry about working up a sweat when she had nowhere to shower.

But she told herself not to be ridiculous. Surely there had to be some other place on the island where she could stay. A motel. Another B and B.

She would ask Jamison while they ran.

"Nope." Jamison puffed as they headed down the strip of beach together.

"No other place to stay on this whole island?"

"Not a one. Guess it sucks for you. Oh, well. You gave it your best shot. Good luck getting this career started in New York."

Gabby watched him go from warm-up mode to high-gear mode. In the space of a minute he was yards and yards ahead of her. Eventually she came to a stop. She caught her breath and kept walking only to realize Shep wasn't plodding along next to her. When she turned around she saw him lying on the sand.

Something about the way he was laid out bothered her though. She called for Jamison but he was out of earshot. No doubt trying to put her as far behind him as fast as possible.

Approaching the old dog, Gabby got down on her hunches. "Hey, are you okay?"

A soft wine and whimper was her answer.

She tried to give him a little nudge up on his feet but the dog only whimpered more. He wasn't moving. He certainly wasn't walking anywhere.

Now what was she supposed to do? Jamison wouldn't

loop back here for at least another forty minutes. She couldn't leave the poor dog sitting on the beach. And she sure wasn't going to wait around while something awful might be happening when she could have gotten him to a vet.

Decision made, Gabby began to use her foot to draw out some letters in the sand. That done she bent down and hauled what had to be forty pounds of German Sheppard into her arms and over her shoulder. As old as he was, he didn't carry a lot of weight, but still he was as much as she could handle.

"Okay, boy, stay with me now."

Carefully she made her way up the incline. Stopping a few times to catch her breath. This workout was way worse than jogging, but fortunately the old dog didn't fight her, just laid over her shoulder with an occasional whimper. No struggle at all in fact.

It made Gabby feel worse. Obviously something was wrong for the dog to be this complacent. Reaching the top, she spotted Jamie's truck. It would be a whole lot faster to use than making her way down the long driveway to where she left her rental car. Taking a chance Jamie was a leave-the-keys-in-the-car person—wasn't that a thing most small-town people did?—she opened the passenger door and settled Shep inside. The poor dog simply curled in on himself and closed his eyes.

Running around the car to the driver side she opened the door and checked the center console for the keys. Nothing. She lowered the sun visor and found nothing there, either. Last shot was the glove compartment otherwise she would have to move Shep again—something she didn't want to do.

Pay dirt. A fat key ring sat in the compartment but the car key was the heaviest and easy to identify. Partway down the drive, she realized when Jamie returned from his run he would need to follow her. She reversed to where her car was parked, dropped the keys on the front seat, then drove on.

She really had to hope the stuff about small towns being safe with low crime rates was true.

"Okay, Shep we're on our way."

Thanks to the coincidental meeting in the café last night, she knew the island had a vet. Of course, she didn't have a clue where his office was located. She figured she could simply drive into town and someone there would help her. If not for her, then certainly for Jamison's dog.

JAMIE KNEW THERE WAS something wrong when he reached his starting point. Shep should have been there waiting for him. Shep was always there waiting for him. And despite the fact he'd told her otherwise, he kind of thought Gabby would be waiting for him, too. He put his hands on his thighs and took some deep breaths. Walking it off for a while he whistled to see if maybe Shep had wandered into the bushes for a spell.

Then he saw the letters in the sand. Big letters hastily drawn that made his heart sink into his stomach.

SHEP TO VET

Running up the hill as if he hadn't finished a five-mile run, Jamie cursed when he saw the truck was missing. She had to know he would follow her so he took a chance and sprinted down the driveway. Her rental sat at the side of the road as if waiting for him. He opened the door and gave a soft yes when he saw the keys.

There was only one vet in town. Tom had been treating every animal on the island for the past five years. Even if Gabby couldn't find his clinic, anyone in town would know exactly where to find him.

PULLING OVER AT Tom's home Jamie felt a spurt of hope when he spotted his own truck already in the driveway. Good girl. Gabby had found the vet and hopefully Shep was being treated right now.

Jamie got out of his car and walked up to the home that used to belong to Tom's parents. They retired a few years ago to warmer climes in Florida, leaving the home to Tom to do with it what he chose. He wondered how they would feel about his decision to convert the place into an animal retreat. Personally, with Shep getting older, Jamie was grateful.

Just starting out and not having the money to keep up with both a home and an office, Tom had transformed the large house so that it now contained a shelter, a treatment room and surgical facility along with an apartment for himself.

With dread in his stomach, Jamie made his way through the empty waiting area and peaked beyond the sliding door into the treatment area. Shep was laid out on the table not moving and Gabby stood over him stroking his coat while tears ran down her face.

Right then he knew.

He knew and wanted to walk out and pretend this wasn't about to happen.

"Jamie, I'm sorry." This was from Tom who saw him in the doorway.

No longer able to avoid the situation, Jamie slid open the door and stood next to Gabby. Jamie took in the vet's sad expression and swallowed. Tom was good with the animals. He'd finished school and had come home to start his practice. Not something many people did after they made it off the island and saw what life on the mainland had to offer.

He was connected to the island and now to everyone's pets. He had a reputation for being kind and gentle. He also knew when an animal had come to the end of his time and he didn't sugarcoat the truth with the owners.

Jamie saw Shep's eyes were open and though he was breathing he wasn't moving at all. Not sitting up with his tongue hanging to the side and his tail wagging to greet his master. Jamie put his hand on the dog's gray muzzle and he felt a small lick on his fingers, but it was followed by a soft sighing whine.

"You knew this day was coming. He's nearly sixteen. For a German Sheppard that's really old. He had a good long life."

"Yep," Jamie said tightly. He looked then at Gabby, who was wiping her nose on her jacket. "What happened?"

"He wouldn't move. He just laid there whimpering. I didn't know what to do. I couldn't catch up to you."

Jamie nodded. "You carried him up the hill?"

"He was heavy, but he didn't fight me."

"That's because Shep knows how to treat a lady. Don't you old boy?" Jamie met Tom's sympathetic face. "Today?"

"He can't walk anymore, Jamie. You might be able to carry him around for a time, but—"

"No. He wouldn't want that. Can I have some time?"

"Sure."

Gabby mopped her eyes then looked as if she wanted to say something, but didn't. The two of them left the treatment room and Jamie said goodbye to the best friend he'd ever had. Even though he'd known this day was coming, the reality of it was way harder than he'd imagined. He knew this was the right thing to do, but selfishly he wanted Shep with him. As he stroked Shep's fur, Jamie said everything he could think of to reassure him, make him understand this would be okay. That *Jamie* would be okay. Finally, when he ran out of words, he called out for Tom to return.

After it was done, Tom told him he would handle the body. Shep would be cremated and Jamie thought he'd spread the ashes on the beach where the dog used to love to run. When he left the treatment room he was surprised to see Gabby still sitting in the waiting area.

His eyes were red and, while he wasn't ashamed to say he'd shed a tear for a fine and loyal dog like Shep, he was guy enough to be embarrassed by it. Clearing his throat he scowled and hoped his voice didn't crack. "You didn't have to wait."

"I thought you might need someone."

"I'm fine." He wasn't. But he would be. Shep had lived a long and good life. It was his time, and, like Tom said, this was inevitable. Jamie just hadn't counted on Shep passing today. He sure as hell wished he hadn't been off running, leaving the dog on the beach alone.

Of course, he hadn't been alone. Gabby had been with him. And she had petted him and soothed him until Jamie arrived. Shep had been comforted and cared for. That meant a lot to Jamie.

"Thank you."

She nodded and with the tissues clutched in her hands wiped her eyes again. "I have extra." From her pocket she pulled out a wad and held it out to him.

It was one thing for a man to cry over the loss of his dog. It was another to actually use a tissue.

"I'm fine. Here's your key." He tossed it over and she missed it, then handed him his key ring.

For a moment he stood not really knowing what to say or do. He'd thanked her and that was all he was obligated to do. Still, he felt like a pile of horse manure. After all, she had offered to give him some company.

"Maybe...maybe you could come back to the house. We can have a drink. A toast to Shep."

"Okay. That sounds like a good idea."

Silently they left the clinic and climbed into their respective cars. For the first time, she drove up the long driveway and parked next to his truck. When he opened the front door an overwhelming sense of wrongness hit him.

Something was missing. Some*one*.

He wondered how long it would be before he stopped expecting Shep to greet him every time he returned.

"Preference?" he asked over his shoulder as he made

his way to the kitchen. He didn't have a fancy bar. Just one cabinet where he put any alcohol he had on hand—usually only a bottle of Jim Beam and that old bottle of single malt Scotch he'd gotten as a Christmas gift one year. He knew he had some beer in the fridge and probably a bottle of wine somewhere. He hoped to hell she didn't ask for something like a margarita.

"Whatever you're having is fine."

He brought back two bourbons in short glasses and handed her one. She raised it in the air with a sad smile. "To Shep. Please tell me you didn't name him that because he was a German Sheppard."

"Alan Sheppard, first man in space."

"Much more appropriate. To Alan Sheppard."

Jamie's throat closed up again, but he nodded and took a deep gulp. The heat and fire running gave him a good excuse to cough out the hoarseness. He sat in his favorite chair and thought how it wouldn't be the same when he reached down to offer a pet because his friend wouldn't be there.

"There was a time when Shep was literally the only friend I had in this whole world. It was me and him against everyone. How do you repay an animal like that?"

"With love," Gabby offered. "I know after we lost our family dog I cried for three days."

"Did you ever get a new dog?""

She shook her head. "I never wanted to feel that way again. I knew Shep for five minutes and I'm sad."

He smiled. "Well, Shep did have a way with the ladies."

For a time they nursed their drinks and kept their thoughts to themselves. Eventually Jamie poured himself another and, without asking, filled Gabby's glass, as well. He had to admit she was good company for a time like this. Not chatty, not trying to say the right things. She was simply there with him and he thought he would be grateful to her for a long time.

Not that he had any plans to tell her. She'd probably try to turn it around and get him to confess his secrets as a result. That was never going to happen. His secrets were his and he intended to go to the grave with them.

"So what are you going to do now you've been kicked out of the B and B?"

Gabby sighed as though she'd just remembered she was homeless. "There really is nowhere else to stay on this island?"

"Nope."

"Not some rental cabins, something?"

Plenty of them, but none he would tell her about. Suddenly it seemed really important she leave now and not later. It was bad enough he'd been fantasizing about her for the past few days. Now he was actually beginning to like her and that would never do. Maybe if she was a regular stranger who wanted nothing more from him than a little time, a little conversation and, with a pinch of luck, some good sex. But Gabby really did want something from him, something big. She wanted to poke around at all that crap he'd locked away.

"Then I guess I'm going to sleep in my car."

"Your car?" Was she really that persistent? If so, what hope did he have of resisting her?

"You think I won't?"

There was a challenge if he ever heard one. "I think it would be uncomfortable and a complete waste of your time. Gabby, I'm never going to agree to this."

"There was a reason you took the advance in the first place. You wanted to tell your story."

She was right. He couldn't lie about that. The idea of a book held a certain appeal. He wanted to put it all down some place, written concrete proof that he'd been here—proof to the world of how far he'd come while, at the same time, offering tribute to the people who had helped him along the way. His life growing up in the backwoods of Maine, how he made his way out and into the Air Force Academy. He wanted to shout from the rooftops about what he'd done. Not necessarily about the rescue in space—he hadn't planned on that rescue and his actions had been a combination of instinct and training.

No, he wanted to talk about the other things in his life, all those achievements that took total mental focus and discipline to push himself to the next level and the next level. Something he'd done time and time again. It felt corny to say, but he'd been proud of himself and wanted the world to know.

Then *it* happened and suddenly all of his accomplishments were nothing more than ashes on the ground. It had been the darkest moment of his life. Worse than anything that had happened to him as a kid, or during his training at the Academy.

He couldn't share that humiliation and pain, that

sense of intense loss and failure. Not with anyone. Certainly not with the world.

"It isn't going to happen, Gabby."

She polished off her bourbon and squeaked a little. "At least now I have you calling me by my name. That's a positive."

"If you think so."

"I'm not going to stop. I'm not some wimp. I may not look like it, but I am tough. Real tough. When my father left us, I took over everything. Paying the bills, keeping our heads above water financially. Working extra jobs and staying in school while I did it. You know how I got through all that?" She stood as though to emphasize her point. "By being *tough*. Your stubbornness is not going to dissuade me."

He realized she was a little wobbly on her feet. Two drinks, no food, probably not very nice of him. "I'm sorry."

She looked at him blankly.

"About your father leaving you."

"Did I say that out loud?"

Oh no, Houston. We definitely have a problem. "You sit. I'm going to make you…" Since he had no idea what he had in his refrigerator he let that trail off. He made his way to the kitchen and was happy enough with what he saw. Ground beef and rolls would make for some pretty good hamburgers. She would probably get upset over the menu, remembering their shared meal from the other day. He would have to tell her they were diet burgers.

She followed him into the kitchen. "I think I'm a little woozy."

"No kidding. Sit," he said directing her to one of the chairs surrounding a small table for two. "I'll make you something to eat."

"That's nice. I only had toast this morning."

No wonder the alcohol had put her on her butt. Especially after the day she had. He looked at her sitting there still dressed in her running outfit, which made her look sporty even though he suspected she didn't have an ounce of athletic ability in her body. But she'd carried Shep up a steep climb and that said something about her heart if not her strength.

He formed the meat into patties. Then he plugged in his countertop grill. Normally, he'd fire up the barbecue outside but this was faster and since it advertised on being a healthier way to cook, it might make her feel better about eating ground beef on a bun. Because he was going to add cheese. There was no way to eat a burger without it.

Before long, the patties were cooked and Jamie added the condiments then served.

"This looks so good right now," she said with a half smile. "But you know I can't—"

"Eat," he ordered and did the same.

Hunger and wooziness must have won out over calorie counting because she took a bite and then another. He watched her and thought about the last time he'd been in this situation. Having a meal in his home with a woman he was attracted to. It felt uncomfortable and good all at the same time. Then he considered what she was feeling in return, if anything.

Did she even see him as a man or only as the means to an end? He recalled making the comment about their meal together at the diner being a date and the way she practically freaked out on him.

It wasn't the typical eyebrows raised look of a woman who simply didn't trust dating a known adulterer. It was more like the reaction of a woman who was simply afraid of men.

"So do you see your father at all?" Jamie asked.

Gabby put the burger down and nodded as she swallowed her bite. "Holidays and such. Not too often though since my half-sister got married."

"Don't like the husband?"

"I liked him well enough when I was engaged to him."

Jamie winced. "Ouch."

"Yeah. It wasn't pretty. In a weird way, I have you to thank for it, too."

This wasn't going to be good. He braced himself.

She finished the last bite, closing her eyes as though to savor the taste of it. The action made him instantly hard. Then she wiped the grease off her mouth with the napkin he held out for her.

"When everything was happening to you and the stories were all over the paper, at first I thought it couldn't be true. Then when it was proven true—those pictures of you at the motel with your wife and that woman... I thought no woman is safe. All men must cheat. So I started paying a little more attention to those late nights

Brad claimed to be working and the sudden weekend business meetings. I followed what turned out to be some pretty obvious evidence and at the end of the trail was him in a bed with my half-sister. At the time I wanted to write you a letter thanking you for saving me."

"That might have been the only letter I received that wasn't hate mail. I would have treasured it." He laughed to show exactly how serious he wasn't.

She looked at him with an expression he knew well. This wasn't condemnation or disgust. This was hurt. As though he had walked up to her and popped her balloon with a pin.

"Why?"

She wasn't the first to ask. And she wouldn't be the last he refused to answer.

"I think you need to go."

She gave him that wounded expression again. He was sorry for it, but he didn't change his mind. She was making him feel things he didn't want to feel. His emotions were a little too close to the surface at the moment. And his best way of coping, of containing those emotions was to get the hell out of this situation.

"You said you could spend the night in your car. Well, you're going to have to. You can't drive anywhere since I pumped you full of booze. And you can't stay here. So, the car it is."

"I can't stay?"

"No, because if you did, I might want to restore my image as a hero in your eyes just to make the hurt you feel go away. And that wouldn't do either of us any good because I'm nobody's damn hero." Yeah, that was true. But that wasn't the entire reason. And somehow he felt as though he owed her his full rationale. "You want to know the real reason I'm kicking you out?"

"Yes. No."

"Because if you stay here for another minute I swear I'm going to have you naked and underneath me."

CHAPTER FIVE

GABBY HUDDLED IN the backseat of the rental listening to the sound of rain hitting the roof. Heavy rain drops falling at a rapid pace. The word *deluge* would not be an inappropriate descriptor. It wasn't helping the headache she was nursing as the effects of the alcohol wore off and the hangover took hold.

Shifting, she glanced between the two front seats to see the clock on the dashboard. Barely after midnight. So much for being tough. Not much of that to be seen in the midst of the cold and fear.

And loneliness.

Great plan, Gabby. Come to Maine. Meet the legendary Jamison Hunter. Get him to write a book. No, even better, write the book yourself. Then maybe everyone will love you again.

What a joke. Instead she'd done nothing more than annoy him for a couple of days, get herself kicked out of a respectable bed and breakfast and his home. Not that it had been anything she'd done, she told herself.

Naked and underneath me.

The words had naturally stunned her. And frightened her. And turned her on. Jamison Hunter wanted her. What the hell was up with that?

A flash of white surrounded the car and two seconds later a crack of thunder sounded in the night sky. If it was possible, the rain fell harder.

Images of the rain turning into a river and the car floating off the island out to sea started to flicker through her mind. Those thoughts were slightly less terrifying than trying to imagine what being naked with Jamison would be like.

It would be awful. Not *him*. She was sure he'd be incredible. A man like him exuded sexual confidence and fierce physicality. No doubt his body was hard and rippled with muscles if the way he looked in his jogging clothes was any indication.

She could see it now, them together in his bedroom, stripping off each other's clothes, really into each other. Then it would take only a flash of her bare skin to remind her of everything she hated about her body. Her breasts were too big, her hips too wide, her butt...

Well, let's face it. A big reason she was huddled in a car on an island off Maine waiting to be swept out to sea by a deluge of rain was the size of her butt. She wondered what her replacement for *Wake Up, Philadelphia* was doing right now. Probably curled in some nice warm soft bed dreaming about how secure and happy her life was. Not even conscious of the day when it would all be ripped away.

Another flash of lightning flickered and Gabby huddled tight waiting for the thunder. It rattled. Then it stopped and she heard a pounding on the car window. Startled, she screamed and watched as the lightning flashed again and illuminated a large figure outside the car.

"Gabby, it's me. Open the door."

It took a moment for the words to penetrate through the adrenaline haze. Jamison was trying to open the driver's door and so she leaned between the seats and lifted the lock.

The door opened and a spray of rain followed him inside. He was wearing a rain coat but even from here she could see the walk down the driveway had soaked him. She'd moved the car away from the house so as not to be tempted to knock on his door late at night. But she hadn't gone any farther than the bottom of the lane in case there did happen to be a murderer lurking about the island looking for defenseless women sleeping in their cars...during a thunderstorm.

"You scared the crap out of me."

"Sorry. Give me the key. I'll pull up to the house. I didn't realize there was going to be thunder when—"

"You kicked me out?"

"Key, Gabby."

She reached into her pocket and handed him the key, but pulled it back at the last second. "Does this mean I'm going to have to have sex with you?"

Jamison was quiet for a moment. "Do you want to have sex with me?"

She snorted. "That's not a fair question. I've been fantasizing about Jamison Hunter for the past ten years of my life."

"Why? Why me?"

Because he was everything to her. Everything she

wanted to believe a man could be and he made her feel
safe. Hell, she even felt safe right now.

"You were heroic. Smart and handsome, brave and
daring. You were larger than life. But I also thought
you still might be someone who a person could sit beside and have a beer with. You made me feel safe in a
dangerous world." She stared out at the night, a little
too embarrassed by her honesty to make eye contact.
"Must seem silly to you."

"It does. What you saw was a fake image of me. A
caricature the news created. If they could have, they
would have had me walking around like a damn super-
hero. But I'm not talking about that guy and back then.
I'm asking, do you want to have sex with *me?* The man
you've known the past few days?"

That question was way more difficult. The answer
that leaped to her mind was something she really didn't
want to think about. So she went with her third thought.

"It would compromise my professional integrity."

For whatever reason he found that hysterical. She
waited until he'd stopped laughing so hard then handed
him the key. He drove up the winding hill to his home.
When they were parked next to his truck, he turned the
engine off and for a time they simply sat listening to
the thunder and the rain.

"You can have the guest room."

"Thanks."

Jamison didn't say anything more but she felt he
wanted to. He wanted a real answer from her and not
only because it might result in him getting laid. There
was something else there, a vulnerability she sensed in

him. And if that didn't make him a little more attractive, she didn't know what did.

He opened the door and made a break for the porch. She wasn't going to worry about her luggage and instead grabbed her purse and followed, squealing as the rain pelted her. Once inside, they walked through the house quietly.

"Do you want anything?"

"Just a bed." It wasn't hard to admit she was exhausted. The emotional roller coaster of the day had taken its toll and it wasn't like she had gotten any sleep in the backseat.

She followed him up the stairs which overlooked the spacious living area. From above she could see everything in one glance and noted it was definitely a man's home. All stark lines and manly colors. It seemed a bit formidable. There were no decorative pillows. A room where people lived needed the softness of pillows. Only the skylights, which were black tonight, suggested any whimsy.

The stairs opened to a hallway off of which were two doors.

"That's the guest room." He pointed. "Should be clean. I have someone who comes in every other week and, even though I tell her not to bother, she's a stickler for cleaning every room."

"Thanks." Gabby started toward the door and stopped. This wasn't going to be a good idea. In her mind she could already see how bad of an idea it actually was. But having your life ripped out from underneath you made a person a little more daring. When there was nothing to lose, there was also no fear.

"Jamie?" She turned and saw him standing there. His face was hard, but also a little sad. A little lonely. "If I were a different person, I would want to...you know... with you. The person you've been these past few days. I like this person. But I've been burned. Badly. And you, you're a—"

"I'm a cheater. I cheat," he said softly, sounding like a man who had spent his life whipping his skin out of guilt.

"Yeah, you cheat," she said. As much as he attracted her and fascinated her she could never let herself be involved with a man who, at heart, she couldn't trust.

"Goodnight, Gabby."

"Okay." She turned her back on him then and entered the guest room finding a light switch on the wall. When she closed her door he was already inside his bedroom. She hated herself a little bit for hurting the man even more. Because what she said had hurt him. She knew that. And no man deserved that on the day he had to put his dog to sleep.

BLINKING HER EYES OPEN, Gabby registered the sunlit room around her. For seconds she had no idea where she was, but really didn't care because she was completely comfortable. The bed was soft, the sheets were crisp, the pillow under her cheek was plump. She wasn't wearing her usual pajama bottoms and tank, instead a sports bra and her panties.

Had she gotten lucky last night?

Instantly the fog cleared from her morning brain and she remembered it all. Carrying Shep up the hill. Seeing tears in Jamie's eyes. Getting drunk with him, getting propositioned by him and then stabbing him through the heart with the truth she would never get involved with a man who she knew had been unfaithful to his wife.

Fun day.

And it wasn't really over. He'd been good enough to allow her to stay in his house rather than try to sleep in the car during a thunderstorm, but according to the sun filtering through her window, the storm had passed and he was probably downstairs waiting to boot her out again.

He wasn't going to let her write a book about him. She wasn't going to let herself have sex with him. Now all that was left to do was say her awkward goodbyes, slink back to New York with her tail between her legs and hope she could beg her boss not to fire her.

Today was looking even better than yesterday.

Groaning she rolled on to her back and wondered what would happen if she stayed in here all day. He wouldn't be so rude to throw her out wearing nothing but her sports bra and panties, would he?

Naked and underneath me.

Those words came alive in her brain and reminded her of his raw side. She figured she shouldn't take the chance. Climbing out of bed, she dressed in her running outfit. Given the long drive back to New York ahead of her, she was going to have to ask one last favor— use of a shower. She would grab her suitcase from the car, shower and change with a promise never to bother him again.

So why was she standing immobile in the middle of the room?

Because none of the options she'd outlined for today were appealing to her. Except maybe the shower.

Her cell buzzed from inside her purse and, as if it were some kind of magic fairy ready to provide some new answer to all her problems, Gabby pounced on it. When she saw Melissa's name hope turned into dread.

This was it. Probably best to give her boss a heads-up as to what was happening. Maybe ask if she would actually consider accepting the advance from Jamie, because Gabby was convinced nobody was ever going to get this story.

"Hey, Melissa."

"So, tell me. How are you doing? Still making progress?"

A hundred responses ran through Gabby's mind and ridiculously, foolishly, none of them were remotely truthful. Well, one was. "You are never going to believe where I am. I'm speaking to you right now from Jamison Hunter's guest room. He's asked me to stay with him."

"What? Seriously? As in stay with him while he tells you his story?"

"I can't think of any other reason he would invite me to stay, can you?"

"No." Melissa laughed. "I mean, why put up with a complete stranger if you aren't at least interested in the idea of having her do your story? Great job, Gabby. Way to get him to open up."

Gabby bit her lip and wondered if there were any lingering bolts of lightning from last night's storm that might be getting ready to strike her down. "Thanks. It hasn't been easy, but I think he's coming around."

Liar! Are you really so pathetic you would put off getting fired again for a few more days? A week at most?

The answer was obviously yes.

"Okay, well, look. We're going to need a commitment at some point. But I don't want to spook him. If he's opening up and working with you, let's go with that for now. Like I said before, I can't guarantee you the job of ghost writer, but any notes and prep work you do on this will be compensated. Does that sound fair?"

"Really fair." Especially since there wasn't going to be any notes or prep work. "Maybe a couple more weeks and I should have something concrete for you." *Like my resignation when I turn up in New York with nothing.*

"Two. I need to justify the expense of having you in Maine. Although I guess if you're his guest, it should considerably cut down on your expenses."

Melissa was laughing and Gabby tried to chuckle along with her, but all she could imagine was spending another two weeks in her car. Was it worth it? Two more weeks of dodging being a failure?

Again, yes. Two weeks would buy her time to think about her next step. Two weeks would give her time to plan. Two more weeks with Jamison Hunter. Gabby shook her head. What the hell was she doing?

"And if you could send me a picture or something, that would be great."

"You want a picture? Of Jamison?"

"Just something that shows you are where you say you are. I'm not doubting you. I'm not. I want to be able to show something to my boss so he can see we are finally making progress."

"I guess." How hard would it be to text Melissa a picture of the man? "Okay. Well, I think I smell breakfast."

"Listen to you. Jamison Hunter—at one point named the sexiest man alive—is about to make you breakfast. Are you freaking?"

Not half so much as when he told her he wanted to see her naked. That was full on freaking. "I'm cool. He's just a man, Melissa. He puts his pants on one leg at a time. Not that I've seen him put his pants on or anything—"

"Don't worry. I know you wouldn't let anything sexual happen between you two. Very unprofessional. Besides, I can't imagine you're his type."

Ouch.

"I'm sorry, Gabby. I really didn't intend to sound as bitchy as I just did. I just meant— I mean— He's Jamison Hunter. He's probably dating supermodels in between having actresses imported onto the island."

"No worries. You're so right. What would a man like him ever see in someone like me? Well, I should go. I'll check in, okay?"

"Okay."

Gabby ended the call and tossed her phone into her purse. It was done. She'd lied and bought herself two additional weeks. She felt as though she was in some weird limbo place. She didn't want to go back. She couldn't see her way forward. She wondered if this was how being a ghost felt.

She knew she couldn't hide out in the guest room forever. She had to have some courage. Opening the door she was hit by the smell of bacon.

Bacon was so good. A man who ran five miles a day could probably eat all the bacon he liked. Bastard.

"Jamie!" The front door opened and closed and from the second floor landing Gabby could see Zhanna glide—there really was no other word for it—across the living room. Jamie met her halfway out of the kitchen. He had an apron tied around his waist. It was yellow and for some reason made Gabby's heart stop.

Zhanna wrapped herself around him and he patted her back. "I'm *so* sorry about Shep."

"It's all right."

"But we all loved him. Even Adel, although she wouldn't let him inside the diner."

"I know. He was a good dog."

Gabby watched the scene and thought about what Melissa had said. She doubted Zhanna was a super-model who worked part-time as a waitress, but with her long, lean body and fascinating face it wasn't outside the realm of possibility. Yes, those two hooking up made way more sense than Gabby hooking up with the guy. Walking into the guest room, she grabbed her phone and tapped on the camera.

As she descended the stairs, she called to the two of them. "Hey, guys, say cheese."

They both turned in the direction of her voice and she snapped the picture. She looked at it as she got to the bottom of the steps, and felt her heart skip a beat. A horrible thud that reminded her she wasn't worthy. They looked really good together. As though they fit somehow.

"What the hell do you think you're doing?" Jamie barked. He moved out of Zhanna's arms and walked toward Gabby with purpose. She didn't even consider backing away because she couldn't imagine what would have pissed him off so much. He took the phone from her hand and started messing around with her pictures.

"Hey, it's just a photo. My editor wanted proof I actually met you."

His face tight, he handed her the phone. "It's deleted. Next time ask before you take a picture."

"What is *she* doing here?" Zhanna asked.

"I had to let her stay since Susan kicked her out of the B and B."

"Yes, Susan kicked her out. I told her who she really was. She lied to Susan and told her she was a fiction writer. What bull."

Gabby winced. She hadn't meant to lie to Susan, she'd simply wanted to spare herself the woman's disapproval. Really, it was the same with Melissa. Lying to seek approval and esteem from others wasn't the best habit to develop, Gabby knew. But apparently her self-preservation streak was alive and well.

"Look, I'm sorry," Gabby offered. "Can you appreciate my life is on the line here?"

Jamie barked a laugh. "No, sweetcakes, I cannot."

Fair enough. The man had been to war. Had risked his life in a space walk to save others. Lying to save her job wasn't exactly on the same level. "Okay maybe not my actual life, but my professional one and it's almost as important to me."

"You leave him alone." Zhanna growled the words in her heavily accented voice.

For whatever reason it was enough to piss Gabby off. She took an aggressive step forward. "Yeah, and what if I don't? What are you going to do about it?"

"Are you two serious?" Jamie stepped between them. "Enough. Zhanna there is bacon in the kitchen. Go make yourself some eggs and eat."

She left with a sulky pout and Gabby thought about what it would be like to slap her, even though she'd never hit anyone in her life before. Not even her half-sister when she was explaining why she and Brad were meant for each other.

"What are you doing?"

Gabby shrugged. "I don't know. I really don't know. I just— I can't go back. Not yet. Please don't make me go back."

He sighed. "Go upstairs and get your purse. I'll follow you to Susan's and I'll talk to her about letting you stay."

Gabby smiled. "You will?"

"Don't get all mushy about it. I don't know what it buys you other than more time away from your boss. I'm not going to do the book, Gabby. I'm never going to do it."

Gabby considered what he was saying. "Can I still meet you on the beach and run with you?"

"You mean for the whole five minutes you can keep up?"

"I was planning on going for six today."

Jamie shook his head. "What is it about you? Do what you want. It's a free country. But stay out of Zhanna's way, okay? I don't need the drama of you two fighting."

"I'm not really a fighter anyway."

"Could have fooled me."

Gabby ran upstairs to get her purse and Jamie called out to Zhanna that he would be back in a few. Gabby considered asking to stay for bacon, but decided she shouldn't push her luck. Then she pulled out her camera again. "About the proof I need—"

"No pictures. I hate having my picture taken. I especially hate it when I don't know it's coming."

That made sense. A man dogged by paparazzi would have some battle scars.

"How about this, then?" Gabby was pointing to the wall. It was the medal he received for service to his country. In a ceremony shortly after the space station crisis it had been pinned to his chest. There had been a brass band, the flag behind him and his wife at his side.

Now the medal was behind glass and looked very formal. She recognized the signature of the president at the time in the certificate below.

He looked at the medal, then quickly looked away as if he was embarrassed he had it hanging on his wall. "Sure. Whatever."

She snapped the picture then put away her phone. She

wondered at his behavior. She wondered about a lot of things when it came to Jamie. Good thing she had another two weeks to try and figure him out.

CHAPTER SIX

JAMIE HIT THE bell on what served as the front desk for Susan's inn. She came out of the kitchen with a dishrag in her hands and a smile on her face.

That is, until she saw Gabby.

"Hello, Jamie," she said stiffly. "I am very sorry to hear about Shep. I'm making you some muffins right now. Apple cinnamon to help you grieve."

Jamie smiled and remembered for the second time that day Shep wasn't sitting in the back of the pickup truck outside waiting for him. He wondered how long it would take to get used to his absence.

"Thanks, Susan. Listen, I need a favor. I need you to take her back."

The older woman huffed. "She lied to me. Said she was a fiction writer. I didn't know she was coming here to snoop on you. I know how you feel about snoops and such. I kicked her right out the front door. I said to myself, 'Susan, are you going to let this person stay in your establishment just because you don't have any other guests right now?' Then I answered myself, and said 'Certainly, I am not.'"

"Yeah, well, she's not a very good snooper. She can't get so much as a secret recipe out of me. She's just someone trying to not to lose her job. She can't stay with me and there's no other place on the island that's habitable this time of year." He still wasn't quite sure why he was helping Gabby. They were at an impasse on all fronts—she wanted his story, which he had no intention of giving her, and he wanted to have sex with her, which she had no intention of agreeing to. Absolutely no winning here. So why not let her go home?

"Can't she go home?"

"Hey, you know I'm standing right here," Gabby announced.

Jamie glared at her. A little less attitude would go a long way to convincing him to continue vouching for her. "You want your two weeks or what?"

"Sorry."

"Susan. As a favor."

Susan clearly couldn't resist. "You know I would do anything for you. If it weren't for you fixing my roof, Jamie, we would be closed for the whole summer season."

"She won't cause you any trouble." He hoped.

"Fine. I'll take her in and I'll feed her breakfast and keep her room neat, but I'm not promising my normal sunny welcoming service."

"I'll live," Gabby muttered.

"Thank you, Susan. I really appreciate this." He shot Gabby another look and mouthed the words *play nice*. "I'm out of here, then."

Heading outside he continued to mull over why he'd made it okay for her to stay here. He wasn't normally such a sucker for female desperation. Okay, check that. He was a sucker. A full-blown sucker.

But he thought he'd been working on it. Honing his bastard persona as much as possible so he would be left alone except for the few people on this island he cared about. Obviously squaring Gabby away with Susan wasn't going to win him any mean metals.

After what Gabby had done, being there for his dog when he'd needed someone, then waiting for him all day yesterday while he had to do the suckiest thing a person could do with a beloved pet, made her different in his mind.

She'd stayed with him. Drank with him.

Then she stabbed a knife through his heart by telling him she might have had sex with him if he wasn't a known cheater.

Yeah, Gabby was different all right.

The worst part was he knew she wanted him even before her hesitant confession. He was a man of a certain age. He'd certainly been around the block more than once. When mutual chemistry happened it happened. And between him and Gabby, it happened.

She wanted him. He wanted her. Period.

But she was letting his past get in the way and he couldn't say he blamed her. He'd had to accept what he did and what people, especially women, thought of him a long time ago.

In fact, he usually relished these moments. When he didn't get something he wanted, he thought it was good for him. A growing experience. A lesson in humility for a guy who, albeit through hard work and discipline, had gotten most of the things he desired.

Jamie had sculpted out an existence for himself that he thought he'd been in full control of. Control was everything in a pilot's world. It's how you climbed into the cockpit of an F-16 fighter and told yourself everything was going to be okay. Because you were in control of the machine. Even though in reality that control was a complete illusion.

Which is why when he was younger and things didn't go his way, he dealt with it poorly. Immaturely. Now as a grown-up, when things didn't go his way he prided himself on accepting it. The experience helped him to become a better person. At least he hoped so.

Only this time, not getting what he wanted—aka Gabby—annoyed him. Mainly because he couldn't stop thinking about what it would be like to get her to lose some of that self-consciousness and let loose in bed. Man, oh, man would that be a fun ride. Like a liftoff into space that rattled your whole body from teeth to nuts.

"Hey, wait up." Gabby quickly approached, her hair swinging.

He stopped as he reached his truck and thought again of what he might do with the long bouncing ponytail.

Let it go.

"So what time were you thinking of heading to the beach?"

He should tell her to get lost. Let her take the next few weeks to figure out what she was going to tell the people in New York and move on. It's not as though she was staying permanently so even if anything did happen between them, it wouldn't amount to more than a few good nights of sex.

A few very good nights of sex. Man, he missed sex.

It was time he stopped kidding himself. The truth was he'd kept her here for a reason. He wasn't quite ready to let this one go. "Usual time, early afternoon."

"Okay. So I'll see you, then."

"But here is the deal—"

"I need a deal to run?"

"You call what you do running?"

She frowned. "Fine, slow jogging. The question still stands—I need to make a deal to torture myself?"

"No, you can do that all you want. But if you want to talk to me, ask me questions, then there has to be something in it for me. You think you're getting closer to me so that I'll agree to the book. What do I get?"

"My scintillating company?" she suggested.

"Not quite the equal trade I had in mind." He looked her directly in the eyes so there would be no mistaking his intent. "I want the opportunity to seduce you."

She snorted. Then rolled her shoulders forward, then made an attempt at laughing.

"I mean it. I know what you said last night. I know trust is probably an issue with you and, on paper, I look like a guy who can't be trusted."

"On paper? How about on TV, on radio—"

"Yeah, I get it. But I'm still putting it out there. I'm going to try to seduce you. The way I see it, either my past is too big of an issue for you and we won't get busy—win for you. Or, if you were telling the truth last night and you do want me, then eventually I'll convince you to trust me enough to sleep with me. Win for me and, if I may be so bold, another win for you. If you're really worried about my past and are afraid I will succeed, you'll stay away. Also win for me."

Gabby glanced around. "I'm sorry. Did I suddenly find myself on the set of a bad romantic comedy? Is this some kind of joke to you? I told you how I felt."

"And I'm telling you how I feel. I want you, Gabby. Like hell on fire. Maybe because I'm a sucker for women in distress. Maybe because I can think of about fifty things I'm going to do with your hair once I get you naked. Maybe because it's been a long damn time and I'm a man and not a damn robot. You want to run with me? Fine. I'm going to use my—" he put his fingers up to make little rabbit ears "—charm on you."

She rolled her eyes and he smiled. At worst she was keeping his mind off Shep. Gabby was nothing if not entertaining.

"See you this afternoon. Around one."

"You think I can't handle a little *charm?* Bring it on. We'll see just how irresistible your *charm* is."

As funny as her trash talk was, he wasn't listening anymore. He was getting in his truck and shutting the door.

"I've interviewed charming men. Did I mention Kevin Bacon? He was very charming."

Jamie started the engine and cupped his hand to his ear as if to tell her he could no longer hear her. Then he held one finger up to remind her of the time.

She was still shouting something at him as he pulled onto the street and left the sight of her in the rearview mirror.

ZHANNA WAS POURING the eggs for the second omelet into the skillet when she heard the door open. "Good. You make perfect time."

"Smells good," Jamie announced as he walked into the kitchen.

"It is. I already ate mine."

"You know you don't have to cook for me."

She shrugged. "I like to cook for you. And you like to eat what I cook, so shut up and do it."

He laughed and sat at the table. They chatted while the omelet finished cooking, then she served it along with a heap of bacon and some wheat toast.

"So…" Zhanna said, sitting across from him. "Her?"

"Don't start with me."

"Why not? I can't help it if I'm protective of you. I mean, we have our thing and it's our special thing alone. But I think it gives me the right to tell you when I believe you are making a mistake."

"She's not a mistake yet. She's just a girl I happen to like who will be staying a couple of weeks at most. It's nothing permanent, Zee. A fling at best. You know I won't go there again."

Zhanna frowned. "So you told me. I think this is also a mistake."

"Well, then it will be my mistake. Like the thousand other ones I've made in my life."

Sensing his heels were dug in, she tried another approach. "What if she starts to really dig into your past, what then?"

"Zee, she's not going to find anything if that's what you're worried about. No one on the island will tell her jack and she's sure not going to get any real answers from me. All she'll get is what's already been printed about me." He wiggled his eyebrows as he took a bite of the omelet. "I'm going to impress her with my space stories."

"Yes, yes. Jamie—the big hero in space. I'm sure that will have her dropping her American panties in no time."

"Hey." He swallowed. "No panties talk. It's weird with you."

"Because you are not a grown-up. In Russia relationships are very easy. We are all grown-ups from very beginning of life. You have to be if you want to survive."

Jamie put down his fork. "Are you happy here, Zee?"

Such a strange question. "Of course I'm happy. I'm in America. I have own apartment, a green card and job. Ask any Russian and they will tell you this is a combination for a lot of happiness."

"Yes, but what about your dreams. What about meeting someone?" She started to protest, but he interrupted. "Yes, I know. We have our special thing. But this is a really small island and there is a very big world out there. If you ever wanted to leave and go see it, I would be okay with that."

She didn't like that his words hurt. She didn't like that, by him simply saying it, she felt a little lonelier. Now that she was here, she didn't want to leave. Didn't like him even thinking she could leave. "You want me to go so you can be with this other woman on your own."

"No," he said roughly. "What you and I have is not related to what I may or may not have with Gabby."

"*Gabby.* Blah. Sounds like a chubby girl's name."

"Zee. I'm trying to be serious."

Exactly. Serious was not for her. Serious was for people not trying to avoid their life, which she very much was. When you had no past and you could see no future it was best to stay in the moment. Zhanna felt there was never a good reason to make the moment too serious.

"I think you are grieving Shep and it is what makes you say all these things."

"Maybe. I'm not going to lie. I'm lonely without him."

"You could get a new puppy.'"

He shook his head. "I'm not ready. Shep deserves a little sadness on my behalf. It will make his life that much more meaningful."

Zhanna thought about her mother and how little time she'd actually taken to grieve. Yes, there had been sadness. There was always the sadness. But spending time and space letting herself be sad, that hadn't happened. There had been too much to do.

It made her feel serious all over again. That was the problem with Jamie. With him she always felt like their *thing* was a like a weight on both their backs. They easily carried it, but it was impossible not to be aware it was there.

"Okeydokey. I will leave you with your grief. But just know with this girl I see something there. In her eyes. She's desperate. And it's never a good thing to mess around with a desperate woman."

He smiled and gave her a wink, which meant he was absolutely not listening to her. Well, he would see and she would do what Adel called an I-told-you-so dance, which she would like very much, she thought.

Leaving Jamie's place Zhanna felt a little adrift. It was her day off and she considered what she might do with her time. Jamie's words about leaving the island and seeing the big world came back to her. Maybe she should take her used car—bought with her own money she was proud to say—and go as far across the country as it would take her. She could see this big place called America that was now her home and—

And what? Feel lost in it? Much like she had back home before she decided to come here. After her mother died there didn't seem any point in staying.

Again, she thought of her mother. Gone too soon from ovarian cancer. She had been a brilliant woman. A scientist. She loved her work and she loved discovery. When Zhanna was a child, her mother would leave her at the daycare and always say she was sad to kiss Zhanna goodbye for now, but there were big things for her to do that day. Answers she needed to find for the world.

Then when the cancer came, suddenly it was like someone had pulled a plug somewhere. Years of treatments, years of bad news, then worse news. Until finally in the end she was drained of everything. First her energy, then her passion, then her hope until finally death claimed her and left Zhanna wondering what to do next, where to go.

That was her past and she didn't want to think about it. Somewhere was her future and she didn't want to think about that, either. Too scary. Too uncertain. For now, there was only here.

With her car and her apartment. Her friends and her Jamie.

A sign on the side of the road caught her attention and she pulled over. She got out of the car and didn't hesitate even though Jamie had told her otherwise. She knocked on Tom's door then let herself inside.

"Hello?"

It seemed odd to her the man would live in a place where the door was always open to strangers. Although it wasn't like anyone on the island was actually a stranger. Still, during the summer season some off-islanders would stay in the cabins to fish and camp. She would tell him he should put a bell out front so people who needed him could ring first instead of walking into his home.

"In here."

The place smelled like animals. A mix of dog and cat and other things she didn't want to name. She could hear the woofs and meows chiming in from what had once been a dining room and was now a staging area for healing animals.

"Look, I've got my hands full. If you want to poke your head around the door—"

She did just that. A little hesitantly as she wasn't sure if she would find Tom elbow deep into some animal. Instead he was wrestling with what looked to be one pissed off kitten.

"Zhanna." She could hear the surprise in his voice and wondered why. After all she liked animals. It shouldn't be strange she might come to see them.

What she didn't like were doctors. Although he was a pet doctor, he landed on her list, too. He was a man who delivered sad news. Who made death happen. When he first started coming into the diner she would turn away from him and make Adel serve him. She didn't want to make small talk with a doctor. She didn't want to know anything about him that might make her rethink including him on her list. She didn't want to know how Mary, who owned the tackle shop, was doing after her precious kitten Teddy Bear had been put to sleep.

After weeks of his teasing her and hounding her for information on the daily specials and always sitting where Zhanna was forced to acknowledge him, however, he eventually wore her down. Tom was a hard man to hate. Still, she didn't like what he did for a living. She liked it even less today.

Maybe that's why it was a surprise to him she should be here.

"Come in. Maybe you could give me a hand. I gave Emily the afternoon off and I forgot what a handful Trixie can be. I need to give her a shot. Can you—"

Moving forward Zhanna took the little hissing bundle in her hands. Judging by Trixie's bandaged leg she'd gone toe to toe with some other predator and lost. Maybe she didn't realize she was small and defenseless. Silly kitten.

"There you go," Tom crooned. "Lean a little farther into me."

Zhanna wasn't sure who Tom was using his soothing voice on, her or the cat. She was leaning over the stainless steel examination table as far as she could. Meanwhile Trixie was butting her head against Zhanna in an effort to communicate how unhappy she was about her treatment.

"One second," Tom took a handful of fur in the back of her neck and slid the needle inside while pressing down on the plunger.

Trixie jerked but other than that held steady.

"All done. Give her to me. I'll put her back in her cage. Then we can talk about why you stopped by."

Zhanna handed over the cat somewhat reluctantly. The feeling of all the warm fuzzy fur pressed up against her chest had been nice.

This she thought was not a good sign. It meant she might be lonelier than she thought she was.

Following him to the other side of the house where the sounds of all the animals in residence could be heard, Zhanna was reminded of how tall Tom was. Taller than her, which at 5'10 was not always the case for most men. He wasn't a handsome man. His face was too long and his chin was too pointy. But he had a way about him that put people at ease.

Since he was often the bearer of bad news, Zhanna figured his demeanor made sense. You didn't want some uptight tense person relaying the news your dear and loyal friend of so many years was about to be taken from you.

Lifting Trixie into one of the second-story cages, Tom gave her a gentle pat on the head and then closed the cage.

There were four animals in residence. One tiny dog with a funny name for its breed, and three ailing cats including Trixie. A fairly robust business for an island of not many people. Then again islanders by nature tended to be loners. And loners loved their animals.

"So what brings you here?"

There was a look in his eye, Zhanna thought. Like he was excited by the prospect of something. She couldn't imagine what it might be.

"You killed Shep."

He winced and she admitted she could have phrased it better. She blamed it on her English, which could be perfect—when it suited her.

"I'm thinking Jamie would like a new dog."

Tom put his hands in his pockets and rocked back on his heels. "Did you talk to Jamie about that?"

Zhanna didn't want to lie. She also didn't want to tell him the truth. "Can't I see the new dogs? I won't make any decisions for him."

"Yeah, okay. I'll walk you out to the kennel." Tom headed for the rear of the house and out the door. In the backyard there was a separate structure, which had probably been a garage but that he used as a kennel. Half the small building was for the cats, the other was for the dogs. He also had a gated piece of land beyond for the dogs to have play time. She could see the yard was littered with chew toys and wondered how much of the money he earned went toward the animals in his care rather than into his own pocket.

"I don't really have many now," Tom said as he led Zhanna to where she could see two dogs currently napping in the sun. "We don't get a lot of strays here like they do on the mainland. All I have are two puppies from Jerry's litter nobody adopted. I was considering bringing them to a shelter on the mainland where they might have a better chance. They're close to a year now and once they lose the cute puppy look, it's a harder sell. But they're good dogs. Real good."

Zhanna saw the dogs wrapped around each other, their snouts in the other's chest, and she ached a bit.

"They're a mix of Lab and Border Collie so they need space to run. Might be a good fit for Jamie if he's ready."

"Why do you say *ready* like that? People are always ready for a new friend in their life."

She could feel Tom looking at her fairly intently. "Are they? I've been trying to make friends with you for almost a year now. But you haven't seemed ready to me."

She scuffed her feet in the dirt. Over her shoulder she could see another structure, short and square with a chain-linked fence around it, too. The crematorium, she knew. The place where Shep had been destroyed.

And Jamie's heart with him.

"I don't like doctors," Zhanna mumbled.

"Good. Neither do I."

She glared at him. "I don't like pet doctors, either."

"Oh. Thank goodness it's the job. I figured it was because I always smell like someone's shaggy mutt."

Zhanna sniffed. He did smell a little wild. Nothing cultured or sophisticated about Tom.

"Anyway, I think a new dog will help Jamie."

"Jamie had Shep for a lot of years. Sometimes you want to take some space to grieve. Your heart is in the right place, though. Maybe in a couple of weeks or months Jamie will change his mind." He paused then turned to her. "Can I ask you a pretty blunt question?"

"Of course. I have no problem with blunt. It's easier than subterfuge."

He nodded as if he approved. "Okay. What is the deal between you and Jamie? I get you are friends. But are you more than friends?"

Instantly she felt the muscles in her back tense. "Why are you asking?"

"Well, if you can get over the fact that I'm a pet doctor, maybe I could take you out to dinner sometime. Some place nice on the mainland."

She heard the words, saw the excitement in his eyes that had been there when he'd first realized who had walked through his door and did what any sane woman who had just been asked out on a date by a pet doctor would do.

She mumbled something half in Russian about being late for work and then bolted.

CHAPTER SEVEN

"AND IN OTHER breaking news, plans are being made to send a rescue shuttle to the now critically ailing space station. The international community responsible for the station is seeking advice from NASA, the only organization to have attempted a mission of this nature before. Many remember Colonel Jamison Hunter's daring rescue of the fourteen men and women aboard the space station almost ten years ago."

A picture flashed on the television screen a couple of days later and Gabby, who was in the process of tying her running shoes, sat on the edge of the bed to watch.

That was the picture all right. The one of Jamison in his Air Force uniform staring intently out at the world. Not a hint of a smile. So serious, so stalwart. Of course he rescued all those people. Gabby had fallen in love with that picture. With the *idea* of him.

Then another picture flashed on the screen.

"Of course most also remember Hunter's fall from grace two years later when he was caught by his wife while at a motel with another woman."

Gabby remembered that picture, too. It was taken by a fan, of all people. A young kid who had recognized Jamie and wanted a shot of him. Instead, the guy got a picture of Jamie's horrified wife and Jamie coming out of a motel room, while another woman in a precarious state of dress looked on from inside.

It didn't occur to the boy why Jamison Hunter might be found in a motel room off the highway outside of Cape Canaveral. After all, he was happy to see his favorite hero.

It wasn't until his father realized the potential money to be made from the picture that the situation all started to snowball. Ending only when a hero had been brought to his knees.

Gabby thought of the broadcast she'd just watched. A report about a failing space station, lives at risk, a rescue mission being formulated all ending with *let's not forget Jamie was a cheater.*

She imagined the second picture would dog him for the rest of his days. Always the story of his heroism to be followed by the story of his downfall—the two permanently linked in the public's mind. It rubbed her the wrong way. Like a piece of sand in her shoe. Annoying, but not really worth the effort of trying to remove it.

Finishing with her shoes she bounced down the stairs of the B and B and stopped when she saw Susan cleaning the windows of the front door. Gabby had managed to avoid the woman since Jamie had muscled her back inside the place. She'd bought a box of Pop Tarts from the grocery store and had been eating those for breakfast. Not exactly the well-balanced food someone trying to start a running regime and get into shape should be consuming, but it was uncomfortable to have a woman who didn't particularly want you in her establishment serving your food.

Of course that wasn't stopping Gabby from frequenting Adel's. She knew it pissed Zhanna off to serve her dinner, but Gabby was taking a perverse thrill in it. It was like poking a tiger. Or perhaps a Russian bear. She had a feeling one of these days her grilled chicken salad with dressing on the side was going to end up on her head, but she couldn't seem to stop herself.

Facing the reality that if she was going to leave through the front door, she was going to have to engage the hotelier, Gabby lifted her chin and threw back her shoulders.

"Morning, Susan. Fine day, isn't it?"

A muttered humph and more squirts from the glass cleaner bottle were the only response.

"I'm going to meet Jamie for a run on the beach. Sort of becoming a habit for us."

This time Susan replied by vigorously wiping what she had recently squirted.

Persistent, Gabby continued. "It's almost like we're becoming friends."

In a flash Susan whirled around with the spray bottle in her hand and aimed it at Gabby. Her finger was pressed against the trigger and ready to fire. Gabby held up her hands in surrender to the woman wielding the window cleaner.

"Don't you talk about friendship to Jamie with me. I know better. You lied to get close to him and now you're going to use him for some sleazy tell-all."

"Susan, I know I lied to you about what I was doing here. But the only reason was because I could tell people were really defensive when it came to Jamie. I needed a place to stay. To work."

"You're darn tootin' we are defensive. We know who Jamie is. We're his friends. And we know what he went through all those years ago. I don't want to see that happen to him again."

Gabby dropped her hands realizing the woman didn't have it in her to shoot. "That's my point. You all know him and seem to have his back. Which makes me think there is more to the man than the cheating adulterous scumbag he's been painted to be."

Susan's eyes narrowed and Gabby could see she had said the wrong thing. She hadn't meant to. She just wanted to get out of the house and go for a run with Jamie. So maybe she could learn about him what these other people had learned and know him the way the world didn't.

Solely for the purpose of convincing him to let her write his story. Only for that. There was no personal gain for her. And if she believed that…

"Jamie said I had to let you stay here. And Lord knows I owe him enough favors I'll do what he asks. But I'm telling you again if you hurt him, you'll hear about it from me." Susan made a jabbing motion with the bottle and Gabby backed away as she stormed off abandoning the windows. Knowing nothing she said was going to make a difference, Gabby trotted off to her car on her way to meet Jamie.

"I'M READY. I FEEL like I can run miles today. Maybe even two."

Jamie shook his head. Newbies. It had been two days

since he declared his intentions toward Gabby. Either he didn't make a compelling case that his seduction methods were near lethal, or she really wasn't interested and thus unafraid. Because she continued to show up, like clockwork and give it her best effort.

She could hang with him now for almost a mile. When he'd told her she made it a mile yesterday she instantly stopped to give herself a round of applause. Then he asked if she wanted to keep going to which she replied "Hell, no," and walked down the beach toward her car.

She was obviously a woman who liked to take the time to celebrate the milestones.

Today she was bouncing around with the energy of a younger woman and she did look ready to take on the world. He probably figured the least he could do was explain how not ready she was. He didn't imagine it would go over very well as a seduction attempt, but at least he would get to do bendy things with her and that was always fun.

"Okay, it's time to take this seriously."

She nodded. "Yes, that's what I'm talking about. I'm ready to go. Let's go. I feel good. Yesterday one mile, tomorrow a marathon. Who knows what I can do."

He didn't snicker. It wasn't cool and women didn't like it. "If you're going to run on a regular basis, you need to learn the basics of stretching. All you do is lift your legs a few times and then jump around. Not that I'm not enjoying the bouncing—it has its advantages in your case—but it's not exactly doing your muscles any good."

Gabby waggled her finger at him. "Is that supposed to be a seduction? Because, dude, telling a woman her boobs are bouncing when she's wearing a sports bra is not exactly going to win you any points."

"We'll call today a seduction-free zone."

"Because I've had such a hard time resisting up until now." She smiled to lessen the blow and he smiled back.

Damn, he was starting to like her. Not good. That's not what quick flings were about. They were about heat and passion and goodbyes. They weren't about jokes and fun and teasing.

"Will you listen to me?" He tried to make his tone stern because, joking aside, she really did need to take care of herself or risk injury.

"If you say something worth listening to."

"You need to stretch. Correctly. I do this up at the house, so you don't see it. First, you want to focus on your hamstrings." He indicated the muscle above his knee that ran the length of his thigh to his butt and watched to see if she actually followed the motion all the way up.

She did. He so had her and she didn't even know it yet. Instruction and seduction in one smooth move.

He stretched his leg in front with his heel up. She copied and he pushed down slightly on her lower back to get her into the correct position.

"Now hold this for a few seconds and breathe."

"It hurts." There was a touch of whininess in her voice.

"Because the muscle is loosening."

He took her through the other leg then they moved

on to calf and Achilles stretching. She grumbled but did what he asked and if he touched her more than was necessary to put her body into the correct position, well, all was fair since he'd told her upfront what his intentions were.

Seduction-free zone. As if such a thing existed.

She looked fine in black spandex bending her body in half to reach for her toes. She might think her butt was big or her hips were wide or whatever, but all he thought was *hello.*

"Why is Susan so loyal to you? What did you do for her?"

The question took him completely off guard. He was thinking sex and she mentioned Susan. The sweet lady who ran the inn and sex occupied such opposite sides of his brain it jangled him for a moment.

"Ah, Susan." What could he say? He certainly wasn't going to reveal any of her secrets—wasn't his place. But sometimes the best way to make a question go away was to answer it. "She was having some financial issues— the roof was leaking. So I helped her out."

"Is that what you do here? I mean, for a living. Do you lend people money or something?"

"Stretch the other calf," he told her and watched her mostly get it right. She was trying to merge yoga or dancing into what was supposed to be a simple stretch.

"So do you?"

"No, my job is not to lend people money. I'm not a bank. Yeah, I had a pretty good income back in the day and I was able to save. And before my reputation went to shit I was doing speaking engagements of up to fifty-thousand dollars a pop. Now I collect a government pension. I don't need to work. Whatever I do around the island I do to keep me busy and help the locals out."

"You don't get bored? You were an astronaut. Going from that to a jack-of-all-trades guy seems like a pretty big step down in the excitement factor."

"Let's go," he said as she shook off the last of her stretches. They started at an easy pace, one catering to her. He wasn't going to kid himself and say he adjusted his pace for any other reason than to keep her with him longer. He liked the company. Especially now Shep was gone. Even if he wasn't going to answer half of her questions, he liked the distraction she provided.

In the past few days he'd come to realize he had relied too much on his dog for companionship. Had Gabby not been around to fill the void left by Shep, he couldn't say how hard he would have taken the loss.

Jamie knew why he'd sentenced himself to life in isolation. He had even convinced himself he preferred it. It wasn't until Gabby arrived that he suspected he was missing something. He should be annoyed with her, but he was honest enough with himself to acknowledge he needed this.

He needed a kick in the butt. Something to push him out of his daily rut. It had taken years to adjust from being an astronaut to, as Gabby so succinctly put it, a jack-of-all trades. Tough mental conditioning to learn how not to miss flying, adrenaline and, even though he was loath to admit it, the spotlight.

It wasn't the national spotlight he craved. But the one shone on him by his peers. He respected the intelligence and talents of the elite teams he'd worked with. Their acknowledgement and recognition he'd done something better than so many others did…yeah, he'd liked that.

It was hard to not miss it. But hard was his wheelhouse. It's where he lived.

"After being an astronaut, anything is a step down. If it wasn't handyman, it was going to be something else equally as unexciting."

She snorted, but because she was breathing harder it came out more as a coughing choking sound. "I don't believe you. You could have stayed with the Air Force, maybe been promoted to general. You could have gone into politics or business. You're a natural leader. That's evident about you."

"Yeah, and now I lead the island." The words came off his lips and when he heard them he realized it was true. It wasn't strapping himself to a volatile rocket and shooting into space, but it had its perks.

Like loyalty. Like acceptance. And a sense of community. All qualities he'd had in the world of space exploration.

However, here on the island, the loyalty and acceptance also came with responsibility.

They approached an aging dock. Jamie did the usual scan of the area and frowned when he got the expected result. He jogged toward where the dock extended over some protruding rocks and stopped.

"Oh, thank God we stopped."

He disregarded his partner's mumbled prayers and shouted. "Bobby Claymore, you get off that dock right now."

"Ah, but Mr. Hunter, Mr. Neely says—"

"I don't care what Ted says. If he's going to let kids try to lobster off the dock, then he's going to have to repair it. It's not safe. Let's go. *Now.*"

The kid scrambled, gathering up his pot and heading for the security of shore.

"Wow," Gabby said bent in half, trying to restore normal breathing. "That was a total dad voice."

The flash of pain ripped through him almost stealing his breath.

"Hey, are you okay? I didn't mean—"

"I'm fine. Just annoyed. I've been telling Ted to either restore the dock or tear it down. I would do it myself, but the man is so damn stubborn and it's his property. I'm sure if he saw me coming with a saw in my hand, he'd have his gun ready. Seventy-five years old and he thinks he can still do everything."

"See, there it is again."

Jamie turned toward the beach. He had another few miles to go. She'd gone nearly two today and would probably be proud if he told her. Some last lingering bit of irritation had him holding back, though.

"Are you done running?"

"Hell, yes. And don't think you can avoid what just happened."

He didn't want to contemplate what she'd said about him having a dad voice. Some things were better left suppressed. He was old-fashioned like that.

"Once again, you're charging to the rescue."

Oh, that was what she meant. "Rescue?"

"You got the kid off the dock."

Jamie laughed. "Big deal. Kids go where they're not supposed to and adults should be around to tell them to knock it off."

Gabby shook her head. "I'm just saying it doesn't fit with someone who did what you did to your wife. And I don't like it when puzzle pieces don't fit."

"Will you stop trying to analyze me," he snapped. "Seriously. There is no grand revelation at the end of this story. I am who I am."

Again she shook her head this time not looking at him, but at the kid who had scrambled past them with a negligent salute. Bobby Claymore thought Jamie was still someone who needed to be saluted.

"I don't believe it. Adel, Zhanna, Susan, they are all so fiercely loyal to you. I sat in my room this morning and watched the news. They talked about you, did you know that? Showed your picture and mentioned the current rescue mission for the space station. Then two seconds later they're showing another picture."

Jamie knew that one. A run-down motel outside of Canaveral. Pain, betrayal, confusion all captured in one very clear picture taken by some kid.

"It's not right the second story should always follow the first. And the more I get to know you, the more I realize how wrong it is. This isn't about me needing to write your story. This is about you needing to *tell* your story. You need people to see who you are so they stop showing the second picture."

He actually believed her. This wasn't about her and what the book would mean to her career. She truly was pissed off on his behalf.

Hands on her hips, ponytail swinging, she was all fired up. The sun was turning her nose red, but the color in her cheeks… That was all from her passion. She wanted to save him. He could see it in her eyes. Either that or she desperately wanted to believe he was somebody else. He couldn't let that happen.

"Gabby, the second picture is as much a part of me as the first."

"That can't be true," she whispered.

"Why? Because it makes it harder for you?" He took a few steps closer until he could capture her red cheek in his hand. It was soft to the touch and made him believe for a second they were two much younger people.

Two kids who didn't have a whole history of shit behind them.

"A person can't be two things," she said stubbornly but didn't pull away from him. "You're either one or the other."

"And what about mistakes?"

He couldn't determine if the sound she made was a laugh or a sob. "Mistakes? Like falling out of love with your wife and in love with another woman? Leaving your daughter so you could go have another one? Deciding you like one child better than the other? Mistakes like those?"

Yeah, there was a whole river of shit that flowed behind Gabby. And she was going to have to wade through it if she wanted to find herself on the other side of it with him. Part of him knew it was unfair. Wrong to make her feel one way when she was so committed to holding on to mistrust and bitterness.

But as she'd said, a person couldn't be two things. He believed that about Gabby, as well. She couldn't be hard and cynical about men when she was so soft under his palm.

She'd stopped talking and was staring at him, waiting for him to move. Her breath came in shallow puffs and he thought if he moved too quickly or pulled her toward him too sharply, she would bolt.

"Gabby." He sighed as he dipped his head a little closer so his lips hovered above hers. Now he could feel her breath on him and almost sense the plump ripeness of her lips. She didn't lift her head to meet his kiss, but she wasn't pulling away, either.

"Do you want this?" he asked, even as he moved in to gently bite her lower lip. He heard her groan. He licked the spot he'd bitten. Oh, yeah, this was going to be good. Hot and delicious and good. "Do you?"

"I…think…maybe…yes."

"Then you're going to have to forgive me."

CHAPTER EIGHT

"Hi, Mom," Gabby said when her mother answered the phone.

"Oh, thank heavens. I haven't heard from you in two weeks. I called your office and they said you were on assignment. I thought, what the hell does an editor go on assignment for. I was afraid you'd been let go again and didn't want to tell me."

Gabby laid on the bed in her room at the B and B and let her mother go off for several minutes while she simply listened. She heard anxiety and worry and she hated she'd added those emotions to her mother's voice. It was one of the reasons she'd avoided calling her since arriving on the island and jeopardizing the one job she'd managed to find. That and she didn't really have any good news to share.

It wasn't that her mother didn't want to hear the bad stuff; they had both been through enough of it to know there was no avoiding it. Gabby simply didn't like to talk about those things with her mother. Somehow it made the situation more real.

"No, I'm really on assignment. In Maine."

"Maine? So you haven't been fired?"

Not for at least a week and a half. "Not today, Mom."

"I'm afraid I have some news, then. I certainly wasn't going to tell you if you were out of work again. It's why I was frantic when I couldn't get in touch with you. I didn't want you hearing this from anyone else."

Gabby sat up and gripped her cell more tightly as the knot in her stomach twisted.

"Kim is pregnant."

Gabby took the blow with relative ease. She knew it was inevitable. Kim had made no secret after she and Brad got married that she wanted to start having kids as soon as possible. That it had taken them this long meant Kim was probably over the moon excited.

When Kim had gone year after year without conceiving, Gabby tried really hard not to think karma was intervening and denying the couple what they wanted as payback for cheating on her. *Really* hard. Because that would make her a bitter person and Gabby didn't want to go there. Bitter people were no fun to be around.

It seemed the karma gods had been sufficiently paid. Kim was pregnant and Gabby made the conscious decision to be happy for her. Happy that Kim got everything she wanted from life even if it came, in part, at Gabby's expense.

"Your father said you would take the news better coming from me than Kim. I told him he's an ass."

Gabby smiled. Years ago Elizabeth Haines had taken the news of her husband's affair and resulting child like a seasoned prizefighter. Emotionally, she took blow after blow without a whimper or a tear as far as Gabby could remember. She kept things sane and peaceful without all the drama usually associated with divorce and she made sure Gabby maintained a relationship with her father, even when she didn't want one.

Where Elizabeth fell apart was the business end of life. Not knowing how to write a check or how to keep track of what bills were due when. How to figure out the amount of money they needed in a month to live so she knew what to ask for in alimony and child support. Elizabeth had married right out of college and went from wife to stay-at-home mom in a year. As she'd put it, there was never any reason to bother with the household bills. That was the man's job.

Until the man left you high and dry for a new family. And the divorce settlement, while fair, left Elizabeth and Gabby struggling to keep their heads above water and maintain the house Gabby had grown up in. Her mother had been adamant about not selling and Gabby did what she needed to do to make sure her mom got her wish.

Beyond the extra part-time work she took on after school, Gabby also learned how to handle the bank account and bills. She took lessons in car repair, basic plumbing and electrical work, too. She could change a tire, replace a leaky faucet and install a new ceiling fan all on a balanced budget.

And Elizabeth always knew when to come in with a pint of ice cream and put her arm around her daughter's shoulder and tell her everything was going to be all right.

They were a team. One, the bedrock of emotional stability and the other just…stable.

Suddenly Gabby felt guiltier about not telling her

mom what was really happening in her life. She was on the verge of losing another job and worse, she was becoming romantically involved with a man known for cheating on his spouse. Not anything to write home about.

"Are you still there?"

"I'm here. Mom, do you think Gram was really unhappy her whole life?"

"Uh-oh."

Gabby winced. She knew bringing up the subject of Gram now was probably not a good indicator she was okay with Kim being pregnant. But this wasn't about Kim. It was about Gabby herself.

Her history with infidelity and what it meant all started with Gram. Gabby would never forget when, after Grandpa's funeral, everyone gathered at the house for lunch and Gram stood in the middle of the living room and introduced everyone within earshot to Grandpa's mistress of twenty-plus years.

Gabby, ten years old at the time, asked her mother what a mistress was. When Elizabeth wouldn't tell her Gabby asked her classmates at school. Fortunately, she had some very worldly classmates.

"No, I think your Gram was angry."

"Isn't that the same thing?"

"Not necessarily. She wanted to hold on to her anger. She wouldn't let it go, which means it must have brought her some satisfaction and that's not unhappiness."

"You figure that's why Dad thought it was okay? Because his father did it meant he could do it, too?" Not that family tradition made it right. If your father robbed a bank, you would have to know it wasn't an okay thing to do.

"I think your father fell in love with someone else. It's really as simple as that. He didn't let it go on for years. He could have. I sure wasn't aware of what was going on. He met another woman, fell in love and wanted to be with her more than me. It says something that he's still with her now."

Gabby rolled her eyes. "How can you be so serene about it? It was wrong and unfair. He fell in love with you first."

"Hon, I know you're going to have a hard time believing this, but I'm happier because your father left me than I would be if he'd stayed with me while loving someone else. That's the truth. I've moved on and had relationships with other men who I have really enjoyed. Who made me feel good. Can you imagine trying to stick it out with someone who doesn't want to be with you? *That's* unhappiness."

"You never remarried," Gabby pointed out.

"Yet."

This made Gabby smile. Elizabeth Haines: ever the optimist.

"Are you going to be okay?" her mom asked.

"I'm fine." At least with the news regarding Kim and the baby. It was the truth, too, which felt good. "I'm happy for Kim. She really wanted this and I'm glad it all worked out."

"You're going to have to be there you know. For all of it. The baptism, the first birthday, high school graduation."

Good point. Maybe all moms had the skill to lay out the truth in a way where you couldn't look away from it. Gabby couldn't look away from a future of holidays and birthday parties with Kim and Brad and their child. The happy family. She swallowed, then sucked it up.

"I get it. Aunt Gabby. That's all I'll be now. That's all I should be. I was sort of getting tired of the role as the jilted fiancé anyway. Made everything so awkward. This will be better. Babies fix everything."

"I raised a really good kid."

"I had a really good mom."

After some more chatter about meaningless things like a leaky window and electric bills—Gabby still worried about her mom when it came to the day-to-day stuff—they hung up.

She felt stronger somehow. More ready to face whatever was coming next.

So strong she thought she was even up for a meal at the diner.

Only Zhanna was apparently not up for verbal sparring. The girl was walking around the tables, serving food like a zombie. The smile and hellos were so disconnected she didn't even realize she was smiling at Gabby at one point.

Until Gabby said something and immediately the smile turned to a frown.

"Haven't I been rude enough to you to make you not want to come here?"

"You have. But this is the only place on the island that serves a decent meal besides breakfast. I need to be strong. Not that I think I need any ammunition to-night. You look a little worse for wear. Are you okay?"

She wasn't sure why she asked. Zhanna had made her disdain for Gabby very evident. And it was possible she was sparring with a woman who could be her rival for Jamie's affections.

If she were interested in romance with Jamie.

Which, of course, she shouldn't be. Even though her mind, her body and her freaking heart were telling her differently.

Argh! Gabby shouted silently in her head. At least she hoped it was silent. She didn't appear to be startling any of the other diners so that was a good sign.

Zhanna plopped onto the booth seat opposite Gabby, her pad and pen sprawled on the table. "I'm not okay."

Awkward. Gabby looked around for someone more appropriate to listen to the woman's problems. Someone like Adel. Or maybe Susan would come in. Or, hey… was that Tom who just walked in? He seemed like a nice enough person. A good listener.

But when Zhanna looked up at the sound of the bell, she made a squeaking noise, which suggested Tom was not someone she wanted to speak to. She shrugged as if to indicate he could sit anywhere he liked.

He smiled.

She scowled.

Gabby didn't know what to think. "Guy problems?" Because, let's face it. With women, nine times out of ten men were usually the source of their issues. She was a rarified exception to that. Since Brad, she'd built her life around making sure her problems weren't guy problems. Until now.

"Why do men have to be men?"

"To avoid being women?"

Zhanna's eyes narrowed. "You tease me now? When I tell you I am unwell?"

"Look, if you're having problems with a guy…with guys," Gabby corrected thinking about Jaime, "you're talking to the wrong person. I don't have any good advice."

"I don't need your advice. Or anything. I don't need anything from anyone. Why would you even think I did? I was tired and I sat for a moment. Excuse me."

Before the woman could stand Gabby reached out and touched her arm. "I didn't mean it like that. I didn't mean to say I wouldn't listen, only that my advice would be questionable. I'm not very good in the guy-problem department."

Zhanna was clearly suspicious.

"Look, clearly something is bothering you. If you want to tell me, you can and I'll listen."

"I can't speak of this to anyone else on this island. Everyone on this island knows everything, hears everything, sees everything. You're an outsider."

"I get it. You need to talk to someone who isn't going to tell Tom you've got a crush on him."

Zhanna yelled an inarticulate sound trying to stop the words from traveling farther than the booth. She whipped her head around quickly to see no one heard and Tom was still safely seated at the counter. Adel had come out and was taking his order. "*Crush.* It is a silly word."

"No, it's perfect. Nothing sounds good about a crush. It reeks of falling, pain and breaking on a massive scale."

"You are correct. You are no good at this."

Gabby smiled. "Why is it hard? Do you not think he likes you? I mean, the guy is in here all the time. Could be he likes something more than the food."

"Like you said, there is no other place on the island. But yes, I think, maybe he eats at the counter always because I usually handle the counter customers. And I think maybe he likes me because he wanted to know about Jamie. Everybody always wants to know about me and Jamie."

Add Gabby into that mix. She definitely wanted to know about Zhanna and Jamie.

"Also I think he might like me because he said he wanted to take me on a date."

"Okay of all the things you mentioned, that last one right there…that's a pretty clear indication he likes you. So this is easy. You like him, he likes you. Go out on a date and let everything take its course."

"Is that how it works for you?"

Gabby actually laughed. Laughed until she snorted. Until she almost felt like crying. "No, that's not how it works for me. I don't trust people." The words left her body with a whoosh of air and she wondered why, of all the times and places and certainly people, did she finally admit the thing she knew to be true about herself since she turned fourteen years old. In front of Zhanna, no less.

"I don't, either. They die."

"They leave."

Zhanna shrugged again. "Then there is nothing to say. Do you want salad tonight for dinner with all things on the side?"

"Okay."

Gabby watched Zhanna move around the counter. She could see Tom lean forward trying to get her attention, trying to get just a little closer. But Zhanna kept her welcome brief and paid him little attention other than to plop a plate in front of him and turn away before he could even say thank-you.

Did Gabby appear like that with people? Always feinting left or right and out of reach? Is that how people, men in particular, saw her? She could count on two hands the number of times she'd been asked out since her breakup with Brad. She liked to blame her job, her busy schedule, her less-than-perfect figure.

All she had to do was watch Zhanna and know none of her reasons were the truth. The don't-touch-me shuffle was a hell of thing to behold in action. And it was a bit humbling to know exactly how well Gabby had perfected its art.

The chime of the bell over the door rang again and instinctively Gabby turned to see who entered. She tried to pretend she wasn't looking for him in particular. She told herself that every time the bell chimed and she looked toward the door.

Until the fourth time when it really was him. Seeing him made her happy.

She was a fool.

JAMIE WALKED INTO the café and paused for a second when he spotted Gabby in one of the booths. Her head was turned toward the door as though she was waiting for him. He wasn't expecting her to be here, although he wasn't sure why given that this was the only place open for dinner.

Maybe his subconscious brought him here looking for her.

Or maybe he was simply hungry and hadn't felt like making his own meal. He didn't really want to over-think things.

Except as soon as he saw her expectant expression, the words from the other day came back like a sonic boom in his ear.

Forgive me.

Jamie still couldn't believe he said it. His own harshest critic, he'd spent the years after the scandal broke walking around with figurative mirrors surrounding him everywhere he went so he couldn't look away from himself, couldn't ignore who he was and what he'd done. He'd wanted to pay for his crime. But, once his self-flagellation was over, then he'd wanted people to forgive him for his actions.

At first it started with him wanting the world's forgiveness. Not an unlikely thing to want after becoming the scoundrel of the twenty-first century. It didn't take him long to see that wasn't going to happen. Most strangers he met knew too much about him—or thought they did—and instantly judged him. Nothing he could do or say to change that judgment.

Instead he concentrated on his family and friends, the people who knew him, the people he'd shamed by his behavior. Some came around. Some didn't.

Then, of course, he'd had to ask forgiveness from his ex-wife, Paula. He had no right to expect it, but he wanted it anyway. As strange as it was, of all people, she'd given it most freely.

So had his parents and his closest friends. So had the people of Hawk Island when they realized, deep inside, he was one of them.

It wasn't until he recognized how miserable he still was after all these years that he realized the one person he forgot to ask forgiveness from was himself.

It had taken time, but eventually he got there. Once he finally achieved that, he promised himself he would never ask for forgiveness from anyone else again. It was pointless because he was the only person who needed to forgive himself. If other people granted it, he didn't believe it. If they withheld it, he had nothing more to say to them.

Until Gabby. Gabby was different. He felt differently about her.

He hadn't spent the years since the scandal broke being a monk. There had been a few women. More in the beginning. Women who wanted to sleep with a legend more than they cared about his reputation. Women who felt morals were sticky things, so did without.

Not women he stayed with for very long. Not women

he respected very much when it came right down to it.
But they were the only women he thought were still
available to him. He'd joined the ranks of the dishon-
orable and so it seemed only right they should mingle
amongst them.

Hell, Zhanna was the really only admirable and eligible woman he'd met in the past eight years. The only
woman he'd gotten to know and had let her know him.

Now there was Gabby. With her big eyes and hope-
ful expression tempered by so much caution. She was
such a contradiction. The way she struck out on her
own, made herself a career and then remade herself
when she needed to. She showed up every day on the
beach ready to do battle like a Valkyrie yet when he'd
gotten close, too close, she'd shrunk inside herself so
far he wondered if she wasn't a turtle.

Today had been the first day she hadn't met him on
the beach. He missed her.

Decision made, Jamie slid into the booth across from
her. He wasn't sure where to start and, for the first time,
found himself hoping she might take the lead.

"Hey."

Not a bad opening, he decided. "Hey."

"Sorry for bolting like I did the other day."

"You call what you did *bolting?*"

She tilted her head and glared. "I'm getting faster
and I'm running farther, I'll have you know."

"Yes, you are."

"But I will admit to not being the fastest runner."

"Not even close."

"What happened to you wanting to seduce me? Do

I have to remind you that insulting me is not the best way to go about it."

He did want to seduce her. He wanted her naked and underneath him. He wanted to fill his hands with her breasts and plunge into her so deeply she would take away all his loneliness.

And where the hell had that come from?

Stranger still, as much as he wanted all those things from her, he wanted something else, too.

"We should go out on a date."

"A date?"

"Yes. An off-island-nice-napkins-restaurant date. I'll pick you up, we'll ferry to the mainland and we'll eat lobster. That kind of date."

"A date so you can continue to seduce me."

"Well, that is part of the purpose of the date and I'm not saying I won't be trying the whole time. But also a date is a chance to sit and talk and eat. Get to know each other. I don't mention taking you to bed because it would be considered ungentlemanly, even though I'm thinking about it. And you don't talk about the book that I'm never going to agree to write with you. A date."

He could see her struggle. Could see the debate she was holding in her mind. Worse, he could tell immediately when she decided to say no.

Quickly, he reached across the table and grabbed her hand. "It's a date, Gabby. Not a lifetime commitment. While I understand I have a certain reputation, you can be damn sure I'm not going to run out on you in the middle of it, or do some other woman in the bathroom during it. Okay?"

She leaned forward with urgency. "You don't understand. I don't want to like you. I don't want to like you...more."

He smiled. "You like me."

"Just barely."

"I haven't been on a date with someone who liked me in a long time. If I consent to let you talk about the book I'm never going to agree to write, will you come?"

"This is a huge mistake." She sighed.

He was breaking her down, which, if he thought about it, didn't do much for his ego. No, he hadn't taken out anyone who liked him for more than a good screw. But he also hadn't had to browbeat anyone into spending an evening with him, either.

"Come on, Gabby. You know you want to. Dinner, candles, tablecloths and lobster with extra butter."

"I refuse to wear a bib," she said finally caving.

"Deal."

"And just so you know, I haven't forgiven you. I guess I need to say that."

Jamie ignored the ball of lead in his stomach. "Haven't forgiven me...yet."

CHAPTER NINE

THE KNOCKING WOKE her up and Zhanna growled into her pillow. It was Monday morning and the only day she was allowed to sleep past 6:00 a.m.

Somebody better be dying. No, that upset her. Somebody better have the most wonderful news ever.

Opening an eye she glanced at the clock and registered that it was already nine. She'd slept way beyond what she normally did. Perhaps because she had been awake most of the night tossing and turning and thinking.

Always thinking.

It was Tom's fault.

The knocking started to falter as if the person on the other side was no longer confident somebody was home.

"I'm coming!" Zhanna tumbled out of bed and looked down. Cotton shorts and a tank top. Not naked. She flicked a hand through her hair to push it off her face and made her way from the bedroom to the single room that made up the rest of the apartment.

She could smell coffee and bacon wafting up from Adel's below and the aroma was enough to give her the jolt she needed. A little shoulder wiggle and some smoothing of her hair down around her back and she was ready to face whoever was on the other side of the door.

More than likely it was Adel asking for help. She probably had a crowd of customers—unlikely on a Monday morning—and needed another pair of hands. Zhanna would pout and remind Adel this was her day off. Then she would shower and go help.

There wasn't anything Zhanna wouldn't do for Adel. She wondered if the older woman knew that.

Opening the door, she framed her lips into a premature pout. Only it wasn't Adel.

"Hi," Tom said.

Zhanna tried to recall what her hair and pajamas looked like. But knowing she wasn't naked and she'd made an effort to smooth her hair was all she could remember.

She swallowed. "Tom."

"I woke you. Shoot. I knew you had this morning off, but I wasn't sure if you were an early riser or late one."

What did he want? Why was he here? Hadn't she made enough of a fool out of herself the last time they spoke? These were all very good questions she could be asking him. Instead she crossed one leg over the other and turned her shoulders in on the hope he would see less of her pajamas, which for some reason were making her blush.

She would not blush.

"I was thinking of you and wondered… Oh, hell." He reached into his jacket and pulled out a ball of white fuzz.

Purring white fuzz.

"I wasn't sure if you were a cat person or a dog person. You were pretty good with Trixie, I thought. Plus, I didn't really have any small dogs and large dogs aren't great in apartments. They really need a yard to run around in. But I thought maybe a kitten… Please say something."

The urge to touch it was nearly irresistible. But if she touched it, she would hold it. If she held it, she would love it. If she loved it…it would die.

"I can't," she whispered.

"Allergic?"

She shook her head. "I'm not supposed to have pets."

"I don't think Adel would give you too much grief over a little kitten. She's the smallest of the litter so I doubt she'll grow to be very big. And, well, her mother died and her siblings have all been adopted so she's got no family left."

Zhanna blinked then and stared at the fuzz ball. "Why did her mother die?"

"I don't know. The family who brought the kittens in found them with the mother, but the mother was already gone so they didn't bring her to me."

"She's got no one?"

Tom smiled. "I guess she's got me. I just thought for company— You talked about wanting to get Jamie a dog and I thought you could use a pet, too."

"Shep died."

Zhanna knew she wasn't making much sense. Her fingers were twitching and she could feel herself weakening. Then the little white fuzz ball moved and opened its tiny eyes and squeaked.

"Give me." Zhanna held out her hands and Tom carefully transferred the tiny animal to her. She brought it to her chest and kissed the tiny head. The kitten purred louder, then snuggled in for a nap.

"Love. I knew it," Tom said smugly.

Since she couldn't refute him, she made no comment. "Is that all you wanted?"

He looked at her for a moment and she couldn't look away. "For now. You're going to need supplies. I brought some stuff from my office you'll need. The litter box, a food dish and kitten food. I'll go get it."

"You were very confident, no?"

"I was. Love beats fear every time."

He jogged down the steps that ran along the outside of the diner to his car. She watched him pull out bags of supplies from the trunk.

"He thinks he's won, but I'm made of sterner stuff. I can resist his manly charm. I hope. For now, we must name you little one." Zhanna stepped out on to the deck. "Tom, what is it? Boy or girl?"

"Girl."

"I should have known," she said to the kitten. "You're too pretty to be boy."

He returned with two large bags in his hands. She watched him warily as he went inside her home with more ease than he should have.

"You're going to want to find a private spot for the kitty litter. Cats apparently have a little shame when it comes to doing their business, unlike dogs who will just drop their butts anywhere they please. Sometimes a little curtain around it—"

"I'm not going to sleep with you," Zhanna blurted.

Tom straightened from where he'd been unloading the bag. He crossed his arms over his chest and ducked his head. "Is that what you think this is about?"

"Isn't it?" She cradled the fuzz against her cheek and the animal purred so loud it shook. Zhanna would never tell him but she'd slept with men for worse reasons.

Seemingly at a loss for words, he eventually burst out laughing. "You know, I suppose it is. I wanted to do something nice for you so you would like me. I want you to like me because I like you. And yes, I hope maybe someday you'll like me enough to sleep with me. Who knew I was such a cad?"

"I do not know *cad* and I do like you. But—"

"You're scared."

"Reserved," she corrected.

"Shaking in your boots."

"Cautious."

Tom shook his head. "You going to tell me who it was? Who made you so...cautious."

No, because he wouldn't understand. Nobody ever did when she told people. "Thank you for Mary."

"Mary, is it?"

"Good American name. I want to acclimate to my new country."

"She'll be good company. If you ever want people company, you know where to find me. And in two weeks you need to bring her to the clinic for a checkup and shots."

Zhanna nodded and Tom slowly made his way to the door. She could see he was reluctant to leave, as though he could find some magic words which would make her ask him to stay. Only there weren't any words. There was only fear…like he said.

"See you."

Crazily, she felt tears well in her eyes. "Of course you will see me. You come to eat at my counter almost every day."

"Yeah, I guess I should probably start learning to cook. Take care, Zhanna. And remember, two weeks."

He trotted down the stairs and she watched him get in his car and then watched him drive away until she could no longer see his car on the road.

It was what she wanted. It was essentially what she'd asked him to do by not asking him to stay. His only option was to go. So why did she feel so sad?

"Come, Mary, let's go inside and make you up a nice bed. We can be lonely together."

NIGHT HAD FALLEN on the island, but as Jamie pulled up in front of the B and B, Gabby realized how early it really was. Not even ten o'clock.

Pathetic.

Together they sat silently for a minute until the tension thickened to the consistency of pudding. Finally, she couldn't stand it anymore.

"So, that was awful," she announced.

Jamie tilted his head back and laughed. A true belly laugh with lots of power behind it. Gabby wasn't exactly sure what was so funny.

"Yes, it was. You were completely uncomfortable.

There was a brief second I actually thought you might throw up right there on the table."

He had no idea how close they'd come to that actually happening. However, Gabby was not going to take all the blame. "It's not like I didn't tell you a date was a bad idea."

"Then why did you agree to go out?"

Because she was an idiot. "Maybe I couldn't pass up a chance to have a date with Jamison Hunter."

"Bull. Try again." He turned to her in the confines of the truck. The cab seemed smaller and the overcast darkness that surrounded them made the world seem far away. "Why did you go out with me?"

She wrapped her arms around herself and tried not to look at him. She imagined this was what the do-not-touch shuffle looked like when performed in a car. Her insides were shouting at her to hide, to run, to stay away. Her mind was backing all that up. But some other instinct kept her butt firmly planted in the passenger's seat waiting to see what he would do, what move he would make.

His fingers brushed the side of her cheek. "Gabby, talk to me."

"I knew you wouldn't back off. I wanted to show you how ridiculous a date between us would be."

"Another lie. You better watch it. I hear bad things can happen to your nose if you keep doing that. The question then becomes why can't you be honest? You wanted to go out with me, I know you did, despite all your reservations. Then we got to the restaurant and you panicked. Hell, you might have been panicking from the moment I picked you up."

He was correct. The panic had happened minutes before he arrived. She'd stood in front of the full-size mirror on the back of the closet door in her room, looking at the person she'd become. She hadn't liked the way her jeans fit—too snug. Or how her top fit—too booby—and it was like all the insecurities she'd ever felt came bubbling to the surface.

She—the one who'd gotten herself fired from TV for being too old and too big—was going out on a date with Jamison Hunter. Ridiculous. If Brad, who was just an average guy, hadn't wanted her, what in the world made her think Jamison, a superstar, would.

Because he said he did.

That silent whisper had pushed her out of her room and into his truck. But seeing him leaning on the railing of the ferry as they sailed to the mainland with the wind in his face and his rugged good looks practically beaming as the sun set, he'd intimidated her all over again.

He was Jamison Hunter. He saved lives. He'd been to space.

She got fired. She got dumped.

Those two people didn't seem to jive. He was staring at her now, waiting for the truth. She tried to think of a plausible lie she could tell him. It would have to be very convincing because he had a built-in lie detector when it came to her. But it also had to bring his pursuit of her to an end. She simply did not have it in her to believe Jamison Hunter would want Gabby Haines.

"Maybe I'm just not into you."

Another deep laugh. Either she wasn't convincing at all or he had a very healthy dose of arrogance.

"Some might say you're full of yourself," she mumbled.

"Not some. Most. You know when I had my first flight?"

Obviously she didn't since personal facts about this man were very difficult to find. Maybe that was why he'd agreed to do the book in the first place. It would be the place where he told all his stories so people wouldn't have to keep digging for his secrets.

"I was fourteen. My dad worked for the Maine Forest Service as an incident commander. During summers I was always at the command center. He taught me everything he knew about firefighting, figuring that one day I would grow up and follow in his footsteps. That was his plan, but I knew fairly early on I wanted something bigger."

"Bigger like an astronaut."

"No, not then. I didn't know what *bigger* necessarily was back then. Anyway it was the middle of summer, hot as hell for Maine, and everyone was out of the center trying to deal with this nasty fire. It had splintered and was moving both east and north so it required two full teams to tackle it. One of my dad's deputies, Big Joe, was left to run the command center and handle communications. We hear a mayday over one of the talkies. A chopper went down. Steve and Charlie were okay but trapped in the center of the fire with no way out. With the winds shifting and the fire moving so fast—"

"You relayed the message to your father and he went to go save them."

Gabby waited for him to contradict her. She knew he would. He hadn't started this story to tell her about a teenager who had done the right thing.

"You know I didn't. Instead I convinced Big Joe we needed to act. There was an old tricked-out Huey chopper my dad had been teaching me to fly with. I was certain I could get it airborne and could get to Steve and Charlie faster than anyone already in the forest. I didn't even need to land. Just get up and find them, lower a cable and let Big Joe haul them up. Once Steve was on board he could take over piloting."

Gabby chuckled. "So you're telling me you were born a hero."

He ducked his head. "I'm telling you I know my abilities. I know when I'm capable of something. I also know when I'm being cocky rather than confident."

"What were you that day?"

"Confident. Confident I was going to get Steve and Charlie. Confident I wasn't going to put Big Joe at risk and confident my dad was going to kill me when he found out. All those things happened. Although the death prediction was replaced by a pretty rough belt lashing."

"But you saved Steve and Charlie. That doesn't seem fair."

"I could have killed us all. I knew I wasn't going to. I tried to explain it to him. I wouldn't have done it if I hadn't *known* I could do it. But he couldn't hear me.

Not that I blame him. That *knowing* has been a blessing and a curse my whole life."

"Why a curse?"

She could see intensity glowing in his eyes even in the dark. "Because when you go through life knowing who you are and what you're capable of, you think the world is at your disposal. That you're a king who sits on top while others scramble to find their place. I *know* you wanted to go out on this date. I *know* you want me. And because I know it, and know you're fighting me and what you feel… There is the curse."

She wasn't going to say anything. She didn't want to give him the satisfaction of being right.

He leaned forward. "Tell me I'm wrong. Tell me you don't want me to move closer. That you don't want me to reach my hand around your neck and pull you into me so I can kiss you."

Jamison Hunter wanted to kiss her.

She wanted to kiss Jamison Hunter.

And the problem was…?

"What if I'm not big enough for you?" It shouldn't have been a question, she thought. It should have been a statement, because it was true. Gabriella Haines was not *big* enough for Jamison Hunter. Not even close.

He scooted along the bench seat until their thighs were touching. He wrapped an arm around her shoulders and tugged her more tightly against him. Then he leaned back and looked out the windshield into the blackness. His relaxation made her relax by default. Not all of the tension dissipated—there was still plenty of the sexual kind—but the awkwardness from dinner was finally behind them. It felt as though they were starting again at a drive-in theater, watching a movie, and it was the moment when the screen went blank right before all the action began.

"You're big enough, Gabby. In fact I don't think you *know* how truly big you are. I think a few things in life might have kicked your confidence a little. But I bet if you go back in time, before the moment when it all started to turn on you, I bet you were a knower, too."

She rested her head on his shoulder and thought about when she was six years old and told her mother while they were watching the *TODAY Show* how she was going to be the co-host someday.

"You weren't supposed to be this person. You weren't supposed to be a good man," she muttered, burrowing a little deeper into him so she could smell his soap. Something piney and manly.

"Sorry. I know you came looking for an asshole. If it makes you feel any better, there are a lot of days when I can oblige you."

She lifted her head "I came looking for a legend. I didn't think you would really end up being one."

"No legend. Just a man who knows himself. The good, the bad and the ugly."

The ugly. It was always there, Gabby thought. In the corner of her mind. The ever present reminder of his sins against women. The danger of allowing herself to get too close. It was there even now as she considered the shape of his lips. This close to him, she could see where he missed the smallest spot on his neck while shaving and she wanted to kiss that spot. She wanted to press her lips to his neck and then maybe bite him just hard enough to leave a mark. A mark on the *man,* not the legend.

She took a deep breath, maybe the deepest of her life. "You were right. I do want you. Take me to your place."

She could feel his body tighten next to hers, feel the muscles harden and shift like an animal preparing to pounce.

"Nah. Not tonight."

"But you said—"

"And I meant it. I want you. A lot. But you don't trust me yet."

She was never going to trust him. She knew it, but she didn't want to tell him.

"Besides, this is our first date. I don't want you to think I'm easy. And I'm sure you don't want me to think that about you."

Gabby shrugged. Easy was not a label she had to worry about.

He lifted her chin and made her look at him. He was smiling as though he'd won a small victory, but the muscle in his cheek was twitching as though he was holding himself back.

"Can I kiss you?"

She nodded, oddly pleased he asked her first.

She felt his lips and thought how nice it was to be kissing someone. She'd almost forgotten it all. The rush of heat through her body, the pulse of her heart as it kicked in to a different speed.

He pressed harder and she sighed, liking the way he encouraged her to open her mouth and offer him welcome inside. Slowly, softly until she thought she might scream he teased her with this lips and tongue until finally she felt him penetrate her mouth. Her stomach tightened and she could feel herself go wet. She thought *sex*.

Heat and gooeyness. Tension and pressure. Urgency. It all felt so raw and at the same time it was like meeting up with a friend who she hadn't seen in years. The patterns and rhythms came back and she was once more in tune with her body and, most of all, in tune with him.

She pushed her tongue into his mouth and heard him catch his breath. She felt the tension of his body where it touched hers. His kiss was sweet and seductive but most of all it was sincere.

The sincerity disturbed her and pulled her out of the moment. A man who cheated couldn't be sincere. It had to be part of the act, part of the seduction he'd promised. As if he could sense her pulling away, he stopped the kiss, running his thumb along her wet swollen bottom lip as if to make sure it was good and covered with his taste.

"Goodnight, Gabby. Sleep well."

She puffed out a breath and reined her body under her control. This had not been a good idea. This thing between them was going to a place she was fairly certain was out of her control.

"I'm pretty sure that's not going to happen," she admitted.

"Then think of me. And do sinful things to your body you think I might like to do."

She turned to him surprised to hear such naughty

language from a man who had kissed her the way she'd always imagined Lancelot might kiss Guinevere. Then he wiggled his eyebrows like the dirty man he apparently was and made her smile.

"Jamison Hunter, you are a pervert."

"Gabby Haines, all I can tell you is I'm going to have some pretty rocking dreams tonight."

She got out of his truck shaking her head, but she was also smiling. She climbed the stairs up to her room and when she closed the door behind her, the goofy grin was still in place.

"Damn," she whispered to a dark empty room. "I'm in serious trouble."

CHAPTER TEN

WHY THE HELL hadn't he taken her up on her offer?

Jamie sat in his kitchen the following morning brooding. As he sipped his coffee and considered his foul mood, he thought of a hundred other endings that could have happened last night instead of the one that did.

Hell, she'd offered!

Take me to your place.

He could have brought her here. They could have messed up the sheets three, maybe four, times over and then he would have gotten whatever it was about her out of his system.

But *no!* He wanted something as ridiculous as her trust, which, in the cold light of day, he was fairly certain he would never have. Not entirely because of what he'd done in his past, but because of how she'd been treated by the men in her life. He was the last person she could ever consider giving her heart to and so here he sat trying to convince himself he didn't want it.

Just her body.

The facts didn't really bear out that assertion. He'd treated her as someone who was important to him. Not a one-night or two-night stand. Not an easy screw he would forget about in a few days' time after she left the island.

He'd been horny and irritated with himself all night. Instead of riding her hard until dawn, he'd gone for a late-night run on the beach and when he got back to the house he was still as tense as hell.

A cold shower, a hand job, then a glass of Scotch had finally put him down for the count where he'd done nothing but dream about her.

Freaking dreaming about her. When he could have had her.

He was an idiot.

The doorbell rang and startled him. He really missed Shep's advance warning. He heard the door open and knew only one person wouldn't bother to wait for him to answer the door.

"Jamie."

"I'm in the kitchen," he called out.

Zhanna walked in and surveyed the room. She spotted the still half filled carafe of coffee and went to the cabinet where the cups were kept. At one point he'd offered to let her move in with him, but she had declined. In some ways he was glad, since he didn't know how he would adjust to living with a woman again after so long. In other ways he thought how nice it was to have someone else in the world know where you kept your coffee cups.

With Zhanna he supposed he got the best of both worlds.

"I'm having hard day," she announced as she sat across from him and dumped teaspoon after teaspoon of sugar into her coffee until it was more hot sweet water than coffee.

"Join the club."

"I need to ask you something and I need you to be honest."

"Okay."

"Do you think it is a good idea to have sex with Tom."

Jamie groaned a little. "Zee, I do not want to talk about guys with you."

"Why not?"

"It's weird. Do you want me to talk about why I didn't have sex with Gabby last night?"

Zhanna winced and Jamie knew she understood.

"We're two grown adults and we are friends," Zhanna said, pointing out the obvious. "We should be able to talk about our problems without it being weird."

Jamie snorted. "That's nice in fantasy grown-up land. In real grown-up land things are weird and awkward all the time."

"But I don't know what to do. He gave me kitten. He has nice smile. I think— I think I like him."

Jamie couldn't comment on Tom's smile, but he knew him to be an okay guy both professionally and socially. And he'd been honest about Shep when he started to see his condition deteriorating. He didn't try to push Jamie into any decisions, instead let him make the call. He figured Zhanna could date guys way worse than Tom.

"So what's the problem. Why not go out with him?"

She gave him a shuddered look and he was reminded that, while they'd grown close in the time they had known each other, there were still parts of their lives they kept separate. Like the bulk of her past.

"You asked my advice," Jamie reminded her. "Here it is. Tom's a good guy. You're a great person. You should go out if he asks or, if you're so inclined, ask him out yourself. Go have a nice time. Because you never know where things could lead."

"That's awful advice."

"Only because you were hoping I would say something else. You want me to play bad cop and tell you to stay away from him?"

"Maybe."

"I'm not giving you an easy out. Besides, if I told you not to date him, you would probably only want to date him more."

She made a noise that was a cross between a sigh and a groan that Jamie didn't know if it was a particular Russian sound or uniquely Zhanna.

"Okay, this was a big waste of time. We might as well talk about you. Why did you not have sex with Gabby last night?"

"I don't want to talk about it."

"You brought it up."

"Only to creep you out."

"Yes and that worked very well. But you sit there with your coffee and your brooding eyes and I know you are not happy. I thought you wanted a simple fling. You said two weeks and she's gone."

A simple fling? That's what he told himself he wanted. He was attracted to her, he knew she was attracted to him. They each had their issues and none of it was going to change. Most importantly she wasn't going to be here much longer. The two weeks were now down to one. Her boss would eventually pull the plug, especially once she realized there would be no biography. And Gabby would head to New York.

Then why hadn't he done exactly what he planned to do and taken advantage of the situation?

It was the answer, one he was totally unwilling to share, that had him making broody eyes out the window.

"I like her," Zhanna said as she sipped her sweet coffee.

That was interesting. He didn't imagine Zhanna ever liking another woman he chose to be with. Her behavior to date sort of proved that. "Really? I have to say it doesn't show."

She shrugged. "I didn't want to. But I think we are alike. And I like me."

"Yes, you do." He smiled. "So a kitten, huh? Are you going to keep it?"

"I did not want to, but it needs me desperately. I named her Mary and she sleeps on my feet and makes soft kitten noises."

"Soft kitten noises are hard to resist."

Only Zhanna looked angry about it. "I don't like it when things get close to my heart. I get scared and I hate being scared more than I hate being sad."

"You let me get close," he reminded her.

"You, I had no choice. The kitten…no choice. Tom…a choice."

"Don't choose fear. Don't let it win. You do, and you'll regret so much."

"You who are fearless then, you regret nothing?"

No, he didn't regret *nothing.* But he promised himself he wouldn't let those regrets rule his life. Thinking over the past few years, though, by committing himself to this solitary life, isn't that what he'd done?

Damn Gabby. For making him want something more from her than a damn fling. For making him think about stuff he didn't want to think about. And mostly for letting him know he wasn't quite as fine with his life as he thought he was.

The answer was simple. He needed to find her now and take her up on her offer. He needed to have sex with her quickly, then let her go. Hell, he'd drive her onto the ferry and off the island himself.

He needed to get rid of her before he did something utterly stupid.

Like fall for her.

"LATE NIGHT?"

Gabby looked up as Susan entered the dining room to refill her morning coffee. They were the most civil words Susan had spoken to her since she'd been forced to take her back. And she was giving her seconds on coffee. Bonus.

Maybe Gabby was finally winning the woman over with her charm…and the fact that she didn't require fresh towels every single day. She was perfectly fine with letting them dry and reusing them, which both helped the environment and spared the woman from daily laundry.

"Yes," Gabby answered tentatively. She wasn't sure

how the protective mother bear would take to knowing she'd gone out to dinner with Jamie. No doubt Susan would think Gabby was trying to use her seductive wiles to get his story out of him.

Fat chance that would work given that she had offered herself up on a silver platter only to find out he wasn't dying of hunger. Although his kiss had suggested hunger. It teased at hunger…until he pulled away. Or she pulled away. She wasn't really sure who ended it first.

Just one of many things that kept her awake the whole night.

"You were out with Jamie. I know. So does the whole town if it matters to you."

Swell.

"Not that you would have been able to keep a secret. Doug, the ferry boat captain, gave you away. Or maybe it was his first mate, Eli. Regardless, everyone knew you two were headed to the mainland on a date. And if that didn't do the trick sitting in Jamie's truck outside the B and B didn't exactly scream discretion."

"It was just one date."

Susan sat across from Gabby and Gabby braced herself for what the woman was going to say. Rather than wait, she decided to head her off at the pass.

"Look, I know you don't approve. You probably think I'm a slut in a chubby woman's body bent on seducing him for my own nefarious purposes. But trust me, Jamie is a grown man and can take care of himself. I'm fairly certain he can withstand the charms of little ole me."

He did withstand her charms. Then he kissed her and made it all better.

Blasted man.

Susan sighed. "You know, this time I don't think I'm worried about him. I think I'm worried about you."

There was an interesting statement. Gabby wondered if finally someone on this island was going to cop to the fact that Jamie wasn't the greatest man on the planet.

He was flawed. Seriously flawed.

"Because he cheats on women?"

Susan nearly growled. "No. What happened between him and his wife is something you and I are never going to know about in full. But I can tell you this, whatever happened between them broke him in a fundamental way. The man who came to this island looking for sanctuary was devastated and more than a little emotionally closed off. After time he came to trust us. Mostly because we needed him so desperately, each in our own way, and because of his nature he was always there to help. But in all this time he's never gone so far as to have a real relationship with someone. Yes, women have come and gone. Never for long, and never in a way that changes his habits or thoughts on the possibility of getting married again."

"Not even Zhanna?"

"His relationship with Zhanna is different. If you see them together you'll see they're still guarded with one another. On his side and hers, too."

Gabby shook her head not even knowing why she was asking questions. She wasn't going to have a real relationship with Jamie. Any day now, her editor was going to call and ask for a status update and Gabby was going to have to come clean. There was no book. No story. No special connection with Jamie.

She was going to be fired. Again. And, unlike the last incident, this time she would deserve to be. She wasn't doing her job and she didn't have the publisher's best interests in mind. Losing the job would mean she'd probably have to move in with her mother for a while so she could regroup and think of a new, new profession. A new, new life.

Really, the smartest thing to do right now would be to go upstairs, pack her stuff and head to Philadelphia before things got awkward or embarrassing. For her, for Jamie, for her boss.

Instead, Gabby continued to sip her coffee as she sorted what Susan was saying in a logical pattern. "You're worried about me dating Jamie because you think he might hurt me because he's never opened up to a woman since his divorce."

"That's about right."

"What makes you think I would open up to him?"

Susan smiled in a way that reminded Gabby of her mother. An expression that said people her age knew more about everything in general.

"Honey, you are a walking heart, waiting for someone to love. Now, maybe you think you're protecting it. But I think, deep down inside, you want to hand it over to someone. The right someone."

"I am not," Gabby snapped. "I am closed, guarded and overly self-protective. I don't want to give my heart to anyone. I also don't particularly want it stolen." Which she was in danger of letting happen.

Susan shook her head. "I'm sorry. I don't think so. Maybe you've closeted yourself away from the world to protect yourself, but you don't have the kind of walls I've seen in other people. There is nothing hard or brittle about you. You'll fall in love with him. Don't be too upset, dear, most of us already have. I just worry that he can give you what you need."

The piercing fear that Gabby might have already started her descent into a pit of emotions over Jamie made her feel nauseous. "I'm not going to fall in love with Jamison Hunter."

"Okay. Well, don't say I didn't warn you."

The woman picked up the carafe and turned to leave but Gabby had to ask one more question. "Susan, what did he do for you? You said you all needed him each in your own way. Why?"

Gabby could see the hesitation in the woman. Whatever it was she certainly didn't want to talk about it and Gabby was about to let her off the hook, when she put the pot on the table and once again took the seat across from Gabby.

Slowly and deliberately, like a person getting ready to do an interview on camera who didn't want to make any odd movements, Susan crossed her legs and linked her hands together. It all added to the solemnity of what she was about to say.

Gabby almost didn't want to hear it. Except she was riveted to her chair. In an instinctive move she reached across the table and put her hand on top of the woman's hands. Susan pulled one hand away, patted Gabby's and smiled.

"See, no walls for you. You don't keep people out. You let them in."

"You don't have to—"

"No, it's okay. I don't mind telling it now. I told you the story of my ex-husband George. How he left me."

Yes, Gabby remembered how easily the woman told the story, too. As though they were two casual friends who had decided to go their separate ways with no hard feelings. How stupid Gabby was to think that could have been even remotely true. Divorce always left scars.

"It wasn't a surprise when he finally asked if he could leave. We had grown apart the way people who have been married too long and take it for granted do. But I never thought— Anyway, he left. Found another woman and divorced me. We never had kids and this business with him was basically my life. I felt lost. Like I didn't know where to turn, so naturally I did the most clichéd thing imaginable and started to drink. Drink and take pills. I drugged my way into a full-scale problem, which culminated with me getting into a car accident. The other driver wasn't hurt, and I was only banged up a little when I drove my car off the road. Of course, when the police found me, I was drunk and high on whatever pills I had taken that night. Naturally, I was arrested. It was the single most humiliating moment of my life."

"Oh, Susan, I'm so sorry."

"I had one call and I said to myself, 'Susan, who can you call? George is gone. You have no family. Who is the one person who might come and bail you out and not tell you how disgusting you are?' I thought of Jamie. Jamie would help."

Gabby squeezed the woman's hand as the tears welled up.

"He came to the mainland and found me sitting in a holding cell, hung over and reeking of whiskey. He never said a word. He talked with the police, posted my bail. He got me an attorney and he hooked me up with a support group for divorced women. I had no license for a year, so he drove me once a week to the grocery store on the mainland so I could do my big shopping for the B and B. And all the little things that go wrong in this big old house that I used to rely on my husband to fix, he would come to put right. More importantly, he showed me what he was doing so I could fix it myself the next time."

"Why?"

"I know, right? Why would someone do all that? He didn't know me very well. Only casually from meeting in town or at the diner. Sometimes I would host a town brunch and he would come to that. Jamie loves my French toast. All I really knew of Jamie Hunter when he came to the island was the scandal. But when I met him, and saw the person he was, the man he was, I knew there was way more to the story than anyone knew. I wasn't going to press him, though, and maybe having a few people in his life who didn't ask him any questions was all he needed."

"You thought he would save you, didn't you?"

Susan nodded. "I knew he would. I sat in the cell

and thought what I need is a hero. A knight to come rescue me. Since I happened to have the number of one in my cell phone, I used it. He came and he did exactly what I needed him to do. He saved me. When I tried to thank him, he brushed me off and reminded me no one is perfect all the time. Sometimes people do things they don't mean to do or even want to do. The trick is to forgive themselves for it. Sounded like he knew what he was talking about."

You're going to have to forgive me.

When he'd whispered those words, she'd thought the task impossible. At this moment, though, she didn't know. Maybe the hard part of forgiving him wasn't accepting what he'd done, maybe it was a fault within herself. Her inability to accept that people weren't perfect. Like her father, her fiancé.

"You said others on the island needed him, too." Gabby could only imagine how many ways he'd changed people's lives—big and small. Something she now knew he'd been doing since he was a teenager.

She thought about what was happening on the space station. He'd been so quick to dismiss it and the possibility of NASA calling, but she realized it was probably something he thought about all the time, wondering if he could help in some capacity. If his experience might be of service. He wouldn't call them. But would he answer if they called him? She could say without a shadow of doubt, absolutely he would.

"I'm not going to tell you everyone else's stories," Susan said. "But know that in the years since he's been here there might have been a person with a gambling problem who needed saving from some scary collectors, or a person with an abusive spouse who needed someone to step in. Jamie was that person. It's who he is. At his core."

Gabby thought about him flying the helicopter because he *knew* he could do it. He was a hero. A real life hero.

"But heroes don't cheat."

Susan shrugged. "This one did, apparently. I mean, that's what all the newspapers and news shows said, wasn't it?"

Gabby watched Susan leave the room and thought about her last comment. Yes, it was what everyone knew. There was a picture. Two women and one man outside a hotel room. The one woman who was not Jamie's wife was barely dressed. The facts were indisputable—the picture didn't lie. More than that, Jamie never once suggested the media's spin on events was anything but the truth.

He'd accepted the guilty verdict passed down to him by the media and he'd publicly admitted his mistakes. Tried as an adulterer, convicted by the American people and sentenced to Hawk Island for the rest of his days.

It was getting late in the morning. He'd be preparing for his daily run. Gabby finished her coffee and went up to her room to change. She had some questions to ask him and she wasn't going to let him get away with evasive answers. This was way more important than some stories for a book she might write.

As she reached her room, she realized she wasn't

winded from her quick jog up the stairs and thought about how far she'd come in only a week. Progress.

Now she thought it was time to make progress in other areas. There was a story there about Jamison Hunter and the photograph that changed his life. She knew it and, damn it, she was going to pry it out of him.

Not for her career. But maybe for the sake of her heart.

CHAPTER ELEVEN

ZHANNA DROVE TO Tom's place and turned off the car. She looked to her partner in crime.

"Make it convincing," Zhanna told her.

Mary let out a weak meow.

With each step she took Zhanna tried to fortify her courage and with each step she found herself wanting to turn around and go home. There was no reason she had to do this. No reason why she needed a man in her life. No reason to date or kiss anyone if she didn't want to.

She was here on this island to create a new life for herself. To rebuild a world that had crumbled with the death of her mother. It was enough on anyone's plate. Love and happiness, they were such ephemeral things.

Still she continued walking, then knocked on the door. She realized she was doing a weird convulsive swallowing thing that needed to stop before actually letting herself inside.

"Zhanna."

She gulped one last time surprised to see him answering the door when usually he shouted for people to enter. She held up her kitty carrier. "I think she's sick."

"Okay. Come in. I've got no appointments."

She followed him to the exam room and thought

about what it would mean to come back to his place after a nice date. Her dress would be covered in animal hair. Any kissing would be witnessed by the animals in residence. She wasn't sure if he kept more cages upstairs in his apartment. Did he keep the wine next to the rabies vaccination in the refrigerator? That didn't sound very appealing.

And consider the noise. The barking and squawking and meowing. No woman was ever going to have Tom alone. Zhanna would always have to share him with a house full of furry creatures.

Gently, he extracted Mary from her cage.

"Why do you think she's sick?"

"She sneezed. A couple of times."

Like the best friend she'd quickly become, Mary took her cue and scrunched up her tiny face and sneezed.

Tom smiled. He held the kitten up and checked her eyes, then ran his fingers carefully over her little body.

"Oh, I wouldn't worry about that. She's got no congestion in her nose I can see and her eyes are clear. Is she eating?"

"Yes, wet food. And dry food. And maybe sometimes ice cream."

Tom frowned. "Go easy on the ice cream. It's not so good for them and you don't want to spoil her on human food."

Zhanna nodded.

"But if she's eating okay and drinking, I'm sure it's nothing more than an itchy nose. Keep an eye on her. If her eyes start to run or you can see some discharge from her nose, then you can bring her back. Otherwise I'll see you in a week for her shots."

He put Mary in the carrier and scratched underneath her chin until she purred helplessly. Apparently Mary wasn't immune to Tom's charms any more than Zhanna was.

"I was thinking about what you said last time," Zhanna said in a rush.

Tom said nothing. She didn't blame him. There was no reason for him to make this easy for her, not when he'd been so open and she had been so shut down. Still, a little help right now when her throat was doing the convulsive thing again would have been nice.

"I was an only child." It wasn't what she intended to say but they were the only words that came out. "I did not know my father growing up. So it was my mother and me. We were very close."

"How did you lose her?"

"Cancer. Ovarian. Many doctors, many years, many fights and many losses. I did everything I could to care for her, to ease her pain, to make her live. But always the doctors came into the room with the bad news. Until the last time when they told me she was gone forever."

He reached across the exam table and squeezed her hand. He didn't say he was sorry or offer platitudes about how her mother was better off rather than living in pain. Zhanna hated when people said those things. She didn't fault them for it when their intentions were sincere, but nonetheless she thought all words in the face of grief were stupid.

Grief wasn't something that could be cured by any words.

"I had no good friends back home. I spent too many years taking care of my mother. I was the mother and the nurse. She was my world. We didn't have close family. It was just the two of us and when I lost her I didn't think—"

"You didn't think you could still go on."

"No, I didn't. I didn't see how it was possible. The sadness, it consumed me. I tried for a time to live. To do what people said and move on with my life. I took lovers thinking men would make me feel better, but I only felt empty. I was not— I was not…good. Then I saw this silly commercial for McDonald's. You know we have them in Russia, too, and it made me think of America. In America people can start over and so I came. And it has been very good here. I have people now. There is Jamie and Adel."

"And me."

He was smiling, smugly she thought. "And you. But I am scared. I am always scared now when I wasn't before."

"I know." He nodded. "Now I know why. But you came here with a healthy kitten because you wanted to see me. So maybe there is something inside you that's stronger than the fear."

Of course it's what she'd done. She'd known Mary wasn't sick. Her precious kitten would not do such a thing to make a nervous mama worry. But Zhanna knew she had to come to him. He had made his declaration and would not make another. She sensed this much about him.

"I like talking to you while you eat," Zhanna admitted.

"I like talking to you while I eat, too. You know what else I would like. I would really like for both of us to go eat some place together and talk. So you wouldn't have to leave me for a moment whenever a new person walks into the diner."

"That is a date?"

He nodded and squeezed the hand he'd been holding this whole time a little tighter. "That is a date. If you accept."

"I accept."

He gently tugged her hand to his lips and kissed the inside of her wrist. It made her body flutter and she was sure her cheeks were flushing.

"You're beautiful when you're nervous."

"And you are a flatterer. Now we will go out on this date, will you come back to the diner? You haven't come for many days."

He lowered his eyes. "It wasn't a punishment. I didn't want to push you."

She knew it, but still she missed him. "Come, Mary, we will leave the busy vet to help the other truly sick animals." She picked up the case and smiled at him. "And you will come to the diner tonight as Adel is making meatloaf."

"I love meatloaf."

"Yes, I know it is your favorite. And I will make the

fattening macaroni and cheese you like. Then we will talk about when our date will happen."

"Soon, Zhanna. I promise."

There was a sensuality in his tone. A lower timbre that promised more than soft kisses on her wrist. Zhanna could feel her cheeks heating again and turned her back on him quickly. She knew already someday they would go to bed together, and she knew from how he made her feel with that simple kiss on her wrist that sex with him would not leave her feeling empty.

She did not say this, though. After all, a girl did not want to be too obvious.

"Who are you?"

Jamie looked around on the beach. Since it was only him and Gabby, he thought the question rather odd.

"I mean it. I want the truth," Gabby persisted as she made her way toward him. She was pulling her hair into a ponytail and for some reason the way she handled all those luscious strands so easily turned him on. He told himself not to think about it because A, he knew from experience running with the hard-on was not especially comfortable and B, he still wasn't sure where he stood on the whole sex with this woman front.

His body said yes to the sex. His rational-thinking brain agreed. Sex was good. Sex was all he should or could want.

It was the other area of him that was the hold-out. That weird floating soft spot in his gut which sometimes moved to the region of his heart that said she was worth more than sex.

She's Gabby.

And she could hurt him. It was stunning to realize after having spent so much of his life making sure he never hurt anyone that he was suddenly the vulnerable one.

He didn't like it.

"Are you a good guy? Just answer me. Yes or no. Would you consider yourself a good person?"

Jamie had no idea where this was coming from, but he saw no reason to not answer truthfully. "I'm neither. I'm both. I've done good things and I've done bad things. I try to make sure now I'm more good than bad, but I'm never going to stand in front of anyone and say I'm perfect."

"That answer totally sucks."

She was so disappointed in him it was comical.

"Come on, we'll run and have a philosophical conversation on the differences between good and bad."

"Oh, joy. Running *and* philosophy. Doesn't get much more fun than that."

He took her through her stretches—real ones she finally did correctly—then they started off at an easy pace. One she was able to easily keep up with.

"I hear so many stories about you and I'm trying to put those together in my head with what I know."

"What do you know? What's fact?"

"Fact, you were my hero. My first crush. You did an amazing thing people will talk about forever. Then you got caught outside a motel room in Florida by your wife with another woman. That's a fact."

"There is a picture of me and my wife and another

woman outside a motel room in Florida, it's a fact I can't change."

"Fact, you helped Susan out of a jam when she needed it."

"She told you about that?" It surprised Jamie that Susan would confide in anyone who was a non-islander, but he liked it. It meant Gabby was getting to them. All of them—Zhanna and Susan—were liking her despite themselves.

"Fact, you've won the loyalty of women young and old. You've become the leader of this community. It's clear people trust you despite what they know, and it doesn't compute."

"Because you can't forgive what I've done. Maybe you can't forgive anyone anything. That's not my problem, it's your problem."

He was pushing her at a little harder pace. Not as a punishment but maybe because he didn't want to hear what came next. Maybe if she ran harder, she wouldn't have the breath to say it.

"You don't need my forgiveness." The words puffed out of her.

"No, I guess I don't. I guess I could have taken you up on your offer and brought you to my place after our date, screwed you silly and watched you leave the next day without a backward glance."

"But you didn't. See, that's my point. You're acting like a good guy again. Pretending I mean something to you."

That stopped him in his tracks. He was barely winded while she was trying to suck in oxygen like there was a finite amount. She would have to listen to him then because she couldn't run anymore.

"Pretending? You think all of this is *pretending?* Lady, I could have had you every which way from Sunday by now and don't bother telling me otherwise. What I'm doing here, what I'm trying to do here is—" What was he trying to do?

"What?"

"I'm trying to tell you I like you. I like who you are. I want to have more time with you. I want to go out again."

"Our date sucked."

"No, I liked it. Liked that you were nervous around me because you like me, too. I liked the way your hair fell around your shoulders and I liked when you talked about your mother. I like that I feel normal with you. I'm not on a stage. I'm not Jamison Hunter, Astronaut, with you. And I'm not Jamison Hunter tabloid star, either. I'm just me. I'm Jamie and I like that, too."

He could see the wariness in her eyes. He could also see he was right that she did like him, too. She was fighting herself and he needed the right part of her to win the argument. The part of her that was still willing to take a risk.

He moved forward and wrapped his hand around her neck. "We can do this. We can like each other and let it grow into more. If you let yourself."

"You don't know," she whispered, "how badly I want to try."

Trying wasn't bad. Try was better than *can't.*

"We're going to finish this run and then we're going to my place to shower."

"Together?"

He loved the raspy quality in her voice and reminded himself he would be a good boy. "No, definitely not. But we will make dinner and talk all night and then I'm going to make out with you. A lot. Because people who are trying to get to know each other don't start with sex. They finish with it."

Her lips twitched—maybe on a smile or maybe in anticipation. He wasn't sure. "Don't think you can always tell me what to do."

"Gabby, anytime you want to tell me to do something to you, you let me know."

"Okay, then kiss me now."

Jamie had no problem obeying that order. He was leaning toward her to do just that when something caught his eye out of the corner.

Damn it. Bobby was out fishing off that damn dock.

It was as if the fear of what might happen suddenly turned into a bubble in his head. A picture of a dock collapsing into the cold water and taking the boy down with it. Only he wasn't seeing the bubble in his head. He was watching it happen out over the water as the supports of the short pier started to crumble beneath the not so insignificant weight of the ten-year-old.

Jamie could hear Gabby talking. Something about here he went again, but his legs were already in motion heading closer to the water, his body churning as he realized what was about to happen.

The dock would fall into the water, it would take

Bobby with it, possibly trapping him under broken beams of wood. It was April, not January, but still the water would be freezing. The shock of it would paralyze him and prolonged exposure would put him at risk of hypothermia.

Jamie could hear Gabby again but this time it was a muffled sound, like she was swallowing a shout. The sound of a yelp came to him from forty feet away as Bobby slid into the water while the dock came to pieces around him.

Jamie had three minutes.

"Don't follow me. The water is too cold." He didn't bother to turn around as he stripped off first his shirt, kicked off his sneakers and shucked his running pants. "Keep that dry. We'll need to warm him when I bring him in."

When I bring him in. I have to bring him in.

Jamie didn't issue another order. He waded into the rocky shore line, inhaling as the frigid water flowed around his ankles and calves and the broken shells and rocks dug into the bottom of his feet. He thought of breaking into a swim, but he knew he could make up more ground up with his legs than by pulling himself through the water with his arms.

The weightlessness combined with the heaviness of the water instantly brought him back to his training days, submerged in a pool for hours a day as his body learned to move and function in the different gravity environment.

He didn't remember freezing his balls off back then though.

The dock was now completely broken down in the water. Nothing more than large floating pieces of driftwood. He could see Bobby's head pop up amongst the flotsam with a panicked jerkiness of movement, seeming to search for help.

"Bobby hold on to something!"

Jamie wasn't sure if the words penetrated but he needed the kid not to go below the surface where it would be harder to find him or to get stuck under the floating wood planks. Too deep now to walk, he pushed himself off the bottom and began to swim as fast as he could, heading into the debris.

As soon as his hand came down on a piece of dock, he knew he'd reached the destruction area. He picked up his head in search of his target, but didn't immediately see him. Breathless from the cold rather than the exertion, it took him a half a second before he shouted his name.

"Bobby!" It sounded harsh and raw to his ears and he could only hope the sound carried.

"There!" Glancing at the shoreline he could see Gabby at the edge of the water bouncing up and down pointing at something as she shouted. Pointing at something more to his left. He looked that way and saw a particularly large bit of the dock bobbing in the water.

Two small hands, bone white, clung on top, but it was all he could see.

He put his head in the water and pushed with his arms and legs forcing himself to make up the distance.

How long had Bobby been in the water? How long

had Jamie himself? Not three minutes. Not yet. He was a fast swimmer.

Reaching the small life raft Bobby had found for himself, he saw the kid's body was completely submerged. Only his hands held on to the wood while his head barely cleared the surface. His lips were blue as he struggled to keep his chin out of the water.

Getting behind the kid in the water he lifted him, so his body flopped onto the piece of dock that was just big enough for him to get his chest out of the water if not his legs.

Jamie didn't issue instructions. There would be no point as the kid was half in shock. He simply started to push against the planks, kicking with all the energy left in his body. As soon as he knew he was close enough to set his feet on the ocean floor, he stood. Leaning over the kid he pulled him up and then lifted him over his shoulder.

He wasn't sure what Molly Claymore was feeding this kid, but he might recommend a little less butter with any lobsters the boy had been catching. Making his way to the shore he stopped, momentarily rattled by the fact that Gabby was wearing nothing but a pink bra and some hip hugging panties.

"You said he would need to get warm. You do, too. Put him down." It seemed she was now the one issuing the orders. That was okay with him. He was sapped.

"Lad-d-dy...I can s-see...your...b-bra." Bobby's teeth were chattering as the two of them used Jamie's shirt and Gabby's running jacket to rub him down. They removed the long sleeve shirt he wore and Jamie managed to pull off his jeans, but Bobby balked at having his underwear stripped.

"S-s-he's a g-girl," he stuttered through blue lips.

Gabby pulled the spandex over the boy's legs and Jamie concentrated on not thinking about how close to naked she was in the mid afternoon light. Their combined focus was on the boy.

Once he was fairly dry and his lips were a little less blue, they wrapped him in Jamie's long sleeved T-shirt and started their hike up the hill.

Choruses of *I'm sorry, Mr. Hunter* was the prevailing theme as they climbed to the top of the hill with Jamie and Gabby still clad only in their briefs as neither wanted to put on their wet clothing.

As soon as they reached the house Jamie put Bobby in his truck and turned the heat on high. Running inside he grabbed a couple of athletic pants and thick sweatshirts. Stripping himself of his wet briefs he dressed and shuddered as he let himself register how cold he'd been.

Outside, he got in the truck where Gabby was still talking to Bobby to keep him alert. She took the offered clothes and both males watched intently as she covered up her bra.

Crisis averted, Jamie allowed himself to lock down the visual memory of a mighty fine rack. It helped to warm him up.

"Is there a hospital on the island?" Gabby asked as she shimmied the pants up her legs.

Nothing wrong with those either, he thought.

"No, but I think we're better off taking him home.

His mom is a nurse and she can make the call if he needs to go to the mainland. She working today, Bobby?"

"Not today, sir. Boy, is she going to be mad, too. Her one day off and I had to go and do this. I didn't think the dock would ever fall."

"I told you it was unsafe," Jamie said sternly.

Once more the *I'm-sorry* chorus began and continued for the rest of the ride. Bobby's mom was both grateful and furious just as Bobby had predicted.

After waiting to get her professional opinion on Bobby's physical well-being, Jamie and Gabby got in the truck as Jamie gave a wave to Molly who was still simultaneously berating and hugging her son.

Jamie looked over and saw Gabby still and silent in the seat next to him.

"He's going to be fine," Jamie assured her. "Molly said all he needs is a warm bath and some hot chocolate. He'll be back fishing tomorrow on some other dock. I'm going to have to let Ted know his dock is now drift-wood. Damn it, I don't know how many times I told him he needed to shore it up—"

"Take me to bed."

His mouth snapped shut in a hurry. And he had to swallow before he said, "What?"

"Take me back to your place. And make love to me. Please. I don't want to wait anymore. I don't want to wait for anything."

Please. Well, hell. What was a man supposed to do when a woman said please?

CHAPTER TWELVE

JAMIE PULLED INTO his driveway and turned the engine off. A storm had rolled over the island and the first heavy pelts of rain were starting to fall on the windshield. It was the only sound to be heard in the truck. That and maybe their breathing.

Between the warm clothes and the cranked temperature in the cab, he actually felt himself getting overheated. Or maybe it had something to do with the certainty he was about to make love to Gabby Haines.

She hadn't said a word on the ride home. Had simply folded her hands in her lap and stared straight ahead. Hell, he might have thought he only imagined what she said by the way she was acting. No sly looks, no furtive touches. No foreplay.

Only a request. No, more like a plea.

They didn't move and the rain picked up in intensity. He thought back to the night where he came to get her while she slept in her car. He asked her then if she wanted to have sex with him. She'd never really given him an answer.

"Are you sure about this?"

"I'm not sure about anything. Except that I need you. I'm sure about that."

Need. Yes, it was a better word than *want*. It was more desperate, more urgent, and that's how he felt, too. When was the last time he'd ever taken a woman to bed with this much urgency riding inside of him? As though if he didn't lay himself on top of her and come inside her, he would shatter and fall apart into little pieces.

He opened the door and got out. The heavy drops hit him, soaking him as quickly as the Atlantic had. Only it felt good. The water washed over his face which felt hot and tight. He needed to cool down. He needed something to pull him back from this edge he was on or things would get out of control pretty quickly.

He came around the truck and opened her door. He had thoughts of lifting her out and carrying her inside—it seemed like a silly romantic thing any time he saw it in the movies or television, but now felt right. Like he needed to hold her. Needed to own her in a fundamental way.

She's mine. It needed to be declared.

But as he moved to pull her out of the truck she was already jumping out. Her bare feet covered his as he realized they had left their sneakers on the beach. The sight of their toes, his long and bare, hers tipped in pink polish, mingling together moved him in some elemental way.

She's mine.

Only then she was moving and taking control. Her hand came up and wrapped around his neck urging him down. He needed little prodding and pressed his lips against her warm swollen ones. Her mouth was hot and luscious and the contrast of it against the rain falling around them and on them was erotic as hell to him.

He pulled her close, his hand cupping her ass and hauling her against his body, his erection not bound by any briefs pressed against her belly. He turned them then and pressed her against the front of the truck needing to cover her, needing to surround her.

Her hands clutched his back, her fingers grasping through the fabric of his sweatshirt and he instantly wanted it off so he could feel her touch him. Her skin on his skin. He pushed the material away and then flung the shirt over his head, letting the rain cover him the way he was covering her.

So good the way her hands stroked up and down his back. So good the feel of her tongue pushing inside his mouth as he pushed his tongue against hers. So good the way they breathed together.

"Damn," he said as he backed off, bracing his arms against the hood, trapping her so she couldn't escape. "I'm losing it. And if I don't stop, I'm going take you right here."

"Yes," she said. Her eyes were glassy and her lips were puffy and red. He watched her run her hand along his chest now she had access to it, now it wasn't plastered against her body.

Her thumbs brushed over his hard nipples. He groaned and dropped his head so he could feel her touch him and watch her touch him at the same time.

"Lower," he whispered.

She obeyed and dropped her hands down so her fingers teased the elastic edge of the sweats slowly dipping inside, but not yet taking him where he wanted to go.

"Lower." The word came out on a growl. He wasn't in control anymore. He was going to take her hand and make her stroke him, make her feel what she was doing to him, make her make him come.

But he didn't have to because she was right there, her hand circling him and then tightening in a way that made him want to tilt his head back and shout to the world.

"Yes, damn yes."

But then her touch was gone and he was about to shout again, until he felt her drop to her knees. Before he could blink she pulled the elastic down over his hips and his erection sprang free. Her hand was replaced by the heat of her mouth swallowing the head and he saw stars and wondered if it was possible to faint from pleasure.

It was too much. This was too crazy. They were outside in the middle of the storm in his driveway and he was about to explode. This wasn't how he wanted it. In a bed. Covering her body. That's what he wanted.

With a force of will he didn't know existed within him he pulled himself away from her. Tugging the sweats up, he bent and lifted her to her feet, then in a single motion slung her over his shoulder.

She squeaked and then let out a whoosh of air as her midsection hit his shoulder, but he was beyond caring at this point. He cupped her bottom to hold her steady and made his way into the house. He thought about taking her on his couch because it was closer, but he didn't want anything restricting his movements. And he wanted her on his bed. On his bed sandwiched between it and him. He'd imagined it for long enough. Time to see the real deal.

He started up the stairs and thought she was saying something as she was bent over his back but he didn't want to listen and he certainly wasn't going to stop.

He reached his bedroom and dropped her on her back on the bed so she was sprawled across it. Her wet dark hair streaming against the white duvet nearly crippled him. That hair, he was going to do things with that hair. But not now. Later. Now, it was too late. She had pushed him too far.

Quickly he stripped her of the pants then took a little more time to pull off those hip-hugging panties. He knew she was sensitive about her weight but he had no time for it. All he saw were lush hips and a slightly rounded belly that would make his ride more enjoyable.

"Take off the top," he ordered as he was once again pushing down his sweatpants and kicking them out of the way. He walked over to his nightstand and opened a drawer extracting a condom he was in the habit of keeping there even though he hadn't needed them in a very long time.

On board with the plan apparently, Gabby had already taken off the sweatshirt and undid her bra clasp. As she wiggled out of the garment he started counting the seconds until he could see her breasts.

One, two, three…. Ah. There they were. Round and white with hard little pink nipples he was going to suck on at some point. At this moment, however, he could only think of one thing. He climbed on the bed and pushed his hips between her legs.

"Ready?" he asked as he moved himself so his erection was starting to press inside her. He could see her eyes widen, he heard her breath catch but it was too late to give her more time. She needed to be ready.

She nodded her head and held on to him, but he waited another beat. He could see she was nervous, not practiced or smooth like a woman who did this on a frequent basis. So he took another breath and slowly pushed himself inside instead of thrusting hard and taking himself deep the way he wanted to.

Her body fought him, but only for a fraction of second and then he was inside and on top of her and his world was suddenly right in a way it hadn't been since he'd been flying.

She wrapped her legs around his hips and he bent his head so it rested on her forehead. He had this crazy urge to thank her for letting him inside, but his body taken over and it had its own plan. Slow and easy he started to ride her, listening for the catch of her breath and for the tightening in her body letting him know this felt good to her. Once she was there with him, he moved faster letting his body dictate the rhythm.

"Jamie, oh, please. Yes…yes."

There it was. That special sound a woman made when she was close. He thought about tricks he might do to prolong the pleasure. Pull out and turn her on her stomach so he could take her from behind. Make her climb on top of him and ride him until she reached her peak.

But this wasn't the game of sex. This wasn't teasing and pleasure and fun. This was serious. What he was doing now felt serious. Like a mission or a quest to transport them to some other place. Besides, his body wouldn't let him leave her. So he plunged forward harder and with more urgency, and he felt her fingernails dig into his shoulders, and he felt her mouth on his neck. And then he felt her whole body tense and she let out the sweetest sound he'd ever heard.

He'd done it. He'd succeeded in his mission and now it was time for his reward. In seconds he was plunging inside her so hard and deep he was sure he would be lost forever. When the pleasure hit, she held him. When he collapsed against her body, she held him. And when he finally separated their bodies and turned on his side, she followed along and held him.

She held him as though she would never let go.

Despite the lethargy, the lingering pleasure and his giddy happiness, he knew eventually, when she came back to herself, she would.

Whether he could handle it or not.

SHE'D JUST HAD SEX with Jamison Hunter. Jamison Hunter had had sex with her. She and Jamison Hunter had made love. Gabby wasn't sure how to process that.

Her body had no problem with it. Her body was fluid and relaxed and...*right* in a way it hadn't been right in a very long time. But her brain kept circling what she'd done. What she'd asked him to do.

She rolled over on her side. Half his face was pressed into the pillow but the one eye she could see opened.

She knew as a general fact about him that his eyes were brown but had never really considered the color in any detail. With the afternoon light filtering through the windows she could see hits of bronze and gold in the chocolate depths.

He was so beautiful to her. She should tell him.

"You're going to leave now, aren't you?"

Leave? No, that was not what she'd been thinking. But the vulnerability in his question startled her and made her feel self-conscious.

"Do you want me to go?"

"No." He sat up and she felt a thrill go through her body as she admired the smattering of salt and pepper hair on his chest. "I want to go downstairs and make us some food then I want to spend the rest of the day and night making love."

That sounded like a plan to her.

"But you're going to start thinking any minute and remembering who I am and what I did. Then you'll be upset with yourself for allowing yourself to do it. You'll leave."

"Sounds like you have experience in this sort of thing."

"I do. But it's been a while. A long while since I let myself be with anyone who didn't know the score."

"Ah, I see. Jaded women only for you."

"It's worked out pretty well. Then you had to show up."

This was fascinating. This was definitely not what she expected. Smiling, Gabby turned even more on her stomach and rested her weight on her elbows for some reason completely unashamed he was getting a full view of her ass. "Wow, you really like me."

"Of course I like you. What the hell do you just think happened?"

"Well, I knew you wanted me. And I knew you respected me enough to want to seduce me, but I didn't think you liked me, liked me."

"Look, Sally Field, for the record, up until the scandal I only ever slept with women I liked. After, it became too much of an ordeal."

"Because the women didn't trust you."

"Why would they? In order to trust me, they would have to think I had changed. Most people don't think others are capable of change."

"Yet you made an exception for me. So either you do think I can believe you've changed or—"

"Or I wanted you that badly. Let's keep it simple for now, okay?"

Gabby shrugged. "Okay. But here is the thing I think makes me very different from the women in your past. I don't need to believe you've changed. I'll take the man who is in this bed right now."

His eyebrows lifted and she could see the skepticism. Her Jamie, her hero, was a wounded man. Go figure.

"Yes, I'm quite happy with the man you are. The person I've seen you be. The man who helped Susan when she needed it or saved an abused housewife or rescued a boy in freezing water—"

"Jeez, will you stop? Those are things any decent human being should do. There is nothing heroic in any of it. Don't turn me into something I'm not."

Gabby disagreed but she wasn't going to argue the point. Jamie was something special. His actions since the time he'd been a kid shouted it to the world. Which is why she knew she didn't need to forgive him, or believe he was different than he was.

Everything had become crystal clear. "Tell me what happened that day at the motel."

As if she'd poked him with a cattle prod his whole body reacted. He spun out of bed and she was graced with a beautiful back-end view before he reached for the sweats he'd kicked off earlier.

"What the hell are you getting at, Gabby?"

"I want to know what really happened. I remember the story. I saw the pictures, but now I want the truth."

"You think it's not the truth because you want to believe I'm someone I'm not."

"I know it's not the truth, because I know you."

Gabby also stood and for a moment she didn't reach for the sweats or try to cover herself with a blanket. She stood in front of him naked, with all her insecurities and all her faults. He looked at her then, and even though she could tell he was annoyed, his eyes still took in all of her. If the tent forming in his sweatpants was any indication, he liked what he saw.

"You're reaching because you can't accept who I am."

"You're hiding something you don't want the world to know."

"Oh, it's the world, is it? And what are you going to do, Gabby? Hunt down the truth, expose my secrets and write a tell-all biography? Will that make you feel better about your life? Like you're not quite the failure you think you are?"

That hurt. He'd done it deliberately and no doubt to push her off her course. She wasn't going to let herself be swayed though. She knew she was on to something.

"Why can't you tell me the truth? What are you afraid of?"

"Gabby, the truth is I'm not a perfect man. The truth is I made mistakes. The truth is if you want to stick around for a while, we can probably have a good time for a couple of weeks. But that's all I'm good for when it comes to relationships."

That hurt worse. The thought of leaving him. That she could be this happy but only for a few weeks didn't seem fair.

"Is that what you want?" She had a hard time asking the question. "A couple of weeks of sex and good times and that's it?"

He ran his hand through his short hair and paced like a man on the defensive. "No," he snapped. "No, I think— Damn it— I think I might want something more. But I know what it means. It means forgiveness and acceptance and I don't know if you have it in you."

"You want me to forgive and accept something I know you didn't do."

He shook his head and she knew he was done arguing. "Do you still want some food or something?"

"No." She didn't want to waste another minute standing here when the truth was something she needed to learn. She would call Melissa and tell her what her thoughts were. She was going to need a little leeway and maybe a bigger expense budget to handle airfare, but she was on to something big.

"Then I guess we're done." He bent to pick up the oversize top and bottoms along with her underwear. "You should leave."

"Leave. You make it sound so final." Which made her hands shake and made stepping into her panties much more challenging.

"It has to be. I can't do this, Gabby. I can't have a fling with you and call it a nice time. What happened here was…intense. So let's end it. Now. Before anyone gets hurt."

Yeah. As if having him for the brief time she'd had then walking away wasn't going to hurt. "I don't understand why you're doing this. Maybe it's because no one before ever did what I'm about to do. Maybe you don't believe anyone can. I'm standing here telling you I believe in you."

He stepped toward her as she finished putting on the sweatshirt. He cupped her face and when she had the courage to look into his bronze eyes she could see sadness and defeat.

She knew he wanted to say something. When he opened his mouth no words came out. Instead he kissed her on the forehead. "I'll walk you out."

Numb she paddled barefoot down the stairs, out the door and got into the rental car she'd parked in his driveway before they'd gone for their run.

It was as though she'd been hypnotized because she didn't struggle. Didn't say a word as he opened the door and waited for her to get inside. But once the door was closed he motioned to her to roll the window down.

She hit the button and the electronic buzz of the window sliding down echoed in the car, because she still couldn't say anything.

Leaning in he rocked a few times on his heels. "I'm sorry this couldn't work out."

"I don't know what's happening." It was the truth. She'd made this great discovery in realizing he was innocent of whatever scandal people thought he committed. They had made love and everything was going to be great, because she didn't have to worry he would break her heart by cheating on her.

Except he was breaking her heart anyway by making her go.

"You need to go back to New York or wherever your life is going to take you. And you need to forget this. Forget me."

So not going to happen.

"Remember this though, Gabriella. You're no damn failure."

She looked at him then. "I'm failing at this."

"No. No, you're not. I failed you first."

Pushing away from the car, he turned and walked to his house. She watched him until she couldn't see him anymore and then she continued to sit there. For how long, she couldn't say.

The sun set and darkness started to fall and she wondered if she was going to spend another night in her car simply because she found herself immobilized. Not able to go back inside and fight him, not able to leave him, either.

She still didn't understand what happened. Why weren't they celebrating? Why wasn't he telling her the truth about what happened that day?

Finally she thought of the ferry, the one that would take her off the island, the one that would lead her to the people who would tell her the truth if Jamie wasn't going to do it. She knew if she hurried, she might catch the last one for the night.

CHAPTER THIRTEEN

"TELL ME AGAIN why I shouldn't fire you?"

Gabby smiled at Melissa with what she hoped was confidence, but what she feared was actually desperation. "Because I think I might have a new angle on the Jamison Hunter scandal that, once exposed, will make for an immediate nationwide bestseller."

Sitting on the edge of the chair in her boss's office, Gabby contemplated the questionable ethics involved with her plan. True, she did believe there was more to the story than anyone—than Jamie—was admitting. If she was right, and the truth about what happened that day wasn't what the world believed, then absolutely the story would sell millions of books.

People remembered the scandal of Jamison Hunter the way they did the stories about Monica Lewinsky and Tiger Woods. As much as everyone wanted to celebrate heroes in all forms, watching those same people fall from grace was even better. It was good entertainment. And even better entertainment? The redemption. To find out there was more to the story, of course people would want to read it.

The question was whether she would feel comfortable giving away Jamie's secrets once she knew them.

She had this crazy idea that once the truth, whatever it was, was finally uncovered, he would see the light and recognize that a book chronicling his life and releasing him from his secrets was the best thing for everyone.

Maybe a follow-up interview on *20/20* with his biographer at his side wouldn't hurt, either.

As desperate as she was, even she didn't believe it would ever happen. As angry as she was at him for kicking her out of his bed and out of his house, she would never knowingly betray him, either. Any book that came out of these events would have to be Jamie's idea.

Still, Gabby was going to find the truth. Jamie would simply be the one to decide what she would do with the information she uncovered.

As for Melissa… Gabby decided her role was on a need-to-know basis only.

"So? Don't leave me hanging. What's the big revelation?"

"I don't think what happened that fateful day outside the motel in Florida really happened. I think there was a misunderstanding."

Melissa rolled her eyes, which Gabby wanted to point out wasn't the best look for her.

"Gabby, come on. The man was called out before the world as an adulterer with a capital A. He didn't deny it once. You think he would have let people believe it if he was innocent. If it was all some crazy misunderstanding among friends like a bad episode of *Three's Company?* I don't think so."

He would have if he'd been protecting someone, Gabby thought. The one thing she knew about him

from their weeks together was that he'd always sacri-
ficed himself to protect someone he cared about. So she
needed to talk to the people involved and find out once
and for all what he'd done and who Jamison Hunter was.

Other than the man she'd foolishly given her heart to.

Since she had already confirmed Jamie wasn't going
to talk that left two other people.

"Look, we're talking about two trips. A couple of
days each at most."

"Where you plan to do what? Find Cheryl Hillerman
and get her to speak about what happened? Something
she has never once done for any journalist, television reporter, any news organization? Even more closed mouth
than her is Hunter's ex-wife. The only comment the
woman has ever made was to check the box citing ir-
reconcilable differences on her divorce decree. It isn't
going to happen."

"I can be very convincing." Gabby could use a little
of that convincing power right now.

This was important. Having the backing of a publisher might make her more reputable to the two women
involved. Showing up as an unemployed talk show host
who happened to be in love with Jamie Hunter didn't
seem like a way to win them over. Acting in an offi-
cial capacity as his biographer gave her more cache and
hopefully would persuade them to open up.

Even if Gabby's reason for being there was a lie.

Gabby squirmed a little in her chair and tried not
to think about how she was using Melissa and McKay
Publishing for her own ends. Except, they knew the
risks. As an industry, publishing thrived on a gamble.

All she was asking was they step up to the table and roll the dice.

What happened after would be anyone's guess.

Melissa tapped the ends of her fingers together, making her long nails click. Gabby was reminded slightly of Cruella DeVille, but forced herself to keep her expression neutral.

"Let's look at this from the ten-thousand-foot view, shall we?" the senior editor began. "You're not a writer. You're not a print journalist."

"I was," Gabby interrupted. "At the start of my career."

"You wrote articles for fashion and entertainment magazines."

"Yes, but some of it was really...hard-hitting stuff." Gabby thought about her first interview with a local Philadelphia actress who she made cry after she confessed to having had breast enhancement surgery—something she'd repeatedly denied in the press up to that point.

"That was then. This is now. Now, you're a new editor who failed in the first assignment I gave her. And you want me to sign off on this exploratory mission of yours to prove Jamison Hunter—a self-confessed adulterer—is innocent of cheating on his wife?"

Gabby closed her eyes. When put like that, it didn't seem likely Melissa would agree to her plan.

In a last ditch effort, she played her trump card. "Both Cheryl Hillerman and Paula Hunter will talk to me. I know it."

"Why?" The skepticism rolled off Melissa's tongue.

"Because we have something in common. We all are, or were at some point, in love with Jamie Hunter. They'll talk to me because they'll see I care about him."

Melissa fell back into her chair. "You've got to be kidding me. I send you up there to get a commitment on a biography and you fall in love with the damn guy. Is that what this is about? Some romantic hope he isn't the creep he's reported to be."

Gabby leaned forward until her hands were braced on her boss's desk, her urgency a very real thing exploding in her chest.

"Melissa, I'm telling you this guy isn't who the world thinks he is. I know it deep down inside. He's a hero and an American icon. His name and reputation were trashed, possibly for no good reason. If Cheryl and Paula ultimately refuse to talk to me, then fine. It's my dime and you can fire me as fast as you like. If they do talk, you need to let me tell the story and you need to listen to it. I know I'm right. The country needs the truth."

I need the truth.

"You're right, Haines. You're very convincing." Melissa shook her head and smiled. "'The country needs the truth.' You sound like a bad movie. Okay. I'll authorize the trips but you get your expense check only if we get a book. Even if we can't get Hunter to talk, I'll still bite if either of these women are interested in coming forward to tell their side. You've now got three chances to get me one book. I assume you know where to find both women."

Gabby did. Although they did everything to keep a low profile, the internet had yielded the names of the towns they both called home. From there it was simply a matter of finding the right people who would point Gabby in the direction she needed to go.

"Okay. We'll make sure you have what you need. But this time, Gabby, if you don't bring me back the book, any book… You know there will be no third chances."

She wasn't going to need a third chance. She was sure of it. One of the women would talk to her. Even if she had to shake the truth out of them.

"GABBY!" JAMIE BOUNDED up the steps to the B and B. The sick feeling he'd been left with all night grew darker. The reality that he'd pushed her away for good sank in some time around midnight.

He'd let it stew for a good couple of hours, telling himself he'd done the right thing until about 4:00 a.m. when he was certain he'd made the biggest mistake of his life. There had been another hour of stewing because, even though he knew he'd made a mistake, he wasn't entirely convinced he could fix it if he wanted to.

Now the sun was coming up on the island and he was here with the hope he could make everything better. But no one was responding to his shouts, until finally Susan came out of the kitchen, looking slightly disheveled.

"She's gone, Jamie."

Yeah, he knew it. Her car wasn't parked out front and somehow the island felt a little lonelier. He needed to see the proof for himself, though.

"She came back early last night and threw all her stuff together and took off for the ferry. I could see she was in a state and I told her to wait until morning, but she wouldn't listen to me."

Because he had told her to go. He had told her to get out. Standing there half naked listening to her tell him she believed in him… It was too much. He'd been overwhelmed at the same time feeling stripped and raw and more vulnerable than he'd ever been in his life.

Maybe that was the real reason he kicked her butt to the curb. It had nothing to do with protecting her, or preventing her eventual heartache when she learned the truth about him. Instead, it was *his* heart he'd been protecting. Because he felt her belief in him straight to his core. He wanted to hold on to it. Treasure it. He wanted to believe he could really claim it and call it his own.

He wanted to believe it would last forever.

"I blew it, Susan."

The older woman nodded then tugged on his hand. "I'll make you some coffee and you can have a fresh muffin."

Unthinking he followed her into her kitchen. This room was sacrosanct for Susan. No guests ever came in here. But she sat him at a large, family-size table and put a hot blueberry muffin she'd pulled out of the oven in front of him along with a cup of coffee.

"What happened?"

"I told her to leave. Why did I do that?"

She nodded and sat with her own coffee. "Love can be a very scary thing."

Love. The word had him sitting straighter. "I don't love her. Why would you say that?"

He didn't love her. He liked her a lot. He liked her

company. Her presence in his life, which felt a lot fuller when she was around. He liked that she didn't take herself or him too seriously.

Okay, he loved her body. He loved her body *a lot*.

"Maybe you can't admit you were headed that way. Maybe you think it will be easier to get over her. Take it from me, honey, it won't. Our feelings are what they are. You can't change them, or wish them away. This is going to hurt you, Jamie."

"I can make her come back. If I told her something, I could make her believe in me… I could make her come back."

"I don't think you should do it," Susan said. "I'm sorry you're hurt, but the truth is, I don't think you were ready for Gabby."

Her words jerked him out of his own depressing thoughts. "What do you mean?"

"You haven't let anyone get close to you since I've known you. Not really close. You keep everyone at arm's length and it wouldn't have worked with her. Gabby, I could tell, was a person who needs to be all the way in. That's the only way she feels safe. I was worried for her."

"Worried for her? I'm the one sitting here looking like a fool."

"Because you pushed her away. Because you're not ready."

Was Susan right? It was scary to think how many different ways he could have played out the scene in his bedroom. He could have told Gabby everything. He could have accepted what she had to offer and tried to build on it. He could have kept her close.

Instead, he told her to get out. And not for the first time. Now that he thought about it, he had to wonder why she kept coming back. Every time he pushed her away, she rebounded like a puppy who didn't understand it didn't belong. Was it for the story? Or was it for him?

If it was for him, he had to agree with Susan. Maybe he wasn't ready. On the heels of that acknowledgment was the crazy feeling he wanted to be. Never had his solitary world seemed so dull, so depressing. He wanted Gabby's light, her energy…he wanted *her*.

"How does a person get ready?"

Susan patted his hand. "That is a very good question and one I have no idea how to answer."

He grimaced. "You're not helping me out here, Susan."

She shrugged. "How about another muffin?"

"CHERYL HILLERMAN?"

The woman with the long blonde hair turned around. She was in her early forties and still had a complexion fabulous enough she could leave her house without makeup on.

No one in Ryan's Port, Florida, would give Gabby her address nor was it listed in the area directory. After hours of speaking to the locals it was clear Cheryl was a treasured member of the tight-knit community and they protected their own. Gabby figured the only way

to find her would be to hang out at all the usual gathering spots until eventually she came into town.

The most central of spots was the coffee shop. In
typical fashion it was where people got their gossip and
coffee in one stop.

Yesterday, Gabby had heard the young girl behind
the counter call out to the blonde by name as she handed
over a smoothie. Although it had been almost eight
years since her picture had been plastered on every
newspaper and tabloid in the country, Gabby easily recognized the woman at the heart of the scandal.

She had come and gone so quickly, Gabby couldn't
catch her without chasing her down the block. Not the
easiest or most effective way to make an introduction.
Besides, she hadn't actually worked out what she would
say. Finding the woman had been paramount. Convincing her to open up about the past was an obstacle Gabby
figured she would conquer after she met her.

She'd told Melissa she could be convincing. Sitting
around in a coffee shop, hoping Cheryl needed her daily
fix of smoothie didn't feel convincing. It felt nerve rack-
ing. Those nerves had kicked into high gear as soon as
the blonde woman once again walked through the door.
It took Gabby five seconds to gather up her courage,
but she knew it was now or never.

Gabby waited until she ordered the banana and
strawberry concoction then stepped in front of her before she could leave. The woman had an easy smile and
a graceful figure she covered with a tied-dyed cotton
skirt and white cotton blouse.

"You are Cheryl Hillerman?"

"Can I help you?"

Not having thought of any convincing lie which might get the woman to talk about the past, Gabby's only play was the truth. "My name is Gabby Haines and I work for McKay Publishing—"

And just like that the easy smile was gone and Cheryl was walking out the door. Gabby followed her out onto the street thankful she'd worn practical shoes since she practically had to jog to catch up to the woman.

"Please, Ms. Hillerman if I could have just five minutes—"

"Go away!"

"I'm here because Jamie sent me."

That stopped her in her tracks. Slowly, Cheryl turned, her face a mask of skepticism.

"You know Jamie?"

"I do. I'm writing his biography."

The woman laughed harshly. "Bull. No way Jamie ever tells anyone about his life. He's too damn ashamed of it."

"Well, it's been a while and maybe he feels the world is ready to finally hear about what really happened that day."

"What really happened?" Cheryl's eyes narrowed, but at least Gabby had piqued her interest.

"I'm looking for the complete story. I want to hear what happened from you directly, in your words."

Cheryl shook her head. "Nope. Don't believe you for a second. Jamie will never talk about that day. Not with anyone. It would hurt Paula and he would cut off his arm before he did that again."

"I've spent time with Jamie. I know him." *I'm most likely in love with him, which really sucks if I'm wrong about the past.* "It doesn't take a rocket scientist to know the story told by a single incriminating picture could have been misleading. I'm looking for the truth."

Cheryl didn't speak for a moment and Gabby wondered how close she was to considering Gabby's proposal. Hope spiked, but then Cheryl shook her head, her decision obviously reached.

"Believe whatever you want. I'm not talking. If Jamie got on the phone and told me himself he okayed this farce of a biography, I still wouldn't talk. I've spent the past eight years trying to make the people of this tiny community forget I was the nation's *other woman.* I'm not going back there. Ever. You want to tell his story, then end it before that day ever happened. It would make everyone's lives a little easier."

The figurative walls in front of the woman were so thick, Gabby knew she wasn't going to penetrate them. So much for being convincing. She held up her hands in surrender and took a step backward. "You win. I'll leave. Can I ask one last question?"

"You can, but I won't answer it."

"Did you love him?" Gabby couldn't say why she asked the question especially considering how hostile Cheryl was to her. But something in Gabby wanted to believe if it did happen, if Jamie had cheated on his wife and this woman engaged in adultery with him, then it was about more than sex.

She expected the woman to turn and walk away. Instead a small smile played about her lips as though she was remembering a joke someone told a long time ago.

"Did I love him?" she repeated. "No, I can honestly tell you I did not. For whatever that's worth. Now leave me alone or I swear my next trip is to the police station. Surely there are laws about being harassed in the street."

Gabby took another step back. "I understand. Thank you for speaking with me."

"You're not welcome." Cheryl rushed her steps and a block away turned a corner so she was out of sight. Gabby thought about what she didn't learn and probably should consider her efforts a waste of time.

Only she didn't. If anything, she felt more strongly than ever the three people in this play were hiding something. Jamie wasn't talking. Cheryl certainly wasn't talking.

That left only one cast member.

It was time for Gabby to meet the ex-wife.

CHAPTER FOURTEEN

"MRS. HUNTER, I can't thank you enough for taking the time to talk with me."

Paula Hunter had short dark hair she wore in a sleek bob around her face. Her smile was soft and elegant. Her clothes were Audrey Hepburn chic from her slimming dark capri pants to her crisp white collared shirt.

She was the picture of class and understated beauty. A modern day Jackie O. Gabby felt like an ungainly elephant in her presence. In her defense, she had to imagine most woman would feel the same.

She had been much easier to locate than Cheryl since her name and number were actually listed in the local phone directory. She was still Mrs. Paula Hunter after all these years. She lived in the same home she'd purchased for herself after the divorce. With a generous divorce settlement plus an inheritance from her mother, she lived comfortably in the upscale Connecticut neighborhood.

"I was surprised to receive your call. It's been so long since anyone has asked me for 'the story.' There are days I can almost forget it ever happened."

Gabby watched the woman's delicate fingers form

air quotes around the words and thought she even made that gesture look classy.

"Mrs. Hunter…may I call you Paula?"

"Of course."

"I think you'll find I'm not here to dig up dirt or create more scandal. I'm only trying to put all the pieces of the past together. Because, in looking back at what happened, I think the puzzle was incomplete. I believe in my heart there was more to the story than the people ever knew."

"Why do you believe that?"

It was a fair question. Gabby wasn't sure how Jamie's ex-wife would respond to the answer. But she had taken Gabby's call. She'd invited her into her home. It seemed only fair Gabby was as truthful to Paula as she wanted Paula to be with her.

"I know Jamie. Pretty well, I think. I've spent a lot of time with him. I've seen the man he is."

The older woman nodded sagely. "Of course. Now you know him, you can't imagine a man like him would do something as…crass…as cheat on his wife."

"It doesn't make sense. I've watched every piece of media coverage from that time and knowing him as I do, it looks to me like…like…"

Gabby struggled to confess what she'd seen because she knew it could put the woman she was talking to in an awkward position. The way he took all of the attention on himself, it was amazing to watch. The more he put himself out there, the more he confessed, the more questions he answered regarding his honor and his integrity, the more both Cheryl and Paula faded into the background. Eventually it was as though the two women had never been part of the story. Yes, he'd been the person in the spotlight to begin with, but the way he controlled the media after the story broke appeared to be planned or, at the very least, orchestrated.

"Like what? Say it."

Gabby took a deep breath. "It was like he deliberately fell on some invisible sword. One he shoved deeper into his chest with every remark he made. The more he shoved, the more people ate it up."

Paula didn't speak immediately. She sipped the tea she had poured. She looked across the yard. It was a beautiful spring day in Connecticut and they sat together on a covered porch filled with comfortable lounge chairs for reading and couches for napping. All done in muted colors to accent the beautiful garden around the perimeter of the porch.

Gabby could practically see Paula out there among the flowers, planting and pruning. The image came complete with a wide-brimmed hat to protect her face from the sun and sturdy gloves to protect her perfectly manicured fingers from the dirt.

A woman of means and leisure. A woman who loved her quiet existence. Was she what she appeared to be? It was hard to say.

This was who Jamie had married. This was the woman he took to bed and made love to…except when he made love to someone else. No, something didn't fit. Like an instrument out of tune. She couldn't imagine him running his hands through this woman's hair and tugging hard while he thrust deep inside her.

Gabby reached for her own cup of tea to hide her blush. How wrong was it to be thinking about incredible sex with Jamie while his ex-wife sat across from her?

Wrong, Gabby. Very, very wrong.

Oblivious to Gabby's inner turmoil, Paula leaned back in her chair and sighed.

"An incomplete puzzle. That's what you said. Yes, that's an apt description. Ever since your call, I've considered whether or not I would speak to you about what happened. I thought about calling Jamie, but I know what he would say and frankly, I didn't want to listen to him say it. It's been eight years and many lies. When you called I thought…yes. Now is the time."

Gabby found herself on the edge of her seat waiting for the words she knew would exonerate Jamie. The words that would make it okay for her to love him, or, more accurately, make it okay for him to believe she could love him.

"I was twenty-one when Jamie and I married. He was a very mature twenty-two. Recently graduated from the Air Force Academy he was being transferred overseas to Germany and it made sense for us to marry and that I should go with him. My father was an Air Force Officer and was teaching at the academy in Colorado. That's how we met."

No, Gabby thought. She didn't want to hear this part. She didn't want to know about their married life, and how happy they were, or why they didn't have children or any of it. She only wanted the story of what happened in the motel. Why was Paula there? Why was Cheryl? What did it all mean?

"My parents were very old-fashioned. No living to-gether in sin. No trying out the waters before marriage, so to speak. I was a virgin on my wedding night as any good girl should be, according to my parents. So it was a...surprise...for me when Jamie made love to me the first time. He was not a virgin."

I'm going to have you naked and underneath me.

The earthy words came back with stunning clarity. Jamie was intensely sexual. He'd proven it to her by the way he'd taken her, as if she was the first, last and only woman on earth. Like he couldn't get inside her fast enough or deep enough.

Imagining the twenty-two-year-old version of him on his wedding night was both sexy, because she could only imagine his virility, but also weird because she could see Paula in a prim white nightgown with her eyes closed waiting to be deflowered.

The two pictures didn't jive.

"I was a failure as a wife. I thought I was a failure as a woman. I simply didn't care for...it. I went to special-ists. I saw therapists. I took medication..."

"Paula, you don't have to—"

"No. This is, as you say, part of the puzzle. It's im-portant to understand who we were so you can under-stand how we got to the motel."

But Gabby didn't want to go where Paula was taking her. She didn't want to discover that, at the end of the day, the woman was frigid so she had let Jamie have an affair. Maybe it made him less culpable if he wasn't doing it behind her back, but it didn't exonerate him. If his wife had issues in the bedroom, he needed to help her, not abandon her.

"I was a wreck and Jamie was as supportive as a man can be. Of course we spoke about divorce, but I knew my parents would not react well. I begged him not to consider it. I used his career as leverage. He was climbing the ranks and getting more and more opportunities. I convinced him a divorce would not look good to his superiors. The one thing Jamie and I did together very well was look good."

"I think I understand," Gabby said. "Your marriage was a sham."

"It was. I held it together in a tightly closed fist. I did that for a very long time. Then everything changed the day I met Cheryl."

Gabby waited for more, but Paula had paused deliberately as if she were waiting for something to click with Gabby. *The day I met Cheryl*... Not the day the picture was taken.

A rush of clarity hit Gabby. She thought about the almost amused expression on Cheryl's face when Gabby asked her if she loved Jamie.

"Oh, my goodness." The air seemed to leave her lungs and she felt a little light-headed. "All this time and you never told anyone."

"No. Jamie wouldn't hear of it. He knew it would permanently separate me from my parents and, despite their strong beliefs, we were close so it would have devastated me to not see them. But they would not have tolerated their daughter being a lesbian. So we all stayed silent." She paused for a moment, once again staring out over her garden. Then she sighed. "They have both since passed—my father just this past year. It seems silly now to have lied to them all that time. They thought I was distraught over what Jamie did to me, which is why I never married again. It was a convenient lie to let them believe."

Fury like nothing Gabby had ever known filled her body actually lifting her to her feet. "How could you? You let him take the fall. You let him become America's whipping boy. You were the cheater that day. You were there with Cheryl and he caught you two together."

"He was, to say the least, upset. However, after some time and a lot of talking, we both realized my sexual preferences explained a great deal about why our marriage didn't work."

"I'll say! A man like Jamie... A man like him and he was married to *you.* You should have told him. You shouldn't have tried to hide it from him all those years. It wasn't fair, to either of you."

Paula held her hands up. "I didn't know. I didn't know until I met Cheryl and had these feelings for the first time. I didn't understand what sexual attraction even was until I was with her. You have to believe me, I never would have committed myself to a man had I had any inkling. But growing up, sex was not something one talked about openly in my home. I didn't date, I didn't flirt or tease. My whole world was about meeting a nice boy from the Academy and marrying him. That was my goal. Sex didn't enter into it."

"You know what the press did to him. They vilified him. They made the American people believe that he was less than what he was. He was a hero and you took that from him. You took it from everyone."

A sad smiled played across Paula's lips. "Yes, he was a hero. Is a hero. And so it shouldn't be any surprise to you he decided to rescue me no matter the cost to him."

"You should have stopped him."

"I thought you said you knew Jamie."

Gabby's fury evaporated rapidly, leaving her feeling wobbly. She fell back down into the chair as she considered what Paula's story meant to her own past and her future.

"I was so disheartened. You ruined my greatest crush."

"As I did for many women. But all you knew about Jamie was the public image he presented. You didn't know him. We made the decision together to tell the story most assumed was true and, in a way, it freed us both. I was able to divorce him with my parents' support. He was able to go live his life with whomever he chose."

"Only he didn't," Gabby snapped. "Instead he took himself off to an isolated island. He's been there ever since and he's never once let another woman get as close because he never thought any of them would believe in him again."

Paula smiled. "But you did."

"Yes! I did. I believed in him and he sent me away." Gabby considered his actions. "Why did he do that?

Why did he do that if he knew the truth? Maybe he didn't believe me. Maybe his ability to trust is so shattered— All this time…you took his life away."

"I think Jamie would disagree. We weren't the greatest lovers, but we were good friends. We accomplished a lot together. I was the one who pushed him to apply for the astronaut program. I was there each time he blasted off into space, never knowing if it was the last time I would see him. I was the reason he was a hero the day he saved those men and women on the space station. I gave Jamie his life. I gave you, your crush. Then I gave him his freedom."

Gabby wanted to argue, but really, what was left to say? The truth was out and there was only one thing she cared about doing.

"Thank you," Gabby said as she stood again, this time to leave. "For telling me. I needed to know."

"And what are you going to do with this information? Are you going to tell the world in a book?"

"Is that what you want?"

The woman tilted her head and waited a beat before answering. "I wouldn't mind it, no. I feel like I freed Jamie the day I divorced him. I told myself even while the press was attacking him I was doing a noble thing. But I haven't been free these past eight years. Instead, I've clung to a lie. With my parents gone, there's no reason to stay hidden in this life anymore. It's time for me to move on, too."

Gabby swallowed. She wouldn't feel any pity for this woman. "Good luck. I'll let you know what happens."

"Thank you. And when you see Jamie again tell him…I'm sorry. For so many things."

Oh, Gabby would tell him. Right after she socked him in the nose for lying to her all this time.

JAMIE ENDED THE CALL and put his cell back in his pocket. It was done. Paula had finally given someone the truth and, of all people, it had to be Gabby. The implications of what that meant were staggering.

Most importantly, she would be coming back to the island and to him. That he knew. But what was he going to tell her?

"What's wrong?"

Jamie looked up at Zhanna, whose arms were filled with plates of food. None of it for him. "Go deliver your orders and then we'll talk."

"Uh-oh. You have serious-talk face. I don't want to do serious today. I have hot date with Tom in a little bit. He's coming here to get me."

Jamie cringed. In a way he was glad she was dating. In a totally different way he didn't want to hear about it.

"Oh, no," Zhanna said. "I can see in your face this is not good. Give me one minute."

He watched her serve the plates with speed and grace. She moved quickly and efficiently throughout the tiny diner and made sure everyone got a smile along the way. She was a natural and he couldn't help but feel a burst of pride in his chest. She was an amazing woman and he was glad to call her a friend.

After a once-through with a pitcher of iced tea and hot coffee she topped off any and all drinks for the customers then returned to his booth. She laid her hands on the table and turned her palms up in a gesture that said *so talk*.

"I think Gabby might be coming back to the island." No thinking about it. He knew it, deep in his gut. If only to tell him to go to hell for lying to her. He thought about the book she was so desperate to write. It would be the start of a new career for her. A chance to rebuild her life. She certainly had a new angle to present to her publisher.

What they wouldn't do to get their hands on the story. It would be hard for her to turn something like that down.

"Uh. Her. I guess if she comes back I must find a way to like her."

"You already do like her. You told me so."

"Of course this is true, but I like to keep it a secret from her. It is more fun this way. But I don't understand. You like her, too."

He did. He might more than like her. The L word pounded in his head and suddenly his chest felt tight.

"You should be happy she's coming back. Only you don't look happy."

"I don't know if I'm *ready* for her. Does that make sense?" It had made so much sense when Susan said it, but now he thought it sounded a lot like TV talk show psychobabble.

Zhanna reached her hands farther across the table and wiggled them in a way that told him she wanted to hold on to him. He wasn't really a man who held hands with the women in his life. Crazy, but it seemed so intimate. Like they were connecting themselves out in public for the world to see.

"I know what it means to not be ready. When Tom first asked me out I was definitely not ready."

"Okay. What did you do to become ready?"

She pressed her lips together. "This is a good question."

So he'd been told.

She squeezed his hands and smiled. "I did nothing. I'm probably still not ready. I'm scared. I'm nervous for what is going to happen. I almost wish I didn't like him because then it would be easier. The only thing I changed was I said yes. I said yes to him and so whether I am ready or not, now I must go."

"Fake it until you make it."

"I do not know this saying."

Jamie smiled. "That's okay. I get your point."

"Good. Although I'm not sure I made one."

Tugging her even closer toward him he kissed her knuckles, once on each hand. "I don't know what I would do without you. Thank you for being in my life."

"I do not know what you would do without me, either." She smiled back.

"Zhanna?"

Jamie turned not realizing someone had approached the booth. He watched Zhanna's eyes light up and a blush creep across her cheeks. She did like this man. Jamie could see it and told himself he was happy to let her go. Tom was a good guy.

Although even as the thought formed in his mind, he could see the younger man's eyes falling to where Jamie still held on to Zhanna's hands. Jamie dropped them, but the look of uncertainty in Tom's eyes remained.

"You ready, Zhanna?"

Zhanna laughed at Jamie and Jamie could see Tom's body tighten visibly. "See, this I don't know. But I will go with you anyway."

"Look, if now isn't a good time—"

"No," Jamie interrupted, sensing the man's withdrawal. "She's ready. Aren't you?"

"Yes. Let me get my purse." Zhanna slid out of the booth and the two men watched her flit across the dining room giving a negligent wave to her customers who were no doubt thrilled to be watching her go out on a date with the most eligible man on the island.

The most eligible man after Jamie, that was.

"She's a special girl." He could feel Tom tense at his words. He probably should attempt to put him at ease. "Hey, I'm not trying to cause any trouble."

"Then don't." Tom gave him a hard look the likes of which Jamie hadn't seen since his days in the military from commanding officers.

Who would have considered Tom, the man who took in stray dogs and desperate kittens, a badass? In a way it made Jamie feel better knowing the man had it in him. A little badass never hurt anyone, and Zhanna needed someone strong enough to stand up to her large personality.

"Have a good night, Tom."

"Thanks. You, too." Tom straightened but then ruined some of his fierceness by offering a half-hearted smile.

Zhanna was in good hands. It was time for Jamie to go and deal with his own love life. Because he had a feeling it was about to come down on him like a freight train.

ZHANNA CAME OUT OF the ladies' room wearing a new outfit, freshly brushed hair, pink lips and a glow she knew she had no control over. This was her first date with Tom. Her first date with anyone in so long and it felt good. As though her life was finally starting over now.

She didn't want to think about her sadness. She didn't want to think about her fear. She only wanted to eat food someone else had cooked, served to her by someone else. Tom was taking her to a nice restaurant off the island and she'd worn high heels that she worried might make her slightly taller than him, but when she approached him she saw it wasn't the case.

Maybe because he was standing straighter.

"Wow, Zhanna. you look great."

She looked around him to the now empty booth where Jaime had left half his meal and some cash on the table.

"Where did he go?"

"He left. Is that a problem?"

His voice sounded different. A little strained. And his cheeks were flushed a bit. Zhanna considered all this as she looped her arm through his. "No. We can go now. Adel has me covered."

Tom didn't say any more. Instead he led Zhanna to his car. It wasn't fancy. A Toyota sedan, but she could tell he'd had it washed and the inside vacuumed for their date.

This made him considerate.

He was still quiet as he opened her door first, then walked around to the driver's side. Zhanna waited until he had climbed in.

"Okay, what is it? You are not happy already and I have not even had a chance to show you my charming self."

Tom's head bent. "What is it between you and him?"

"Him, who?"

Tom's eyebrow raised and Zhanna realized immediately what his problem was. Or rather *who* the problem was. "Jamie? He's my friend. You know this."

"Yeah, but it's like you've got this connection. Something different. I'm not going to lie, it doesn't thrill me."

Interesting, she thought. "You are jealous."

"Of course I'm jealous. He's a damn astronaut! An American hero. You know that part right? He's not just the guy on the island who helps people when they need it, or rescues Bobby Claymore when a dock collapses. He freaking went into space and saved people on the space station. I can't compete with him, Zhanna."

"I don't want you to compete with him. I like you. I'm here with you. Jamie and I are…"

"More than friends," Tom stated.

"Maybe. But I am not going to the nice restaurant with him and I am not going to kiss him goodnight at my door tonight."

That made him smile. "You're not?"

"No. I have plans with another man… His name is John, of course. I'm meeting him right after you."

Tom chuckled and Zhanna reached over to take his hand in hers. "I like that you are jealous. You know what it means?"

"I'm an overreacting jackass?"

"Yes. But also you are nervous about tonight. This makes it easier for me since I am nervous, too. I want to have a good time."

"And I ruined it by going all caveman on you to start. I'm sorry. I think you're right. I think I am nervous. I haven't felt this way around a woman in a long time. Maybe not ever."

"It is because I am so beautiful maybe?" She was teasing him and each time he smiled she felt as though she'd scored a point. One date point for each smile. She hoped to have a thousand of them by the end of the night.

Tom shifted in his seat and leaned toward her. "Yes, you are so beautiful."

The compliment, the way he said it, went straight to her heart.

"And since you're saving the last kiss of the night for this John guy, I thought maybe I would have the first one."

He didn't wait. Simply leaned in and pressed his lips against hers. Softly and without too much demand. More of an introductory kiss. It was nice and when his tongue swiped her bottom lip right before he pulled away, she knew it also had the potential to be more than nice later on.

"Yes, I think this will be a very good date. If so, I may have to cancel the one with John."

"Then let's go. The ferry and our night awaits."

Zhanna leaned back in the seat and for the first time in far too long she thought she could see ahead into the future.

Right now it was a very nice picture.

CHAPTER FIFTEEN

IT WAS ALL about the math. After all, Jamie had studied astrophysics during his astronaut training so it wasn't as though he couldn't figure it out.

Paula had said Gabby had left around three in the afternoon. It would take approximately eight hours to drive from the southeast coast of Connecticut to the dock where the ferry left. Maybe seven hours if someone was driving faster than was legal because she was pumped up on female fury.

The last ferry left the mainland at 11:30 p.m. and the ride to the island was about twenty-five minutes.

She would have to push it to make it. Jamie stood at the dock and watched the ferry roll in over the dark waves. Once it was close to the dock, Eli hopped from the deck to tie the boat up.

"Man, I would not be here if I were you," Eli said as he knotted the rope around the heavy-metal moorings.

Jamie didn't have to ask if his assumption that Gabby had made the last ferry had been correct. "Pissed?"

"She spent the entire time standing next to the captain asking him to drive faster. I think I saw steam coming off her head."

"She'll be happy to see me. You wait."

"Yeah, she'll be happy to see you so she can punch you in the nose. What did you do to her?"

"Lied."

Eli shook his head. "You're not supposed to lie to the people you care about." The second in command offered the words as sage advice even though he was barely half Jamie's age.

"You're right."

"You!" The shout echoed against the night and over the lapping water.

"I'm outta here, man. Good luck." Eli trotted off with a wave to his captain who was apparently deciding to hold out on the boat rather than get in the middle of what was going to be a pretty loud fight.

"Me, what?" Jamie nudged her even as he reached out a hand for her to grab as she tried to hop from the edge of the rail onto the dock rather than wait for the gangplank to be lowered.

He caught her as she jumped down, but then was immediately shoved away by a whole lot of angry woman.

"You lied."

"I didn't tell you the truth. It's different."

"It's the same."

She was right, but he wasn't ready to concede defeat. "It wasn't my secret to tell."

"Oh, bull. You know you could have trusted me with the truth."

"Trust you? You want to write a freaking book about me."

"I wouldn't have said anything if you didn't want me to. I wouldn't have. But it was wrong for her to keep the secret and hang you out to dry and damn it, you were wrong to let it happen."

"You don't know the whole story," he said quietly.

"Then tell me. Tell me the whole story." Her voice cracked and he could see she was up against an edge he didn't understand.

He opened his mouth to say…something. Precisely what he didn't know. But she was still ranting so he closed his mouth and let her have her turn.

"I mean, all those weeks of the press berating you and scolding you and vilifying you like you were some monster. Only because you had the audacity to save people's lives and become a national hero and for that you had to pay. I hurt for you. I was angry with you. You should have fought harder. You should have fought back. I *needed* someone to believe in then. I *needed* it."

There it was, he thought, the splinter she'd been living with for so long. Always there, mildly irritating, waiting for something to work it out only to realize how much agony it was truly causing. His heart ached as he heard the crack in her voice. He could feel her suffering and because of it he suffered, too.

"Come here," he said and opened his arms. She fell into him and hugged him so hard he lost his breath. But it felt good to have her wrapped around him even if she was crying all over his neck.

"Why didn't you fight?"

That wasn't her question. Her real question was why he didn't fight for her. Which was nonsensical since he didn't know she existed eight years ago, but she was hurting badly now and he was sure she didn't want to be bothered by facts.

The facts he would keep to himself. For now they were unimportant. Susan told him he wasn't ready and maybe this was about becoming ready. Maybe he had to stop worrying about a history he couldn't let go of and simply be the man he knew himself to be.

That man wanted Gabby. He wanted to hold her and comfort her and tell her everything was going to be all right. Convince her that her father shouldn't have left her when she was a teenager. Prove to her that her fiancé was an absolute dick for sleeping with her sister.

She was better than all of them. For him, she was better than any woman he'd ever known.

He needed to tell her.

"Let's go, Gab. I'll take you home and get you liquored up. Then if you want, you can take me to bed."

She lifted her head and looked at him. "Yes, I want to take you to bed this time."

He smiled as dirty images ran through his mind. "I've apparently been a bad, bad boy. You might need to tie me up and have your wicked way with me."

She glared at him. "Don't get cute. You're still in big trouble with me, mister."

"Yes, ma'am."

"My car," she said vaguely pointing back to the boat where it still sat waiting to be driven off the ramp.

"We will pick it up tomorrow before Doug makes his first run of the day."

Jamie lifted his head to shout out to the captain, although he knew it was likely Doug had heard every word and would be relaying this story to the citizens of Hawk Island early next morning. "Doug, you okay with leaving her car on the boat? We'll be by in the morning."

"Sounds like a plan," he called from his perch in the cabin. "I would be worried the lady is a little too hot-headed to drive right now anyway."

"Okay," Jamie said. "Now let's get you home. I missed you."

"I was only gone for three days."

He tilted his head and smiled at her. "I missed you for three days."

THE DRIVE TO HIS house was quiet. Gabby let the strain of the past seven hours roll off her. She should have been exhausted after the long drive during which she'd had many different practice arguments with Jamie.

In all of her fake arguments each one ended with him falling on his knees and begging her for forgiveness. Which naturally she granted because, at the end of the day, she knew she was in love with him.

In replaying the scene at the dock in her head there had been no kneeling on his part. There hadn't even really been any begging.

Instead he stood there calmly and absorbed the brunt of her fury. Fury which hadn't been directed at him, but at herself. He seemed to understand what was happening to her, but she needed to tell him. She needed to say the words out loud.

"This wasn't about you and the lying. Not really," she said as he navigated the empty roads toward his home.

"Nope."

"I was angry at a legend for falling from grace at a time when I knew— I knew my world was falling apart, too. I knew what Brad was doing. I didn't *know* know. Or I didn't want to know. I'm not sure. But the day the story broke and the picture of you with Paula and Cheryl was everywhere, it was like reckoning time had finally come. At first I told myself I was crazy. You had made me paranoid and I was only going to upset Brad by being some crazed fiancé looking for other women around every corner. I didn't want to believe my gut. I hated my gut back then. Finally, I couldn't stand it any longer. I knew I had to find the proof my heart was pretty sure was already there."

"And you found it."

"Yep. I set a trap, too. Not very classy of me. I think I wanted the worst-possible scenario to further inoculate me from being so stupid ever again. I told him I was going on an overnight trip to interview this celebrity. Even though the show had never sent me anywhere in the year I had been doing it. I waited until I saw her car pull up. I waited until I knew they were in progress… and I walked in on them together in my bed."

"I'm sorry."

"She had her own freaking place, too. There was no reason—"

"Don't. Don't go back there. It was eight years ago, Gabby. There is nothing good to take away from it now. You were hurt. You moved on. Your life got better, even if it doesn't always seem that way."

Gabby dropped her face into her hands. All these years and it was still right there. The memory of walking up those steps so carefully so they wouldn't creak. The feel of her heart pounding so hard she was afraid it would suddenly stop. With each step she knew it was taking her closer to the end of what she'd thought her life would be. It seemed none of it had ever left her.

She remembered the sounds coming from the bedroom. Sounds he didn't make with her. Things he didn't say to her.

"Kim, you're everything. You're everything to me."

He'd never said anything to Gabby remotely close to that in all the years they'd been dating. Not even when he proposed. It had all been very sensible.

"Gabby, I think we'll make a nice couple. We should get married."

They *had* been a nice couple. Nice without the romance. But then she'd never been one to encourage romance. No, Gabby was all about practicality and good sound decisions. She had been since the day her father left her mother. Romance was for chumps.

God, she'd been so wrong.

"He didn't love me. Not when he proposed. Then he fell in love with her. He's been in love with her for all these years. Now they're finally going to have the family they wanted. And I don't think—no, I'm certain, he's never cheated on her. Not with the way he still looks at her."

"Does it upset you?"

It would be awful for her to think it did. Mean spirited to want Kim to suffer the way Gabby had and to know intimately the pain of betrayal. But Gabby had to own it. In some dark corner of her mind it did upset her that Brad had been loyal to Kim all these years, when he hadn't been loyal to her for much longer than a year. Gabby supposed it didn't make her the greatest person on the planet.

One more realization she was coming to grips with tonight.

"Why do you want to have anything to do with me? I'm a mess." It was mostly a rhetorical question, but he answered anyway.

"I want to have everything to do with you. I want to know about every flaw. I want to know every crappy thing you've ever done. Then maybe I can show you how it doesn't matter. How at the end of the day we're all people with good and bad inside of us. It's how we learn and grow that makes us who we are."

"Okay, Oprah, I got it."

He chuckled as they pulled into the driveway and reached out with his hand to capture hers.

"Did I also mention you're the best lay I've had in years?"

She laughed and blushed, which she was sure was his intention. They made their way inside the house still holding hands. It all felt so comfortable. She took off her coat and he handed her a hanger so she could put it away in the closet in the foyer.

He went and splashed two glasses full of some dark liquor and they sat on the couch together in companionable silence for a time.

She yawned and he did, too.

"Let's go to bed," he suggested.

"Shoot. All my stuff was in my suitcase. I left it in the car."

"I've got an extra toothbrush."

"What about a T-shirt?"

"I've got an extra toothbrush."

He was so serious it made her laugh. Together they headed up the stairs and, using the his-and-her sinks in his master bathroom, they brushed their teeth together. Gabby then went above and beyond by washing her face and using his brush to coax her long hair into some type of submission all the while muttering how easy men had it.

Jamie did rustle up a T-shirt with a washed out NASA logo on it that was softer than anything Gabby had ever worn.

As they pulled back the duvet cover on the bed she asked him if the T-shirt was made of special space material only astronauts knew about. He assured her it was merely cotton washed over a thousand times.

She crawled into bed from the right and he stripped himself of the boxer briefs that had made his semi-hard penis appear utterly delicious before getting into the bed from the left. They met in the center, each on their sides looking at each other, seeing each other, even though they had turned out the lights.

"I came after you the next morning."

She smiled in the dark. "You did?"

"I realized I made a huge mistake by sending you away and I charged into Susan's place shouting your name. It was all very dramatic."

She would have liked to have seen that. Jamie didn't

strike her as someone who would make the big romantic gesture. Too undignified for a man like him. She reached out and cupped his face. It was slightly scruffy and she knew it was going to feel so good against her body.

"I wasn't leaving you. I just knew I had to learn the truth. I needed to know the story."

"Now you do."

"You're going to think I'm crazy, but I think Paula is…relieved. I think she was ready to tell someone. Anyone. Even if nothing comes of it."

"Maybe. But I don't want to talk about Paula or the past right now."

"Then what do you want to talk about?" she whispered, shimmying closer to him.

She felt his hand slide along the outside of the T-shirt and then up over her bare bottom. He'd offered a toothbrush and T-shirt, but apparently he was all out of women's underwear.

"I want to talk about how you're the sexiest damn woman I've ever known. Thinking about being inside you can almost drive me crazy. Being inside you is like nothing I've ever felt before."

She pushed a little against his chest as if to suggest he stop with the flattery, but without any words to actually make him stop. His hand stroked her back, then moved around until he was cupping her breast and discovering her nipple was already hard with arousal.

"I want to say how much fun you've brought to my life."

"That's nice," she agreed even as he began to kiss

her neck. Hot, wet, openmouthed kisses along her neck and then little nibbles on her earlobe which made her whole body shudder.

"I want to tell you how amazing you are for taking care of your mother. And how proud I am of you for picking yourself up after getting fired and making a new life for yourself."

"You might get to see that trick again real soon," she admitted thinking about what she was going to tell Melissa. Any thoughts she had of her boss slid out of her mind when Jamie slid his leg between hers.

They were kissing now, his tongue was in her mouth and she was sucking on him, drawing him deeper and she thought about how she had never felt this way with any other man. Never once felt as cherished and as beautiful as she did in this man's arms.

She rubbed her hands along his chest and felt the crinkle of hair under her palms and the heavy beat of his heart and knew a connection she'd never known before. It was like Paula had said, sometimes you didn't know what you were missing until you felt the real thing for the first time.

Gabby brushed her thigh against his and loved the contrast of his rough-furred skin, against her softness. Reaching down, she pulled off her shirt so she could rub her chest against him, as well. She wanted to be covered by him. Consumed by him. She squirmed and wiggled so she could feel him completely and totally all over her body.

Suddenly he pulled back, and looked into her eyes.

"I want to be ready for you, Gabby. I want to do whatever it means to make that happen."

She could see the serious lines along his lips and eyes. He wasn't smiling, he wasn't teasing. He was making a vow and she believed him with her entire being.

Too bad now wasn't the time for vows and commitments. There was so much to hash out, a future they were going to need to discuss eventually. The entire world was going to restart for them both tomorrow. Tonight she only wanted to be with him. To revel in the joy and bliss that he wanted the same thing.

To be with her. Gabby Haines. With her too soft body, her truckload of issues she didn't even realize she hadn't let go of and all the uncertainty about where she was headed.

In what universe did a woman get this lucky to find a man like Jamie Hunter?

He pressed his erection against her belly and she reached down to take him in her hand. He groaned a little in the back of his throat and she thought how much she liked the sound. When they first made love, things had been wild and crazy. She'd been so lost in her desire and her need. It had all felt intense and chaotic and wonderful.

This time she wanted to record everything. She wanted to learn the sound track of Jamie making love and commit it to memory. When she squeezed him harder, he groaned again. When she released him, he whispered no and brought her hand back to him.

"More," he said as he rocked into her hand.

His mouth sucked in the tip of her breast, tonguing

and teasing her nipple until she felt the tug deep in her belly, between her legs. His hand slid there and his finger pushed into her wet sex.

Together they rocked and stroked each other until the need to have him inside became overwhelming.

She felt his momentum push her onto her back and for a second she was willing to go there, to let him come on top of her and take her the way he had the last time. She would be beyond filled with him and he would control the pace and her pleasure and it would be thrilling.

But it wasn't what they had agreed to. This was her turn to take him to bed. Gabby wanted to know what that felt like. To control, instead of be controlled.

She pushed against his shoulder. "No, me on top."

"Yes, ma'am," he drawled, apparently more than happy to roll over. She kicked the covers out of their way and simply stared at him. A beautiful man with a beautiful body. His erection was thick and heavy lying against his hip waiting to find a home. He reached into his nightstand for a condom and handed it to her, allowing her the honors. When it was in place, she leaned back and looked at him like he was a feast she was ready to devour.

Gabby thought about the T-shirt she'd removed. The last time she'd been fully naked with a man while making love was with Jamie, of course, but before then she'd always been partially clothed. The more weight she added the more clothes she kept on.

With Jamie, she hadn't once thought about her body other than to register how good he made her feel.

This time as she straddled his hips and felt his hands

reach up to cup her full breasts, she wondered if her old self-conscious behavior would return. She considered reaching for the T-shirt to have some security nearby.

"No," he said watching where her eyes had strayed. "Naked and on top of me. It's just as good as you naked and underneath me."

Naked and underneath me. She remembered the words and remembered how they made her feel and now it was her turn. She reached for his hard shaft and placed him at the opening to her body and let herself revel in the slow slide as she pushed down on top of him, taking him deep.

Yes, naked and underneath her was a good thing. Had she ever done this before? Had she ever let herself not worry about how she looked or what she did or more likely what she was doing wrong? None of that mattered. Instead she rocked her hips and thought about how she felt.

How good it was to twist and roll and feel his length pressing inside her body. How amazing to have him teasing her nipples, then gripping her hips to make her go faster. How marvelous it was to hear his moans mixed with harsh breaths when she took him harder and deeper.

"Yes, baby, that's it. Ride me. Take me. Whatever you want. However you want it."

She moved one of her hands from the thick muscle of his chest and brushed it over his lips as if to take the words from his mouth and capture them. He sucked her finger deep into his mouth even as he thrust his hips up against her. The simultaneous sensation of part of her being inside him while he was inside her was electric.

His mouth, his tongue. She wanted that, too. She wanted all of him. And she was ready to give him all of her.

She bent down and kissed him, plunging her tongue inside his mouth while she rocked her hips faster and faster. Her orgasm was overtaking her and she almost stopped moving. She didn't want this ride to end. She wanted to be here in this moment forever. Because after the pleasure crashed over them and after they fell asleep, tomorrow would come. And she didn't know what would happen tomorrow.

Now was perfect.

"Oh, yes!" he shouted she could feel him tighten underneath her like a wild animal in the throes of a mindless pleasure.

He thrust heavily once, then again and his pleasure pushed her over the edge. She felt the liquid heat run from the tip of her head all the way to her toes and she wondered if she had ever felt as fulfilled as a woman as she did right then.

She heard him groan again, this time a more languid satisfied sound. He reached up and cupped her head and brought it down to his chest while she disengaged their bodies and lay fully and completely on top of him.

"Don't leave again."

She heard the whisper, heard the almost desperation in his voice.

"No matter what happens just don't leave."

"I couldn't," she answered, kissing his chest and nuzzling more fully into him as she settled into sleep. "I couldn't because I love you."

CHAPTER SIXTEEN

"I FEEL SO freaking good."

"You're welcome." Jamie looked entirely too smug.

Gabby let go of her foot, finishing the quad stretch on her right leg. She was prepared to make a snarky remark but she couldn't. He was right. He was absolutely the reason she felt so good. They had made love last night in a way she'd never done before, giving herself so completely she felt merged or combined or part of something other than herself. As though the two of them had made another entity.

Whatever ridiculous line she could think of from a sappy romantic movie, it was exactly how she felt.

They woke up early to retrieve her car from the ferry and, crazily enough, still had enough energy when they returned to make love again. This time Jamie didn't wait until they reached the bedroom. Instead they started kissing and touching in a frenzy of need as if they hadn't made love intensely enough that they had both fallen into a heap of exhausted bodies mere hours ago.

He undressed her on the stairs and laid her out naked, only pushing down his pants as the minimum he needed to before he took her so hard and fast she had rug burns on her bottom.

She should remind him of those red marks, but she knew it would only make him more smug because she had enjoyed earning every single rug burn.

Still, she felt as though it was her duty to make an effort to keep his ego in check. Otherwise the man could become impossible to live with. If she was going to live with him. In the future. Her thoughts strayed to the future and immediately Gabby stopped herself.

Today. Now. Present. These were the only things she would let herself care about.

"I was talking about the stretching."

He laughed. "No, you weren't."

"No, I wasn't, But you know it wasn't all you last night." It was only fair she get her share of recognition since she'd been the one on top.

"You're right. There was someone definitely there with me. All the way with me. Last night, this morning, on the stairs."

His eyes started to smolder as he took a step toward her and she could feel the inside of her belly turn to jelly. For someone who had gone so long without sex, maybe she was in danger of overdosing. Because right now she wanted him again. On a public beach—even though no one was around—in the middle of the day. Even though she was still coming to grips with her body image, she wanted to get naked and roll around in the sand.

Rocky sand. Hard little pebbles of sand.

"Oh, no, you don't. You already gave me rug burn. I can't imagine what this rocky sand would do to my back."

His smile contained a hint of evil. "Are you suggesting I would have relations with you outside? And on a public beach, no less?"

"Uh-huh."

"Then you would be right. But you know, I don't have to put you on your back. If you want to hop on me and wrap your legs around my waist, I bet we can—"

Gabby held her hand up. "Stop. Just stop. We are going for a run. It's what we said we would do. That and talk."

"Sex is more fun than talking."

It was. She'd never thought so before, but it totally was.

"After we run, we'll need showers."

"Shower. Singular," he said.

Her eyelashes lowered. "I think you mean shower, double."

"Whatever. Let's run and get this over with." He tugged on her hand and they started their slow trot down the beach.

Maybe it was the mild spring sun on her face, or that he was jogging in sync with her or the melodic lap of the water on the beach, but for the first time she was loving the feel of her body. The movement, the pounding of each foot on the beach, the slight pump of her arms. Sweat started to form on her neck and that felt good. Heat was rising under the ball cap she used to keep her hair back and that felt good, too.

She was a runner. She loved running. She wouldn't have known it if not for him. She wouldn't have known so many things about herself if not for him.

Like how she loved stair sex. And how she loved food and wasn't going to be afraid to eat it. And, most of all, how she'd been burying herself in hurt and pain for so long never realizing how much love and joy she'd been missing out on.

Later, she would call her mother. She would let her mother hear her voice and then her mother would know that, for the first time in a lot of years, when Gabby said everything was all right she really meant it. Her mother would hear the voice of a happy daughter and it made Gabby even more happy to think about how good it would make her mom feel.

All because of Jamie. He ripped her open like a bag of chips and ate away until there was nothing left to hide. How was she ever going to thank him? For giving her back her life? Once more a man who knew exactly how to rescue someone.

"So…what happens next?"

Gabby whipped her head around. Jamie was still staring forward not missing a stride in his steps. She'd been too busy thinking about how happy she was and how good she felt. His question bordered on future talk. None of that for her. Not when it might spoil a second of her mood.

"We run another mile? I think I'm good for four today."

"Gabby."

She grimaced. It was his serious voice. She could probably guess what he wanted to know. She had the story of the year in her hands. American Hero caught in cheating scandal and banished from society returns when it's revealed he wasn't the one who had been caught cheating that day.

"I should tell you something," he said unintentionally picking up speed, which made her fall behind a few paces. When he saw she was slower he deliberately eased his pace until she could catch up with him.

"I'm listening."

"When you were gone I got a call from NASA. They've been contacted by the International Space Organization which controls the space station to come up with contingency plans in case the situation deteriorates any further or faster and they can't repair the problem and will need to evacuate."

"And they want you to help them."

"Not to take part in any rescue efforts—I told you, those days are gone. They want me as a consultant."

"Well, if anyone has experience saving the space station it's you."

"It would mean going to Houston. Meeting with officials there. There is news coverage down there as people are watching what's happening and are growing more concerned. If NASA officially gets involved, the press coverage is bound to get more intense."

"It's bound to get really intense with Jamison Hunter involvement."

"Yeah. Maybe."

Gabby didn't say anything for a few steps as she tried to put together what he was thinking and where this conversation was taking them.

"Are you afraid?"

He looked at her sharply. "Afraid of what?"

"Of it all starting again. The questions, the snide comments, the tabloids following you."

"Look, this is a temporary gig. I go down, we spend a few days meeting, then I'm gone. I'm a civilian now. It's not like they can hold me there. How much could any reporter say about anything?"

Gabby snorted. "You don't know what these people are like. News people aren't just news people anymore. They're entertainers. We live in a world with a twenty-four-hour news cycle when, realistically, there is barely twelve hours of worthy news a day. You do the math. Jamison Hunter coming out of retirement will make a splash. Just like the old stories have been surfacing in a vague way every time they talk about the station. And every time they mention your name, the scandal is mentioned. Once you step foot in Houston, the whole story will become front and center again."

Her speech winded her a bit as Jamie kicked up his speed a little and she was forced to do the same to keep up. He was agitated. It was obvious. Again she considered where all this was headed and finally it occurred to her.

She stopped in her tracks and bent over to catch her breath. After a few steps Jamie stopped, as well. Slowly, he walked back to her.

"What's the matter? A stitch? Just breathe it out."

"No," she said, although she did try to take a few deep slow breaths. "Jamie, do you want me to do it?"

He shook his head to show he didn't follow what she was saying.

"I could break the story. I have some friends in the

industry who I could contact. I mean, forget the book for now. Why wait? We can tell everyone what happened in Florida all those years ago. Change the story of you entirely. Then when you go to Houston it won't be 'Here comes the villain again.' Instead you'll be returning as America's Lost Hero. It could be fabulous. If we played it right—"

"Hold on. That's not where I was going with all of this."

"Why not?" Gabby said getting more excited by the prospect. "You've spoken with Paula and you know she's ready to come out with truth. In fact, she wants to finally be free of the lie. She wants people to know who she is. Now is the perfect timing. You can redeem yourself. You can show everyone how wrong they were not to believe in you. You'll look like even more of a hero to the world because you did everything to protect the woman who was your wife even though she was cheating on you."

"Gabby…"

"Of course Melissa will have the exclusive on the book, which she'll have to let me write as the person who actually broke the story," Gabby continued. "It will be perfect! Everybody wins."

Jamie turned away from her and started a slow walk back the way they came. Gabby hadn't made it the four miles she'd hoped, but maybe tomorrow. In the meantime, ideas for who she wanted to bring to the island to break the story circled in her mind. Did they want a hardcore reporter, or someone softer? Maybe more of *Good Morning, America* feel than a *Nightly News* one.

"You don't get it," he said softly. "All I was asking was if you would be willing to go with me. To Houston."

Gabby jogged a few steps until she caught up to him. She reached for his arm to stop him. "Of course I'll go with you. But don't you see this is a good idea. It's the right time to finally tell everyone the truth when everyone will be watching you again."

"Gabby, I don't care about the truth! I don't give a damn if people know what happened that day or not. I know what happened between me and Paula. I know what went down in our marriage. I don't need to share it with the world."

"I get that—"

"Do you? Do you really? Why did you hunt down Cheryl and Paula to begin with? I know you had it in your craw I wasn't telling you the truth. I think I get why it was important to you to find the truth, but I don't know if you do. I need you to say it. Why did you go find them? Did you do it because you knew you would get fired if you didn't have something fabulous to put in this book that is never going to happen?"

He was angry and Gabby didn't understand why. By finding Cheryl, by confronting Paula, she'd finally freed him of this awful lie. He should want to tell the world they were wrong about him.

"I did it for you—"

"Oh, don't give me that bullshit."

"Let me finish," Gabby snapped. "I did do it for you. It's not fair what happened to you. Not fair your legacy is forever tarnished by something someone else did. Maybe you don't care, but I do. And yes, I did it for me. I had to. I was falling in love with you. Don't you get it? You, a known adulterer, and I couldn't stop myself. My grandfather cheated on my grandmother, my father cheated on my mother, my fiancé cheated on me. Do you honestly think I could let myself love *you?*"

"No. I don't."

Only Gabby didn't hear him. "I wanted to love you. I wanted to so badly. I knew you weren't the person they'd portrayed in the media. I knew you were good and kind and heroic. Not just for the cameras, but every damn day. I had to prove it."

"Gabby. I told you, you were going to have to find a way to forgive me. I told you." His face was tight and his eyes were imploring her to do or say something, but she didn't know what.

"But there is nothing to forgive. Don't you see? You were innocent. So everything is okay now."

He swallowed and she could see a shimmering in his eyes that, if he were a normal man, might be a prelude to tears. But Jamie had nothing to cry over. She had liberated him and by doing so she cleared the path to love him. They should be celebrating. Not fighting.

Because this, whatever it was, felt a lot like fighting.

He reached out and took her hands in his, simply holding them and squeezing them for a time while he seemed to search for the right words.

"I thought I wouldn't tell you. I thought maybe it was part of being ready for you. Letting the past go and not hurting you or pushing you away intentionally. But I can't do that. I can't be someone I'm not."

"I don't understand. Jamie, you don't have to be anything besides who you are. You're this amazing wonderful man and I love you." So why did she want to cry right now? Why did she feel her breath coming faster than it had when they were jogging? Why was he looking at her as though he was about to break her heart?

"But would you forgive me? If it had been true? If I had cheated?"

"I— I don't know. I don't have to, so what's the point?"

"The point is eight years ago in Florida I found my wife in bed with another woman. I was shocked and startled and mad as hell. Mad, because it explained a lot about our sex life. Mad, because of what I thought she made me become. I was twenty-two when we married. That first year, when things became clear it wasn't going to be…easy…between us, I got restless. Bored and resentful, too. Everything else you might imagine a hotshot, hotheaded egocentric pilot might become. I started cheating on Paula not fourteen months after we were married. *Fourteen months.* I met a woman in Germany. She was a scientist from Russia working on a program with other American scientists…."

Gabby felt her knees give out. He was still holding her hands but she was now kneeling on the beach feeling the tiny stones dig in through her spandex not really sure how she got there. She pulled her hands free and sat back on her calves.

"Zhanna," she breathed.

Jamie sat in the sand next to her. Not touching her. Not looking at her. "I didn't know. Elia returned to Russia and I never knew. Zhanna showed up here two years ago and told me she was my daughter and her mother was dead and I was to take care of her." He laughed at the memory. "Just like that. She explained how she was a grown woman at twenty, and would have her own place and her own job, but ultimately I was responsible for her well-being."

Gabby thought about the young woman's face. Her beautiful chiseled face. "She has your jaw line."

"She does. And my stubbornness."

The weight on her chest was crushing. This was the truth. The *whole* truth. "You are a cheater."

"I told you I was," he said calmly. "I never lied about it. I told Paula, too. She knew there were others and wanted to pretend there weren't. Elia was one of many. I wasn't out whoring with a different woman every night, but there were affairs. I needed Paula to know. I felt like it was okay and my conscience was clean if I told her. All I did was hurt her.

"Because the kicker is she loved me in her own way. She was funny and sweet. She always represented herself well at any event we attended. She was a great cook and baker. Every holiday she would stuff me with fudge, cake and cookies. And gifts. Anniversary, birthday, Christmas, it didn't matter. Paula always knew the perfect gift for me. Some off the cuff thing I might have said months prior and she would remember it and spin it into something wonderful. She was a good person. And she wanted to be a mother so badly. But I could tell she just dreaded it…and so I couldn't with her. Not even to give her the one thing she wanted."

Gabby felt tears running down her face. She wanted

him to stop talking. She wanted him to take the words back, but he wouldn't.

"You called me a hero? Isn't that what you said about me? That I was good and kind and heroic? I was scum. I was pissed my wife didn't want me in bed and I did the most selfish thing I could do because of it."

"She could have told you," Gabby said trying to defend him, but in her heart she couldn't. The same way she hadn't taken pity on Paula when she'd tried to explain. The same logic was true for Jamie. His actions were wrong and there was no defense for them.

"She didn't know. She was so sheltered as a kid. It didn't occur to her to know how she should feel when I kissed her or touched her. She thought there was something wrong with her. She went through therapy and took pills and—"

"I know. She told me."

"She tried so damn hard," he said, shaking his head. "And every couple of months I would go away for a weekend and come home and say...sorry. I needed it. I would ask her if she wanted a divorce. After every time. I wanted her to know she could walk whenever she chose. She would never agree."

"You did this...for years." Gabby counted the exact number. They had been married nearly fifteen years. Fifteen years of him cheating on a wife who didn't understand she was gay. It was so awful, for two people who liked each other to cause each other so much pain. "What if she hadn't met Cheryl? What if she never figured it out?"

"The deal was we would divorce after her parents

died. The truth is my affairs ended a couple of years before she met Cheryl. I couldn't stomach it anymore. I couldn't live with who I had become. I felt dirty all the time. Finally, I said, screw it. The sex wasn't worth how awful it made me feel. We became this oddly platonic, friendly couple. She was mostly happy and I was sexually frustrated, but it felt better than the alternative."

"And Cheryl?"

"Cheryl was an interior decorator. She came to our house to renovate the place. She was attractive. Beautiful and free. So different than Paula's classic chic style. Naturally, I wanted her. For the first time in years I actually worked up enough anger over my lack of sex— because that's how I justified everything to myself, like I was the victim—to make a move on her."

"Let me guess. You got shot down." Gabby could actually work out a smile.

"I did. Paula started acting funny, though. Like a girl for the first time since I had known her. She'd laugh and giggle and touch Cheryl's hand. She never touched anybody voluntarily. What made me follow her that day, I will never know. Because if you asked me before it all went down if I thought my wife was gay, the answer would have been a big hell no. Paula was such a prude, the idea of sex outside of her preconceived notions of normal, seemed crazy to me. Still, I had this gut feeling something was off. I followed her and I watched Cheryl open the door and I waited outside. I waited a good long time because I thought— I thought…finally Paula is getting some. I wanted her to have that. I wanted her to know how good it could feel. How freaking crazy is that?"

"Why didn't you drive away?"

"The anger came back. I remember what it felt like with those other women. Dirty, tawdry. How shitty I always felt after. The whole damn time, Paula was gay and didn't realize it. I told myself if she'd only known before we married, I never would have become what I did. I wanted to blame her for it."

"You had a choice."

He looked at her then, the first time since he started spilling his deepest life secrets. "I did. I get that now. I could have gone to therapy with her. I could have tried harder. We know now it wouldn't have worked, but I didn't know then. Those years of celibacy because I couldn't stand cheating anymore weren't any more horrible than the years when I was cheating and feeling like crap about it. I could have been a better man for her. It took years of being alone here on this island to figure it out."

"I'm sorry."

"Why are you sorry?"

Gabby couldn't say exactly. She only knew she felt this deep hole in the pit of her chest and thought it must be what it felt like for him, too. For that she was sorry.

"Does she know about Zhanna?"

"No," he said tightly. "Zhanna didn't want anyone to know. It was her secret, she said. Not mine. I'm going to have to tell her I told you. She'll be pissed."

Gabby nodded. They had run for almost three miles but strangely sitting on the beach talking had been infinitely more exhausting. Slowly, she rose without taking the hand he offered. She couldn't.

"What does this all mean, Gabby? Where do we go from here?"

Gabby closed her eyes. "I don't know. I can't think right now. I think— I know I need some space. Maybe I'll grab my suitcase and head to Susan's."

"You're leaving," he said flatly.

"I have to."

"You said you wouldn't."

It was a cheap trick. To hold her words against her when he knew she didn't have the whole story. She looked at him and he closed his eyes.

"Sorry," he said weakly.

Slowly they walked to Jamie's house. Gabby stood outside by the car while he went inside to grab her suitcase. She didn't trust herself to be in the house with him. She didn't want him to say anything that might make her feel better or worse.

She thought about the call she was going to make to her mother. And how it would have to wait.

He emerged with her bag and lifted it into the trunk. She opened the driver side door but he held it so she couldn't escape.

"I'm a better man today than I was then. I know it might be hard to believe. But I didn't just excuse myself, you know. I could have said, hey, my wife was gay and I was entitled. I didn't. I owned every last piece of lousy behavior. But then eventually I forgave myself for it. I had to or it would have eaten me up inside. I'm ready for you, Gabby. I really am."

Tears blurred her vision. He was ready. But she didn't know if she was. She got in the car and tried to close the door, but he still wouldn't let it go. She wanted to close him out. She wanted to isolate herself because she wasn't sure if she could hear one more thing, process one more feeling.

"You're going to have to forgive me. You're going to have to."

Yes. She was. Only she didn't know if she could.

He released the door and she closed it. She looked at him in the rearview mirror for as long as she could until he was gone.

Then she pulled the car over to the side of the road. She was shaking and knew she would need it to stop before it would be safe to drive.

Only the shaking wouldn't stop. She couldn't stop it. She thought she might shake forever.

CHAPTER SEVENTEEN

JAMIE KNOCKED ON Zhanna's door and for a moment hoped she wasn't home. He wasn't positive he was ready to face her anger after having gone through what he went through with Gabby this morning.

He thought about her date with Tom last night and for a second it occurred to him she might very well still be on her date with Tom. The thought made his stomach turn until he reminded himself she was a grown woman and could sleep with whomever she chose.

Besides, it wasn't like he had ever thought about her in terms of his little girl or that he'd ever bounced her on his knee. A man who raised a baby girl to a woman, it made sense why he'd be so distrustful of other men. He didn't want to see the person he'd invested so much of himself into get hurt.

But Jamie had met Zhanna for the first time when she was twenty and the need to not see her hurt, especially when she came to him so wounded and grieving from her mother's death, kicked in immediately.

Maybe it was some built in genetic male instinct that made him want to kill anyone who slept with his daughter.

Glancing around the parking area of the restaurant, he spotted some customer's car and Zhanna's. No Toyotas.

For now Tom was safe.

"I'm coming. Are you bringing me another kitten? I think Mary would like a sibling—" The door opened on a smiling Zhanna whose face changed when she saw who it was.

"Expecting Tom, I guess?"

"He said he would come by this morning for breakfast."

Jamie glanced at his watch. "It's after noon."

"We had a late night and he told me to sleep in. Who are you, the sleep police? What brings you here anyway and why do you have such a sad face."

"I need to tell you something. Something that probably isn't going to make you happy."

"Now I have a sad face." She opened the door and went to sit on the couch, curling her bare feet under her legs. When he saw her like this with her hair a little disheveled and her feet bare he thought this is how she might have looked as a girl.

He thought of all the time he missed with her.

At first when she showed up at his door he was stunned, then disbelieving, then seriously angry. Had he known there had been a child, his child, somewhere out there in the world, he never would have let her exist without him. Nothing, not Paula, or her parents or his reputation would have stopped him from finding Zhanna.

Elia had betrayed him in the worst possible way.

He wanted to rail against the woman who had been

his lover for a brief time, but Zhanna wouldn't have a bad word said against her beloved mother. As Zhanna explained it, Elia's thinking was simple. When she told Zhanna about her father, she also justified her decision to keep him out of their lives.

She lived in Russia and Jamie lived in the U.S. Even overlooking what an illegitimate child would have done to his career as well as his marriage, the reality of trying to raise Zhanna together would have been impractical.

As a scientist, Elia had first and foremost been practical.

Nothing had come easy with Zhanna at first. Just because she chose to find him, didn't mean they had immediately become close. It took time for them to form a relationship. He wanted her to live with him, but she demanded her independence. He wanted to help her financially, but she would take none of his money.

In the end, it probably was for the best. They were able to meet as adults and as equals. He came to love her not because she was his child, but because she was smart and funny and fiercely loyal.

Now he had to let her down and it hurt more than he realized. He used to think of their relationship in terms of friendship. It was easier that way. He could see now there was so much more. She was his daughter.

His daughter. A truly incredible gift.

"What is this bad news?" Zhanna patted the cushion beside her and he sat with his hands clasped together. Like he couldn't look at Gabby when he'd told her the truth about his life, he found the same to be true with

Zhanna. It struck him as cowardly, so he forced him-self to face her.

"I told someone about you."

Her eyes opened wide, then narrowed. "Gabby," she guessed. "She is back?"

He nodded. "She came back last night. This morn-ing I had to explain everything. My life, my past and it included you and your mother."

"Hmm."

He wasn't sure what to make of the noncommittal sound, but she wasn't shouting or throwing him out, which he took as a plus.

"I know you didn't want anyone to know. I prom-ised to keep your secret. Today I broke that promise. While I'm sorry for breaking it, especially if it hurts you, I can't tell you I wouldn't do it again. She needed to know. She is— She was…important to me."

"Was important? Why *was* if she came back?"

"She found out what really happened between my ex-wife and Cheryl. She thought it exonerated me. I needed to let her know the truth."

"Does she know how you have punished yourself in isolation for so many years trying to make what you did right? Does she know how you took me in without blinking and did everything I asked of you? Does she know the actions of an angry young man don't define who you have become? She knows these things, yes?"

Jamie patted his daughter's knee. Fiercely loyal didn't begin to describe her.

"I don't know if she knows those things. I think she does. I hope she does. She didn't leave all the way. She left me, but she didn't leave the island. She's staying at Susan's. I think it might be a good sign."

"I think if she doesn't accept what you have to offer, then she is a fool."

He leaned in and kissed her cheek. "Thank you."

"Hey, Zhanna, I brought muffins for breakfast—" Tom had opened the door without knocking. A sign, Jamie concluded, which meant these two were suddenly very comfortable entering each other's homes unannounced.

His daughter was dating this man. While it didn't appear he'd stayed over last night, most likely those circumstances would change in the near future. The genetic instinct kicked in again and he had to hold himself in check not to charge at the man. Instead he kept his place on the couch and his hand on his daughter's knee.

Tom's eyes fell to Jamie's hand and his face flushed. "Jamie."

"Tom."

They were eyeing each other up cautiously as men do when the possibility of violence exists.

"What are you doing here?" Tom asked.

"I could ask the same of you."

"I'm bringing my *girlfriend* coffee and muffins on her day off."

Zhanna beamed. "Did you hear? He called me his girlfriend. It is such an American word. I like it very much."

"Well, we were having a private conversation. Maybe you could come back later." Jamie said the words intentionally, knowing the reaction they would have on

Tom. He wasn't sure why he was pushing the man's buttons. It could be he was looking for a fight. The idea of working out his frustrations with his fists seemed like a brilliant one. If it also served to let Tom know he better not think of hurting Zhanna, then all the better.

Calmly, Tom set the muffins and coffees on the kitchen counter and walked back to face Jamie with his hands on his hips.

"Who the *hell* do you think you are?" Tom snapped.

Jamie considered the younger man. He didn't launch into attack. He didn't toss the muffins and coffees. Very cool. Very deliberate. Very in control. If a man was going to be sleeping with his daughter, Jamie figured liking the guy was the best he could hope for.

The bad news was he probably wasn't going to get his fight.

Zhanna leaped off the couch. "Tom, calm down. I told you. Jamie is only friend."

"Only a friend, who shows up here in the morning and is patting your knee and kissing your cheek. I like you, Zee, but I mean it. I can't play this game. You're either with me or with him—"

"He's my father." Zhanna turned to Jamie. "There. Now cat is out of bag. Speaking of cat you must lower your voices as Mary is still sleeping. She does not care to be disturbed."

"You didn't have to do that Zhanna." Jamie stood. He knew she'd done it for him. To let him off the hook for telling their secret. Maybe freeing them both from it, too.

She touched his face. "It was time. There is nothing to hide."

"Father?" Tom apparently was still in shock as he looked to each of them then back to Zhanna. "Father? As in *dad?*"

"Father as in dad. Although I can't get her to call me that. She says it's ridiculous for someone her age."

"You are Jamie."

"All this time you've been her father?"

Jamie didn't dignify Tom's bewilderment with an answer. "Thanks, Zhanna. For everything."

"I have one last piece of advice. I know Gabby. I don't think she is a fool. But I think if you let her get off the island…then you are."

Jamie chucked her under the chin and made his way to Tom who was still processing the news.

"Oh, and Tom," Jamie said before he let himself out of the apartment. "Don't think for a second I couldn't have taken you just then. Combat training. Needless to say if you ever hurt Zhanna, if you hurt my daughter— I'm not going to lie, Zee, I really like the sound of that."

She smiled. "Me, too. Now finish your big threat. Very fatherlike."

"If you hurt my daughter," Jamie told him. "I'll hurt you."

Zhanna gave a fake shudder even as she wrapped her arm around Tom's waist and rested her head against his shoulder. "Very scary. You make an excellent frightening father."

Jamie left the couple to deal with their relationship and instead wondered what the hell he was going to do with his own.

GABBY STARED AT THE name on her cell as it continued to ring and wondered what the hell she was going to do. Of course Melissa wanted to know where she was and what she'd learned. She'd let her know after meeting with Cheryl where she was headed next and she had checked in with her again as soon as she confirmed Paula would actually speak to her.

No doubt Melissa was on pins and needles waiting for the big reveal, clicking her nails together in anticipation of a possible bestseller. The make or break moment, the biography to end all biographies.

What a story it was, too.

Gabby could care less about it. What did it matter if he was innocent for a day when he'd been guilty for years?

She tossed the phone on the bed without answering it and listened to the insistent reminder beep, which told her not only had she missed Melissa's call, but also a voice mail had been left. There was no real need to listen to the voice mail. Not when she knew what Melissa would say. *Give me the story or else...*

What in the hell was she going to do? Leave the island, tell Paula's story and redeem Jamie's reputation all the way by not including the early years of his marriage? Or leave the island, tell Paula's story but reveal the truth about what Jamie had been doing years prior with all those other women. He would be somewhat exonerated. Who wouldn't forgive a man who had un-wittingly married a lesbian for having a few affairs?

She would ask to write the book. It would be a huge hit. She would do the book tour circuit. Maybe some-one would see her on TV again and realize she was witty and charming and more importantly see how eas-ily she connected to an audience through the medium of television.

Offers for her own morning show would come in from various networks. She would feature serious in-terviews, her first, of course, being Paula Hunter.

Her life. Back and better than before.

There was just one problem. Jamie wouldn't be in it.

It wasn't as though she had to think about what he would do. If she wrote the book, if she told the world his story after he'd spent all these years protecting Paula, he would never forgive her. Protecting Paula was the only thing he'd done right for her in their marriage.

A soft knock sounded on the bedroom door and Gabby startled. Only Jamie and Susan knew she was here. Susan had left her with a pot of tea and some choc-olate chip cookies she thought might help and Jamie… Well, Jamie wouldn't come after her so fast. He would respect she needed space.

Wouldn't he? Or maybe he'd come to say she was being ridiculous and demand she forgive him. Possibly this declaration could entail lifting her over his shoulder and taking her back to his home where they would live together and be happy in ways she never really thought were possible for herself.

Cautiously Gabby sat up, then made her way to the door. "Who is it?"

"It's me. You need to open the door. Now."

Definitely authoritative, but not who she hoped.

Gabby opened the door to a scowling Zhanna.

"You know you are a big idiot." It was a statement not a question.

"You know you lied to me."

"Pish." Zhanna waved her hand. "We lied to everyone. It was no one's business. People wanted to think things, and we let them."

Gabby let Zhanna sweep inside. She sat on the end of the bed with her long legs crossed.

"I saw him this morning and he is hurting. You are making him hurt. You hurt him. I hurt you."

Gabby considered the threat. While it was true she'd shed some weight after a couple of weeks of consistent exercise, she was still larger than the slender younger woman. "Please. I could so take you."

Zhanna's eyes narrowed. "Yes, but I will fight dirty."

"Yeah, well, I—" Gabby snapped her jaw shut. She was engaging in the ridiculous. "Zhanna, I'm not going to fight you. The truth is, a long time ago I was hurt. My father left my mother when I was a teenager. Then I got cheated on and dumped by my fiancé."

"The people leaving. I remember this is what scares you."

"Then you know why I can't be with him. Why I can't risk it." Or at least why she didn't think she could be with him. She didn't know if she could risk it. She was still working it all out.

"I know what fear is. Bravery is feeling this fear and overcoming it. I was very brave. I'm now Tom's girlfriend."

Okay, maybe she was going to fight the woman. Or at least give her a good slap. Gabby didn't need to have someone else's relationship success rubbed in her face right now.

"I look at you and I think in some ways we are alike."

Young, thin, beautiful and Russian compared to Gabby. She wasn't seeing it. She was, however, seeing more clearly than ever the resemblance to Jamie. It made her feel both sad and oddly poignant. The idea of him being separated from her all those years was wrenching. Zhanna, too, being separated from her father, not because he walked out, but because she didn't know he existed was tragic.

It didn't seem fair. Although why Gabby thought anything in life should be fair after what she experienced, she wasn't sure.

Zhanna continued, "You have it in you to be brave. I see this in you, too."

Did she? Gabby didn't feel brave. Not while she was holed up in her room with tea and cookies. Afraid to talk to her boss, her mother and, most of all, Jamie.

"Did you forgive your mother?" Gabby wanted to know.

Zhanna seemed startled by the question.

"She kept you from Jamie. I don't know if she told you about him growing up but—"

"She didn't. Said nothing of him until the end of her life."

"Weren't you angry? You could have been with him. You could have had a father all those years. She kept that from you."

Zhanna nodded. "Yes, she did. Yes, I was angry when she told me."

"But did you forgive her?" Gabby looked at the woman's expression and it was suddenly like she didn't speak English and couldn't understand a word Gabby was saying even though she knew full well she did.

"Do you love your mother?" Zhanna asked in return.

"Of course. What has that got to do with anything?"

"When your father left, did you forgive her for not being strong enough, not fighting hard enough to hold him?"

The question was absurd. "There was nothing to forgive. It wasn't her fault. He left us."

"Yes, but she had something do with it. A marriage, it is two people. You must have been angry with her for not loving him enough, or making him love her enough to keep him."

Anger spiked through Gabby's body. "My mother did everything she could. She was warm and wonderful and a good wife. It wasn't her fault."

"A good mother to you, yes. But how do you know if she was a good wife? You were a child. You could not understand what their relationship was."

"No," Gabby barked. "She was good to him. She kissed him when he came home from work. She had dinner waiting. She listened to him. I was never angry with her because he left. Never. And it wouldn't have even mattered if I was. Of course I would forgive her."

"Why?"

"Because I love her!"

Zhanna smiled. "Yes. It is the same with me. Yes, I was angry my mother kept me from knowing my father, but it didn't matter. We forgive those we truly love. We do this because we are helpless against this love. The question you have to answer is not whether or not you can forgive Jamie. It is simply whether you love him enough. If you do, the forgiveness will come."

Gabby plopped on the bed next to Zhanna, her energy spent as she considered those words.

"You know, at first I didn't really like you," Gabby admitted.

"No, I did not like you. But I do now. Good thing, huh? Since maybe soon I will call you stepmommy."

Gabby glared at her. "If you ever call me mommy anything in public, then I really will slap you."

Zhanna laughed and stood. "You must think now so I will leave you."

Gabby didn't say anything as the door shut behind Zhanna.

How stupid she had been. Zhanna was right. There really was only one question and one answer.

So what was it?

JAMIE CHECKED HIS watch then looked around the beach. He felt like a fool. He'd given her the space she wanted, hoping a night to think things over would be enough. He came down to the beach at his normal time, expecting her to be here.

When she wasn't, he waited. Then waited some more.

He felt ridiculous. She wasn't coming and his hope that a little space and time would make everything clear to her seemed very naive of him.

How long did it take to decide if you had enough forgiveness in your heart? Obviously longer than a day.

Jamie cursed and kicked at the rocky sand. Zhanna said he would be a fool if he let Gabby leave the island. What good would it do to keep her here if she wasn't with him in his home? In his bed?

They needed to talk more. All the relationship books and couples' counselors said so. Communication. Fine. He would head to Susan's and bring Gabby back here and they would talk and talk until she damn well figured out she loved him enough to stay.

If this involved a little struggle and possibly a kidnapping, then so be it.

Jamie turned then and headed for his house. He stopped in his tracks when he saw Gabby coming down the hill. Her work-out gear on, her luscious hair pulled into a ponytail. He could see she was trimmer than she had been the first day he met her—not that he cared, but he knew it would please her. Anything that pleased her pleased him.

His heart was beating erratically in his chest and he struggled to keep himself in check and not run up to her and shake her and ask her what her answer was. She had come to him. It was a good thing. He would let her take the lead even if it killed him. If she needed to yell at him, or be angry with him for a while, then that was okay, too.

As long as she forgave him in the end, they would

be able to move forward. She was his future. He considered the consequences if she couldn't get beyond his past. He thought about what the future would look like if she left for good. None of it would be pretty.

It would hurt. Like a bitch. But he was still standing here waiting for her to reach him. He wasn't running away or doing anything to stop her from coming to him. It had only taken him forty-five years, but he was finally growing up when it came to relationships.

"You're late," he said to her when she was close enough.

"I know. I had some thinking to do. I figured you would have already started, but I knew I could catch up to you."

"Really? You think you're fast now?"

"I think in the not so very distant future I might even be faster than you. After all, you're getting older, while I'm still in my physical prime."

Jamie tried not to tie too much hope to her use of the word *future*.

"What do you think about that?" She poked a finger in his chest. "Someday you might have to catch up to me."

"I'll like that day," he admitted.

"Why?"

"Because it means I'll get to follow you and watch your ass in black spandex. That's hot as hell."

She laughed and he tried not to put too much hope in that, either. Finally, he couldn't take it anymore. "Gabby, what does this mean? You being here? Are you here to stay?"

"You didn't ask me if I forgive you."

Because he'd never been more afraid of an answer in his life.

"The thing is, it's not the right question. Zhanna was right. There was only one question that mattered. One answer. I'm late because I called my mother this morning. I wanted her to know I was okay. I wanted her to hear my voice and know for the first time in almost eight years I was really okay."

He felt the pressure in his chest lifting. Being replaced by excitement. "Why are you okay?"

Gabby smiled. "Because I'm in love. The real thing. Deep down to the ground in love. A very wise person told me when you love someone, truly love them, you can't do anything but forgive them."

Jamie stepped forward and wrapped his hands around her waist. He pressed his forehead against hers and let himself believe, truly believe, that Gabby was right and everything was okay.

"I will never cheat on you and I will never leave you as long as you want me to stay. I promise."

Gabby looked at him and he could see the love and trust shining in her eyes. It was humbling.

"I believe you. I will always believe you."

He kissed her then, tentatively because he still couldn't believe this was happening. So much happiness, he almost felt a little guilty. As though maybe after what he'd done he wasn't worthy of so much. Then he pulled her in his arms and decided he would focus on the joy instead.

When he let her go, she gave him a little shove. "We

don't have time for monkey business. We've got to go on our run and then we need to pack."

"Pack?"

"For Houston. You said you wanted me to go with you and I'm going. It's time for you to get back to doing what you do best. You're a hero, Jamie Hunter. You've got some people on an ailing space station who might like to have a piece of your wisdom."

"It's going to be a zoo," he warned her.

Gabby nodded. "Yep. But it's going to make an excellent last chapter in your book."

With that she took off at a pretty fast clip. Jamie gave her a head start to make her think he actually might have to struggle to catch up with her. At some point he was going to have to tell her he wouldn't let her write a book about him. But he would wait for the right moment.

Like on their honeymoon.

EPILOGUE

One year later

"I THINK YOU should walk with Armstrong." Jamie was finishing his stretching on the beach and Gabby envied him his fluid movements.

Gabby scowled. "I don't want to walk with Armstrong."

Armstrong, the Golden Retriever puppy, whimpered and rested his face on his mother's sneaker.

"Are you going to leave him behind when you know his legs are too short to keep up?" Jamie asked, knowing the thought of leaving the puppy behind would make her upset.

Gabby shook her head. "I swear, I think you got him now on purpose."

Jamie lifted his hands in the air innocently. "Tom had a litter of puppies, I was helpless to turn this guy away."

Gabby once again looked at the new puppy who was waiting to see which one would stay and walk with him on the beach because he wasn't ready to run for long periods of time yet. His sweet face and trusting expression was a guarantee, it was going to be her. Heck, she felt guilty leaving him to use the bathroom.

"Fine, it will be me. But I'm walking at a brisk rate."

"Honey, you do whatever you want."

"I want to run," she said stubbornly. "Look at me, I'm huge. I need the exercise."

Jamie came around her from behind and wrapped his arms around her waist, his hands joining over her significant belly as he nibbled a little on her ear.

"You're not huge. You're pregnant. And while I know the doctor said it was okay for you to run, I think walking is a much better idea in your delicate condition."

"Aha! I knew it. You don't want me to stay back for Armstrong, you're afraid the baby is going to jiggle out or something."

"Good lord, can that happen?"

Gabby wiggled out of his hold so she could face him. "I'm not going to shatter. Just because I'm a little older than most women having their first child doesn't mean I'm any more delicate."

"What about me? I'm really old to have a baby, too. Think of the stress I'm under. My weak heart."

Gabby snorted. "Your weak heart. It didn't feel so weak this morning when you woke me up for a little… how did you put it?"

"Oh, I put it good," he teased.

"Morning nookie?"

"Don't slam morning nookie. It's almost as good as stair sex."

"I'm only saying I don't want to be coddled. Yes, we're going to be older parents but we're not invalids."

"Got it. We're not invalids. But someone still has to hang back with Armstrong."

Gabby relented. "Fine. It's just I'll have no one to talk to." Armstrong barked. "I meant someone human, baby."

"I can call Zhanna to come walk with you," Jamie offered.

"No. She's worse than you and my mother combined with the fussing. The other day she started doing this weird thing with my wedding ring to see if I was going to have a boy or a girl. She's practically insisting I give her a baby sister. I told her if she wanted a baby so much to go have one of her own."

"Whoa," Jamie groaned. "No need to rush the baby talk. She and Tom have decided on a long engagement and that's fine with me. I don't want to be a grandpa and a new father at the same time."

Gabby considered this. If Zhanna and Tom did decide to have a baby soon after they were married, there would be someone on this planet who would soon be calling her grandma. She was having a hard enough time with the idea of someone calling her mom.

"You're right. No need for Zhanna to rush into motherhood."

"Listen, you'll probably like the quiet time. You can think about the book stuff, figure out what the next chapter will be."

Now Gabby knew he was really laying it on thick. "You hate that I'm writing this book, but you want to give me quiet time to think about it? Talk about a load of bull."

"I don't hate the book," Jamie argued. "If Paula wants to share her story with the world, I'm okay with it. I was sort of hoping you could take out all the parts about me."

"Not going to happen. You agreed I had carte blanche to write about anything Paula was willing to share. That includes you."

Jamie sighed, but he didn't continue to argue. While he wasn't thrilled with the idea of his life being out there on a bookshelf, he'd agreed for Paula's sake. This was about her and her journey. After everything that happened between them, the least he could do was support her.

Gabby had been the only person Paula could even think about trusting with her story. Which made Gabby's former boss Melissa one very happy editor as McKay Publishing won the rights to the book. Gabby had been fired as an editor and immediately hired as Paula's biographer.

Strange as it was, the two Mrs. Hunters had become very close friends through the process of telling Paula Hunter's story.

"Well, go on," Gabby insisted. "I'll walk with Armstrong and think about the book. You run and we'll meet you back at the house."

"I love you," he said as he kissed her on the nose before taking off down the beach.

She watched him jog away and had no worries about how he would handle being a new dad. He was fit and active and more excited by this baby than by anything she could imagine. When they first learned she was pregnant, he said being a dad to this baby was going to be more exciting than rocketing into space. She believed him.

She always believed him.

After he got a few yards away though he stopped and turned around. She wondered if maybe he had a rock in his sneaker or if he possibly turned an ankle.

"What's the matter?" she asked as he approached her.

"I didn't like it," he said.

"You love running."

"I know. But I didn't like leaving you behind. Felt weird."

Gabby decided it was hormones making her eyes mist up and not sentiment. She wasn't that corny. Oh, who was she kidding? Around him she was exactly that corny.

"You could walk with me and Armstrong. Just for the next few months," she offered.

He took her hand and Armstrong hopped around their ankles apparently pleased to have both his parents staying behind with him.

"Sounds like a plan to me. We need to stick together."

"Always," Gabby agreed.

* * * * *

HEART & HOME

Harlequin®
Super Romance

HSRCNM0412

REQUEST YOUR FREE BOOKS!
2 FREE NOVELS PLUS 2 FREE GIFTS!

Harlequin

Super Romance

Exciting, emotional, unexpected!

YES! Please send me 2 FREE Harlequin® Superromance® novels and my 2 FREE gifts (gifts are worth about $10). After receiving them, if I don't wish to receive any more books, I can return the shipping statement marked "cancel." If I don't cancel, I will receive 6 brand-new novels every month and be billed just $4.69 per book in the U.S. or $5.24 per book in Canada. That's a saving of at least 15% off the cover price! It's quite a bargain! Shipping and handling is just 50¢ per book in the U.S. and 75¢ per book in Canada.* I understand that accepting the 2 free books and gifts places me under no obligation to buy anything. I can always return a shipment and cancel at any time. Even if I never buy another book, the two free books and gifts are mine to keep forever.

135/336 HDN FC6T

Name	(PLEASE PRINT)	

Address		Apt. #

City	State/Prov.	Zip/Postal Code

Signature (if under 18, a parent or guardian must sign)

Mail to the Reader Service:
IN U.S.A.: P.O. Box 1867, Buffalo, NY 14240-1867
IN CANADA: P.O. Box 609, Fort Erie, Ontario L2A 5X3

Not valid for current subscribers to Harlequin Superromance books.

**Are you a current subscriber to Harlequin Superromance books
and want to receive the larger-print edition?
Call 1-800-873-8635 or visit www.ReaderService.com.**

* Terms and prices subject to change without notice. Prices do not include applicable taxes. Sales tax applicable in N.Y. Canadian residents will be charged applicable taxes. Offer not valid in Quebec. This offer is limited to one order per household. All orders subject to credit approval. Credit or debit balances in a customer's account(s) may be offset by any other outstanding balance owed by or to the customer. Please allow 4 to 6 weeks for delivery. Offer available while quantities last.

Your Privacy—The Reader Service is committed to protecting your privacy. Our Privacy Policy is available online at www.ReaderService.com or upon request from the Reader Service.

We make a portion of our mailing list available to reputable third parties that offer products we believe may interest you. If you prefer that we not exchange your name with third parties, or if you wish to clarify or modify your communication preferences, please visit us at www.ReaderService.com/consumerschoice or write to us at Reader Service Preference Service, P.O. Box 9062, Buffalo, NY 14269. Include your complete name and address.

HSR11

The heartwarming conclusion of

from fan-favorite author
TINA LEONARD

With five brothers married, Jonas Callahan is under no pressure to tie the knot. But when Sabrina McKinley admits her bouncing baby boy is his, Jonas does everything he can to win over the woman he's loved for years. First the last Callahan bachelor must uncover an important family secret…before he can take the lovely Sabrina down the aisle!

A Callahan Wedding

**Available this May
wherever books are sold.**

*After a bad decision—or two—Annie Mendes
is determined to succeed as a P.I. But her first assignment
could be her last, because one thing is clear: she's not cut
out to be a nanny. And Louisiana detective Nate Dufrene
seems to know there's more to her than meets the eye!*

*Read on for an exciting excerpt of the upcoming book
WATERS RUN DEEP by Liz Talley...*

THE SOUND OF A CAR behind her had Annie scooting off the
road and checking over her shoulder.

Nate Dufrene.

Her heart took on a galloping rhythm that had nothing to
do with exercise.

He slowed beside her. "Wanna ride?"

"I'm almost there. Besides, I wouldn't want to get your
seat sweaty."

His gaze traveled down her body before meeting her
eyes. Awareness ignited in her blood. "I don't mind."

Her mind screamed, *get your butt back to the house and
leave Nate alone.* Her libido, however, told her to take the
candy he offered and climb into his car like a naughty little
girl. Damn, it was hard to ignore candy like him.

"If you don't mind." She pulled open the door and
climbed inside.

The slight scent of citrus cologne, which suited him,
filled the car. She inhaled, sucking in cool air and Nate.
Both were good.

"You run often?" he asked.

"Three or four times a week."

"Oh, yeah? Maybe we can go for a run together."

Her body tightened unwillingly as thoughts of other
things they could do together flitted through her mind. She

shrugged as though his presence wasn't affecting her. Which it *so* was. Lord, what was wrong with her? *He* wasn't her assignment.

"Sure." No way—not if she wanted to keep her job. As he parked, she reached for the door handle, but his hand on her arm stopped her. His touch was warm, even on her heated flesh.

"What did you say you were before becoming a nanny?"

Alarm choked out the weird sexual energy that had been humming in her for the past few minutes. Maybe meeting him on the road wasn't as coincidental as it first seemed. "A real-estate agent."

Will Nate discover Annie's secret?
Find out in WATERS RUN DEEP by Liz Talley,
available May 2012 from Harlequin® Superromance®.

And be sure to look for the other two books
in Liz's THE BOYS OF BAYOU BRIDGE series,
available in July and September 2012.

INTRIGUE®

**MISSION: TO FIND AND PROTECT...
BEFORE TIME RUNS OUT.**

DEBRA WEBB

**BEGINS AN EXHILARATING
NEW MINISERIES.**

Colby Investigator Lyle McCaleb has been assigned to find
and protect the long-lost daughter of Texas's most notorious
serial-killer couple. What Lyle doesn't expect is his first love,
Sadie Gilmore, to be the woman he's looking for. Now the
stakes are the highest he has ever faced, but can he convince
Sadie to trust him with her life...and her heart?

Find out this May in

COLBY LAW

May is Mystery Month!

With six titles to choose from every month, uncover
your love for breathtaking romantic suspense
with Harlequin Intrigue® today!

HI696 k